Fractured Heart

Re Della Strada

Book Two

Samantha Barrett

Debbie,
My Irish queen, I fucking love you so much and for the love of God don't you dare send me any fucking eye emojis!

TRIGGERS!

Note to reader, this book is a cross over from the Murdoch Mafia, Memento Mori and Godfathers Of The Night. You DO NOT need to have read those series before starting this one.

This book contains some scenes that may be triggering, This book is not for the faint of heart, be warned.

Sexual assault

Rape

Kidnapping

Mental abuse

Emotional abuse

Physical abuse

Loss of an infant (stillbirth) – **Chapter Thirteen**

Maiming of an infant – **Chapter Thirteen**

Brutalization of an infant – **Chapter Thirteen**

Attempted suicide
Suicidal thoughts
Blood play
Coprophilia
Kink shaming
Bully
Medical manipulation
Drugging
Sexual manipulation
Forced Proximity
Dub con
Torture
Murder

If you find something triggering that has not been listed please email authorsamanthabarrett@gmail.com. I do endeavor to include all triggers but what I may not find triggering others will so please be kind and reach out to me so I may include those triggers here.

The List

Karl

Nolan

Fin

Donald

Ed

Stephen

Mike

George

Daniel

Frank

Len

Lionel

Jackson

Tom

Thomas

Jones

Aaron

Ron

Preface

Fear.

Four simple letters. They mean nothing when they are separate but once you put them together, that single word can mean so many different things. Fear of the unknown, fear of losing someone you love or fear of failing. I never felt any of that before year one, I was happy, loved and adored by the boy who wanted nothing more in this world aside from seeing me smile.

Alexander Grayson was my Robin Hood, he stole my heart and I never wanted it returned, I wanted him to keep hold of it for the rest of our lives and cherish it. That all changed in the blink of an eye when I chose to save my best friend, my soulmate.

Fear.

That word finally meant something to me.

If you think this is going to be a story about how a girl was adored and loved by everyone and found her prince charming then close this fucker and move along. This is a story about a girl who was broken and grew to become a fucking queen. She stole her fucking freedom back and went after all of those bastards that wronged her, including her family who stopped looking for her because it was easier to believe she was dead than continue to hunt for her.

My name is Doxy Da Luca and I am the bitch your mother warned you to stay the fuck away from.

Year One

Fear is a constant, it's my only friend, I find comfort in its presence and know I'm not alone. It amazes me how one emotion could incite such an irrational feeling inside someone but that feeling is the only thing that reminds me I am alive. I wish I wasn't.

The moment I woke up in this strange place and found myself chained to a table, my hands bound to one end while I was bent over the edge with each of my ankles strapped to the legs. The second I registered I was naked, I knew what would happen. That's when that one fucking emotion took flight inside me, *fear*. I tried to remain strong and prayed that my family and friends would find me in time but a prayer is as useless as wishing upon a star. They all assumed I was dead but I still held a sliver of hope that my brother, Xander and my best friend Lake wouldn't give up on me, that they would never think I was dead unless they found a body.

The first time Karl raped me I was a wreck, he shattered something within me the instant he slammed his cock inside me. The innocence of my youth was ripped away from that very moment. I screamed and fought with everything I had only for him to punish me with the bite of his whip, splitting open the skin on my back to *teach me a lesson*. He allowed his men to use my body as their own plaything and even introduced them to me by name so I would feel comfortable—he's a sadistic fuck.

Any sound that came from me or if a tear should fall I was whipped, some of the men liked to cut me and use my own blood as lubricant to rape me. They said I should be thankful they aren't fucking my ass dry, like they were doing me a favor and I should be fucking grateful. They tore away my humanity and turned me into a pet, a doll of sorts. I was treated worse than a dog.

I thought being raped and beaten was the worst of it, until four days of being chained up meant I had no choice but to piss myself *and* I couldn't hold it any longer, I also soiled myself. Then and only then did the final man, who hadn't laid a single finger on me, come for his turn. He used my shit as lube, smeared it all over my open wounds and used it as body paint, then forced me to eat it while he watched. Ron has a coprophilia kink and I fucking hate him nearly as much as I hate Karl, they are at the top of my list.

"That's right, you're nothing but a useless cunt who takes our cocks!" I block out Ron's words and focus on the crack in the concrete wall, the same crack I stare at every time any of them come to me. I hate it when Ron comes the most. I hate myself for shitting. I fucking try as hard as I can to hold it so I don't have to see him but I can't. I've been here for what must be months now. Tears silently roll down my cheeks. Every sound I make I'm punished for, my back is still raw and bleeding from being whipped yesterday. If I fight, I'm whipped and beaten, if I cry or make a sound, I'm whipped and raped again. Karl–*Master* as I'm forced to call him—watches every time his men take their turn, he says until I can be trusted to behave he won't allow me any privacy. He thinks allowing me to be alone with each of these vile fucking rodents would make me happy. He is the worst type of fucking human.

"Those tears are costing you space on what used to be flaw-less skin, Doxy." I cringe and bite down on my lip trying to force my tears to stop falling at the sound of his voice. I know my family will be searching for me, I just have to hold out until my brother and our friends come for me. I know Xander won't stop looking until he finds me, he promised he would always be there when I needed him and I need him now more than ever.

My mom told me a dream is a wish you make with your heart, my heart must be in default setting because my wish of freedom and a painless death has yet to come true...

Year Two

I'm starting to lose hope that no one is coming for me.

You know how you can feel it inside your heart and soul when something is off? I feel that in mine. I know they aren't coming for me but I can't give up. The moment I do, they have won and I can never fucking allow that.

It's been two years, two fucking years of this hell and I want to die. I want it all to fucking stop and no longer exist, I fucking hate it. How the fuck can people go to church every Sunday and praise God. If there is a fucking God, why would he allow this to happen to me?

I'm starting to learn that fighting gets me nowhere. If I just give in and let them have me, they leave me quicker and don't hurt me as much. Mike and Tom are different, they love it when I fight them, they enjoy the *fire* inside as they call it.

"Come on, Doxy, fight. You know how I fucking like it," Mike shouts and I flinch when he punches me and my head smacks against the concrete wall. I fall to the ground and curl into a ball. Master still watches and regardless of what they like from me, Master will punish me if I don't obey *him*. I must always obey him and no one else, he is the one with the power here not them and definitely not me. Their beatings may hurt but *his* are worse, he gets off on tearing my skin open and making me bleed. "Fucking bitch," he roars as he spits in my face and stomps on my leg. I scream out in pain when I feel a distinct crack.

He broke my leg.

Before the haze of pain can even clear, I'm dragged to my feet by my hair. I scream out when I'm thrown face first against the wall. I almost pass out when my wrists are shackled to the wall and they yank on my legs, securing them to the chains on the floor. I go lax in the restraints, my arms taking the brunt of my weight. I know what this means, I fucked up and cried out so now I'll be punished.

The pain in my leg is nowhere near as painful as what is about to come. I tremble when I hear the whip crack, he does this every time and each time a sick laugh escapes him. This is what he loves, he thrives off my pain, it gets him hard watching my skin tear open and seeing me bleed. No matter how I try to brace myself for these punishments or try to force my mind to a happy place, the bite of his whip always draws me back to the present.

"Oh, I love it when you misbehave and I get to remind you what happens. Master isn't happy with you, Doxy."

My bottom lip trembles. "I-I'm sorry—" My words cut off when the first snap of the whip tears across my back, the unhealed skin splitting instantly and I become dizzy with pain.

"Take it and start counting or I won't stop," Master snarls as he cracks the whip again and again and *again,* until I finally pass out from the pain after shouting *twenty*, the amount of lashes I just received. I relish the moments I black out because I feel nothing, I just fucking wish I never woke up!

Year Five

Doxy

I don't fight, I don't try to escape, I don't even speak anymore. I used to sit in my cell and hum, or make up stories to keep myself entertained but now, I don't do any of that. I just sit in the corner and wait. Master has moved me to a room in the house now. I was good and allowed out of that concrete prison I was held in for years. He says he will train me to be the perfect Doxy so I can show the others he brings home. I tried to train three of the girls but they didn't last very long.

Two died from infections thanks to Ron and his fucking shit kink, I still hate him the most. I hate how he stands in the corner and watches the men take their turns, sometimes he'll even get himself off and blow his load in my face. The Master only lets him play with me once a month now, he won't risk his *pet* dying from infection. Tom and Mike still beat me because I refuse to fight back out of fear of Master's punishment.

When I hear the lock on my door click open, I kneel and place my hands on the tops of my thighs and drop my gaze to the floor. This is the only position I'm allowed to meet Master in, I must never look him in the eyes or I am punished, only worthy people are allowed to gaze upon his face.

"You disgust me," he snarls.

"I'm sorry, Master," I reply on autopilot.

"You reek of shit."

I nod. "I'm sorry, Master."

"Your brother no longer searches for you. He runs all of Canada and has never once looked for you, does that upset you?" His words don't inspire the reaction he hopes for as I hate my brother. Master made sure to tell me the moment he took over the Da Luca family and renamed it the Re Della Strada. Knox has the power and the means to find me yet he doesn't. He's left me to rot in this hell while he moves on with his life never suffering like I do.

"No, Master, I know where I belong." He hums his approval. I wait for him to cross the room and drag me by my hair to the bed like always but time passes and still he doesn't move. There may be a bed in this room I am locked in but I am never allowed on it unless I have a *guest*. I sleep on the floor with no covers or pillows.

"Stand." Without thinking I obey him, not wanting to risk his ire as my back, ass and legs have enough scars on them without needing to add more by being disobedient. My body has been broken many times, you would think I'm crazy but my bones breaking now doesn't cause much discomfort. I pray they break bones so I can focus on that pain instead of what they do to my body. My mother once said that a woman's body is her temple and should be cherished. She was wrong, these bastards bulldozed this temple and destroyed it years ago. I startle when clothing is tossed at my feet, I haven't worn clothes since...

Come to think of it, I've never been allowed the privilege of wearing clothing since I got here. "Put those on." Doing as he says, I yank the sweatpants on and pull the large hoodie over my head, the clothing feeling strange and chafes on my filthy skin. "Kneel."

I drop without thought and bow my head. I see the tips of his shoes and tense. I don't flinch when he grabs my hair but I do still when the sound of buzzing fills the room. I want to protest and rebel against this injustice but I know what will happen so bite down on my lip and slam my eyes closed to keep my tears from coming as he shaves my head.

I stand beside Master with my hood up and head down, the collar around my neck has metal prongs and digs into my skin but I don't dare try to adjust it.

"There, you see her with your own eyes, now you know her brother can never rise against our plans," Master snarls at the men. I know who one of them is—Percy Deveraux but I haven't the slightest idea of who the other man is.

"When I announce Lakeland's marriage to Giovani he will come for us. I want men ready and waiting to take him out," Percy says, his nasally voice has always grated on my nerves but it doesn't bother me like it used to.

"The sooner we get rid of that little prick the sooner I can go after my brother and take back the family. Canada will be ours to trade in as we like. Percy's app has been beneficial for all of us," the stranger says. I know the app they speak of. I heard the men speaking about how each of them wanted to buy little girls from there and keep them as their slaves. One day, when I get the fuck out of here I'm going to free them all. "You planning on selling my niece on there?" I snap my gaze to the strange man and stare at him in horror.

"Bitch!" Master roars before I'm met with his fist to the side of my face and sent to my knees. I don't cry out in pain or fight when he yanks the leash, digging the prongs of the collar deeper into my neck. "Fucking cunt wouldn't fetch a decent price. She's worthless except for the fact she can't birth a child." I slam my eyes closed at the memory. I hate thinking about that time—it broke me, stripped me of all my strength and will to fight.

"What happened?" Percy asks. I hate him. He knows his daughter was my best friend and not once has he tried to help me.

"You got lucky with your daughter losing her memories." I suck in a sharp breath, what does he mean Lake lost her memories? "This bitch had her shit removed when she gave birth, couldn't have the cunt pregnant all the time." I fight back the tears, I got pregnant and much to Master's dismay I never miscarried when he sent the men to rid me of the pregnancy. I fought and covered my belly protecting my innocent baby but I went into labor early and gave birth to a beautiful baby boy, who was born sleeping.

The loss of my son is what truly broke me and made me numb, that was the day they won.

Year Ten

Doxy

Common courtesy would be to at least spit on your cock so it doesn't feel like I'm being fucked by sandpaper but no, not these fuckers, they love knowing that once they are through with me and go home to their wives, children, work, or wherever the fuck they go that I will be left here battered and bruised, wearing the marks they left me with. It's Ron's turn next, he always goes last when it's his one day a month. The others say it's too disgusting to fuck me with shit covering my body like what they have done isn't just as fucking sick. One day I will break free and come after each of these cocksuckers.

Five years ago, I decided to stop being meek and started training when I was alone in my room. I started out slow, simple push-ups, sit-ups and that type of shit until I started to shadow box. I watched Knox, Taylan and Xander enough to know how to throw a punch. I refused to remain broken. I won't allow the death of my son to go unpunished. I'm not the greatest and fighting against a shadow is easy but I know I have gotten better, stronger even. I have no weights to lift so I use the wooden frame of the bed in my room to do some deadlifts.

I see some of the guys sparring and take note of how they move, watching their footwork and apply that to my training. I stretch daily and it has taken me well over six months to even get into a split but that accomplishment brought a real smile to my face. I am getting better and I know with a bit more time, I will finally be strong enough and ready, I just have to keep my head down and take each day as it comes. I will not fucking die here!

Karl, Nolan, Fin, Donald, Ed, Stephen, Mike, George, Daniel, Frank, Len, Lionel, Jackson, Tom, Thomas, Jones, Aaron and the fucking worst, Ron.

I picture their faces and say their names over and over again as I train daily, imagining the ways I will kill them. They are the names of the men that have raped me and one of them is my son's father. I will kill them all and bathe in the blood of the ones they love most. They think Karl is someone to be feared but they're wrong, when I am free no one will be safe from my wrath. I am a heartless bitch with no feelings. They killed those things years ago and all I have now inside me is hate. Ed pulls out of me and shoves me into the edge of the desk in the living room. I've now been given the privilege of being able to roam the house but I'm still collared. It has a tracker in it and will shock me like I'm a fucking poodle if I enter somewhere I shouldn't or try to escape, not that I could unless I had some bolt cutters to cut the fucking padlock off. I'm also allowed to shower once a week, and I get fed twice a day now. Still from a dog bowl but at least it's food.

"Don't make me wait," Ron snarls as he passes by, heading toward the back room that is reserved for him and his *activities* as Master calls it. He is the only one with a room dedicated to him. None of the others use that room because they think Ron's tastes are vile. I wanted to scoff when I heard them say that. They can't stomach the thought of what he does but I am forced to be a part of it.

I want to die!

I tried it a few years back. They found me before I could bleed out and stitched me up. I received the worst fucking beatings for weeks after that. My back, ass and the backs of my thighs were split open by the whip but it didn't stop them from plowing their crusty shriveled dicks into me.

Standing up straight, I follow after Ron, cringing when I feel Ed's cum dripping out of me. They never allow me to clean up, saying that having cum on me or in me reminds me of my place and that I am their whore to do with as they please. Ron slams the door closed behind me and points toward the metal bucket in the center of the room. I swallow down the bile that rushes up my throat.

"You make me wait longer than five minutes then you'll be eating mine, got it?" I throw up in my mouth. Swallowing down the vomit, I force my legs to move and carry me forward. He has made me eat his shit a couple of times and when I threw up he forced me to eat that as well—he is sick! I fucking hate that Ron records me every time. He has his tripod set up in the corner ready to capture this. The moment I squat over the bucket he presses record and begins to rub himself through his pants. I keep my gaze on the floor and force my bowels to do their thing. It makes me sick to my stomach to know he is going to use my own shit as body paint and lube. He is a sick fuck and the fact I know he has two daughters of his own is disgusting.

He groans when I finish and assume the position on my

hands and knees as he rushes to the bucket. I retreat inside my own mind as he groans smearing my own mess over my ass and I know what comes next, he's going to force his shit covered fingers inside my mouth and make me suck them clean before he finally fucks me. I fight the shudder of disgust that wants to roll through me when he smears my own mess through my hair, the smell alone has me wanting to gag.

"You taste perfect, Doxy, now suck my fingers clean while I fuck this ass." I force the bile back down my throat as I turn my head to the side and open my mouth. I feel his gaze boring into the side of my head as he plunges his cock into my ass. I lick the shit from his fingers and hate the sound of him moaning at the sight, he gets off on me eating my own shit.

He will die slowly and painfully.

Year Fourteen

Doxy

Time is a meaningless commodity in my life, nothing changes here except for the amount of cocks that force themselves inside me each day. Unlike before when I was chained to the table and raped repeatedly, I'm a good whore now. I can walk freely around the house so long as I keep my head down and obey everything the Master tells me. For fourteen years I have busted my ass to gain the trust that I have. I never complain when the Master and his men fuck me, I take it. I know what each of them likes, some like it when I fight, others like it when I scream but Ron is the worst. Master only allows him to do that once a month still since I kept getting infections from it.

At the sound of the front door opening I quickly shuffle to the edge of the table. I spit on my hand and rub my pussy before I bend over. If the Master has been away for a long trip he needs to be relieved as soon as he walks through the door. I fight the shudder of disgust that rolls through me at the sight of others walking in behind him. They all stare at me. Master says nothing as the men claim their seats and begin to speak in hushed tones. I feel him behind me and wait. I hear his belt and then his zipper before I feel the tip of his cock pressing at my entrance, he groans thinking I'm wet for him. I've learned ways to make this bearable like spitting rather than it feeling like a cactus.

I whimper when he slams inside me. "See this, this is my fucking whore," Master calls out as he thrusts inside me. "Look at the sight of her, waiting and willing to take any cock like a good fucking bitch. I trained the cunt well." He grunts out as he continues to pump inside twice more before coming. He never lasts long and I am always grateful for it. Once he pulls out I stand and ready myself to leave but he grips the back of my head and slams my face down on the table. I cry out and regret making a sound instantly when I hear his dark chuckle. "You know the rules, Doxy. You made a sound so now they all get to take turns instead of just me." Slamming my eyes closed I will my tears not to fall, if he sees me cry it will be worse.

I force my mind to go blank as I hear them all leap out of their chairs, barely registering them raping me until one of them shoves his cock inside my ass without any lube. I bite down so hard on my lip I bite through it, tasting my own blood. Tears gather in the corners of my eyes but I swallow my cries and think of something, anything to distract me from this fucking pain.

Soon, you will get your chance for revenge! Hold on, you can take all these fuckers out and then you can finally go after those fuckers in Canada! They will all pay for their part in this fucking nightmare I have lived in for fourteen fucking years.

"Karl?" someone shouts, and the guy behind me stills as a man I have never seen enters the room. He takes one look at me and pales. "What the fuck is this?" he roars, the guy with his cock in my ass laughs.

"This is called—" He doesn't get a chance to finish before the man pulls a gun, fires a single shot and his cock rips out of me as his body drops to the floor. I hear someone come up behind me and fight the urge to gag, his buddy just got shot but that doesn't put him off? These cunts are all fucking sick! Every single fucking one of them!

"You lay a single fucking finger on her and you'll join your friend." The menace in his tone is clear. I've never heard anyone speak like this to Master or his men. I begin to worry how I will be treated if he continues to anger them. Whenever they are angry they take it out on me.

"What the fuck do you want, Trevante?" Master snaps. The man keeps his gaze on me as he speaks. It's unnerving to have him looking at me, he doesn't see me as a hole to fuck like the others, he sees me as a... person.

"The Americans have aligned themselves with the Canadians and now the Greeks. They even have the fucking Russians and you can't even get Ian back on your side?" My eyes widen at the way he speaks to the Master. I have never heard anyone speak to him like that before.

"Watch your fucking tone boy—"

"The Re Della Strada are going to come for you now that Ian isn't backing you and is putting his hat in the ring with the Greeks. You're on your own!" the man shouts.

"That little cunt Knox won't do shit to me," Master snarls smugly. Hearing his name has deep-seated hatred rearing inside me. I'll have my vengeance against him one day soon, I fucking swear it. They will all pay for the fucking injustice I have suffered for over a decade, for the losses I have had to go through.

"How the fuck can you be so sure?" the man snaps angrily.

I feel Master lay a hand on my bare back and remain still, fighting not to flinch away from his touch. "Because eight years ago, Gio managed to drive a wedge between him and his best friend. Alexander Grayson is gone and no one has seen him since." This is news to me, I had no idea they weren't together anymore. What happened? "And I have a golden ticket that ensures I break him worse than the loss of his best friend."

"And what exactly is that, *Dad*?" My mouth parts in a silent gasp, the Master is his... father. Any hope I had of this man helping me flees and I'm back to feeling despair and praying for the fucking Devil to come snatch me and take me to hell. I would gladly trade him my soul if it means I get to escape this hell that I am living in now.

"I have her," he says, patting my back. "She has been my hidden gem for years, knowing that when the time came for that little prick to try and come for me, I could finally shove it in his face and show him I won the war years ago." The smug tone of the Master's voice has the man studying me intently for a moment.

"Who is she?" he asks quietly but never takes his gaze off me. The intensity with which he looks at me is unnerving and makes me feel uneasy.

"She only responds to Doxy."

The man's face contorts in disgust. "You call her an abbreviation of the word slut?" I slam my eyes closed and fight off the wave of shame.

"Before I named her Doxy, she was known as Waverly Bronson. Meet Knox's twin sister that he thought drowned fourteen years ago, Son." Trevante's eyes widen a fraction as he looks from Master to me. Call me crazy but I can see the hatred he feels toward my Master in the depths of his gray eyes. He shakes his head and runs a hand through his brown hair in clear frustration. Me being naked hasn't bothered me since I first arrived here years ago but now, under the scrutiny of this stranger's gaze, I feel exposed in more ways than I care to admit.

"You stole the sibling of the Don of the Re Della Strada?" he shouts. I don't react to his booming voice, I'm used to being shouted at, fuck I don't even flinch when one of them raises a hand to me anymore. Being fucked isn't even a big deal, it's just normal to me. "The moment he figures out what the fuck you have done, you and all of these pieces of shit are dead." My eyes roll back into my head as pleasure courses through me at the thought of all of them dead at my feet. I want to cut them open just to see their insides. I want to bathe in their blood and sip wine in a bathtub full of their intestines.

"The prick can try but she won't leave me, in eight years she has never tried to escape even though she has had ample opportunity." I want to scoff, the only reason I haven't taken those chances is because I knew they were a setup, he was testing me to see if he could trust me with my freedom around the house. I'm allowed into his office to help him with his business stuff. He thinks I'm stupid and absorb nothing from those times but he's wrong, I have spent the past eight years learning, listening, and watching. The next time an opportunity arises to flee, I'm taking it because I have everything I need to end all of these sadistic fucks before going after the Re Della Strada and killing my brother and all his men.

"You stupid fucking fool, you have no one to back you. No one to come to your aid, you let him get under your skin. While you have been fucking a girl young enough to be your daughter, Knox was forging connections and solidifying his place among the heads of the families. If you try to go after him, they will come to his aid and take you out." The Master makes a growling sound in his chest, I recognize that sound all too well, he's angry.

"Watch your fucking mouth, boy. I can create another one of you in a second," Master snarls, Trevante just quirks a brow and crosses his arms over his chest.

"You've been trying that for twenty years with your whores, how's that working out for you, *Dad?*" This is news to me. I knew he had daughters but I never knew he had fathered a son. I've seen those cruel little bitches numerous times and each time they have scoffed at the sight of me and mocked me, never once offering their help, so they will die alongside their father.

"Get the fuck out, boy—"

Trevante must have a death wish because he cuts my Master off. "Not happening, the heads of the distros and grandpa are coming." I see Master tense out of the corner of my eye.

"Fine, have the car ready, we'll leave in ten—"

Again, he cuts the Master off. "They're coming here so I suggest you scurry off and start sorting shit while I handle dressing... *her.*" I flick my gaze up to meet his, I haven't looked anyone in the eye for over a decade, the feeling of making eye contact is thrilling but it's the cunning look in his eyes that has me tensing, Trevante has ulterior motives.

"No, she obeys me and me alone. She will remain in her room and not be seen." His word is final, without so much as a second glance at anyone I briskly exit and head straight for my room, slightly grateful that I won't have to persevere with them pawing at me tonight. The moment I enter my room, I close the door silently and retreat to my corner, kneeling on the hard floor with my hands flat against the top of my thighs and my head bowed.

Nerves thrum through me, I hate the anticipation of not knowing what is coming. It's worse when you're left waiting and wondering because your mind conjures situations that have your blood pumping. The sick and deranged fucks love leaving me on edge wondering what they have cooked up, it's the nights like tonight that make me crazy and wanting to take a blade to my throat. I would have rather they all take their turns as they walked in, that's normal, that's what I'm accustomed to happening.

Chapter One

Trevante

I always knew Karl was a sick and twisted son of a bitch but I didn't think he was this bad. To kidnap the twin sister of Knox Bronson is suicide as the Canadians have forged alliances with all the other families. They have been playing the long game while Karl has been blinded by rage because he was beaten by a boy half his age. Knox won eight years ago when he took out Giovani and Percy. Karl fled and hid in Ireland and hasn't left unless summoned to a meeting in Switzerland with the heads of the families.

Coming here tonight for the first time I never expected to see a young woman bent over a table with a line of disgusting fucks waiting for their turn to ram their cocks inside her. She looked frail and battered, her back littered with scars, years upon years' worth of scars! I stand here seething with my fists clenched at my sides as I watch two men drag that cunt's lifeless body out of here.

"I should kill you where you stand!" I lazily lull my head to the side to look at Karl, his features taut and I can see the tension rolling off him in waves. My grandfather hates him, he's never found his son deserving of the title *Captain*, in Ireland we don't have dons. Our underbosses are called Clan Chiefs. We also don't call our heads of enforcers captains, we call them Warlords. *I* am the Warlord to the The Solomon Organized Crime Group but we are just known as The Solomon. It's fucking pathetic and sounds stupid but Karl refused to name SOCG anything other than after himself.

"You should but you won't," I say in a bored tone. The fat bastard snarls as he stomps toward me, thinking he holds all the power but he has nothing. He is under the illusion that he is the one who holds all the cards because he sits at the head of the family, but that is all about to change. Karl stands before me with his fists clenched at his sides. I know it pisses him off that he has to look up in order to meet my gaze and I relish in that knowledge.

"You think because you came from my nut sack that I will be lenient with you?" Spittle flies from his mouth and lands on my jacket. I make a show of disgust before I swipe that shit away, loving how the podgy fucker vibrates in outrage.

"No. In fact I know you want nothing more than to see me fail, which is why you have kept me as the Warlord and not allowed me to move up in the ranks and I have never complained, not once." He opens his mouth to no doubt rebuke my claim so I push on. "You have fallen. You no longer control the lands you think you do. While you have been busy chasing after the Don of the Re Della Strada, men have been moving in and taking over your turf. Good luck explaining that to your father," I sneer as I shoulder past him. Much like his own father, I hate him. Karl is the definition of the word *pig*.

I walk aimlessly through the house and get an idea of the layout. As I pass through a darkened hallway I stumble and tense at the sound of metal skirting along the floor. Frowning I dart my gaze around until I spot an empty dog bowl.

Karl hates animals!

My attention is snagged when a door at the end of the hall opens and the woman from earlier stands in the doorway with her head down and hands collapsed in front of her naked body.

"You..." I breathe out. At the sound of my voice she snaps her head up and her eyes widen for a second before she drops her gaze and flops to the ground with the grace of a baby horse.

"Forgive me, I didn't mean to look upon your face." I jerk back in surprise.

"What?" I find myself asking as I creep closer to her, only to still a few feet away when I see how tense she grows the closer I get. I run my gaze over her and fight back the rage I feel at the sight of her on her knees and bowing her head like a dog. "Get up," I snap. She climbs to her feet without complaint and keeps her head down, refusing to meet my stare. "What's your name?"

"Doxy," she replies automatically.

"What's your real name?" I growl angrily, I know Karl already told me earlier but I need her to confirm it. If what he says is true, then this woman is the key to ending the impending war between the families and us.

"Doxy Da Luca," she answers without hesitation.

"I know who the last name Da Luca belongs to and I have a hunch that your father didn't give you his last name." Finally, she reacts in the form of exhaling loudly.

"Doxy Da Luca is my name. If you don't require my

services then I must return to my room until supper." My brows raise as understanding dawns on me.

"You came out when you heard the sound of the dog bowl..." It's not a question, just an observation.

"Yes."

"Motherfuckers!" I snarl. She doesn't flinch at my angry tone. I want to say more but I can't because Karl's men are shouting that cars are arriving, so I rush forward and grip her shoulders. She doesn't flinch or fight like she has clearly been trained to do. "Listen to me, *Waverly*." She hisses at the sound of her real name. "Shit is gonna go down tonight and you need to be ready to leave when I come for you." She yanks free of my hold and finally meets my gaze with an angry glint in her eyes.

"I will never disobey the Master. I am not Waverly, my name is Doxy Da Luca." The venom in her tone tells me she isn't as lost as I originally thought.

"You are not the first Doxy, my mother was." Her brows raise and her jaw unhinges at my words but I don't have time to pacify her, I have a part to play tonight and I won't allow a woman to side track me. "I won't let you suffer the same fate my mother did. Be ready when I come for you." I leave her standing there as I rush back to the main area to wait for my grandfather and the others. I lied to Karl, it isn't just his father and the Clan Chiefs coming, Ian and Andreas are accompanying them to discuss Karl's surrender. I stay back in the shadows of the large dining room, knowing this is where Karl will host them because it's the largest space and it oozes riches, even though the fucker is nearly broke. He has spent millions on trying to buy off the right people to side with him and restart an app Percy Deveraux made to sell women but the moment Knox or the Americans catch wind of it they take them out, costing Karl more money than he fucking has. Our family is suffering because of his greed and from what we can gather, the men Karl has here with him are the only ones being paid, unlike the others.

I remain where I am as they all begin to trickle in. I roll my eyes at the sight of Karl perched in his chair at the head of the table, acting like he isn't bothered by the sight of all these heavy hitters stalking into his luxurious house. It pleases the fuck out of me when Grandpa walks in and Karl stiffens at the sight of him.

"Still a pompous fucking prick I see." Reid Solomon is a fucking force. Grandpa may be old but he's still in shape for his age and exudes power. His gray hair is styled and his green eyes hold nothing but malice as he stares his son down. Karl shifts under the pressure of his gaze, his own green eyes narrow as Grandpa opts to sit at the other end of the table, claiming the chair there. I smirk. This is fucking beautiful to see Karl losing power and control over the room as his own Clan Chiefs as well as Andreas and Ian sit down at his father's end of the table. The mocking chuckle that escapes sets Karl off. He leans forward and pounds his fist on the table, ready to tear into his father no doubt but the words die on his tongue as the last man enters the room.

"You seem surprised to see me." This guy reeks of arrogance, his black hair a rugged mess atop his head and brown eyes darken the longer he stares at Karl.

"Oh, where are my manners?" Grandpa says with a sarcastic tone. "I apologize son, I forgot to mention I was bringing a friend with me." I dart my gaze between the black haired guy and Grandpa as he comes to a stop behind him and rests his hand on the back of his chair like he and my grandfather are old friends.

"I bet your Don would love to know that you aren't dead like he hoped." The guy just shrugs but I can see his presence isn't welcome by the way Karl is scowling at him. His men have all gone on high alert since he entered the room. Who the fuck is this guy?

"Knox knows where I am. I may be banished from returning home but I have a plan and I believe serving him your head will earn me his forgiveness." Karl's nostrils flare in outrage as he shoves his chair back and pushes to his feet.

"You will fucking die tonight, you little cunt!" he roars.

"Sit the fuck down now, you insulant little prick, before I make you!" Grandpa's voice booms out around the room. Karl glares at him but keeps his mouth closed. "You're lucky I haven't brought the council with me," he warns.

"The council can't do shit," Karl huffs out as he drops into his seat, crossing his arms over his chest. Just the way he sits there with an air of superiority surrounding him makes me ashamed that I share DNA with him.

"They can and they are. We want reports of the past ninety days of royalties and after you deliver that you will also provide us with a breakdown of profits for the businesses." Karl bristles at his father's request and looks uncomfortable but he remains silent. "Alexander will remain here with Trevante and keep an eye on things for me." That has Karl out of his seat and shouting again and before long Andreas and Ian as well as their men are joining in on the argument. When I spy Karl's second Nolan pull his gun and aim it at my grandfather, I rush into the fray.

"Get down!" I roar as I tackle my grandfather and

Alexander to the floor as the first shot rings out. Shit goes from controlled chaos to fucking out of hand in a split second. Alexander and I shove Grandpa out the door and use our bodies as shields as we draw our own guns. "Get my grandfather out of here, now!" I roar as I fire off a few shots at Karl's men as they try to rush him out of the other side of the room. Andreas and Ian rush past us, dashing to their cars.

"No, come with us." I shake my head at him.

"Take my grandfather, Alexander—"

"Call me Xander."

"Fine, take him and I'll meet up with you both later. I can't leave yet." He searches my gaze for a second before he begrudgingly nods and ushers my grandpa out of the house as I race toward the other end of the building dodging gunfire.

I'm not leaving without that fucking girl!

Chapter Two

Doxy

I tremble in the corner of my room as the sound of gunshots ring out through the house, this is my chance. It may be the only one I get to escape this fucking cage. It takes me three attempts to climb to my feet and when I do, I have to lean against the wall because my legs are shaking so hard.

"Pull it fucking together!" I growl to myself, take a deep breath and force all my emotions down into the box I created inside me years ago so I could survive this place, then snag the sheet from the bed, knowing I need to cover up or I risk drawing attention to myself when I escape. I tie it around myself like a toga and once it's secured, I try not to fidget with it feeling slightly weird to have something covering my body. As I inch toward the bedroom door and crack it open, the screams of pain are like music to my ears. The coast is clear, so I push the door open and close it behind myself, then snag the dog bowl from the ground and creep along the darkened hallway. I just need to make it to the back door, then I can slink out the back and make a run for it through the woods.

Fuck!

I reach up and touch the collar around my neck, I won't be going anywhere if I can't take this fucking thing off my neck!

"Doxy!" I still at the sound of Jackson's voice as he comes barging toward me. The rational part of me demands I drop to my knees and weather the punishment but another part, a part of me I always hoped existed but wasn't sure was still inside me, flares to life. When he is within reach, my mind blanks and my body takes over. I strike out, fast and sure with the bowl and hit him right in the throat. He gasps and chokes, dropping his gun to the floor as he grabs at his neck. Without hesitation I drop the bowl, grab his gun and point it at him. His eyes are wide with fear and fuck it's euphoric to see that look.

"Come on bitch, open that mouth for me." I throw his words back at him. The moment he opens his mouth to no doubt curse me out, I shove the gun inside and pull the trigger smiling when splatters of his blood land on me. I moan at the feeling, fuck this feels so good.

I never knew how orgasmic it felt to take a life. I feel fucking powerful and sated. Vengeance like I have never felt before rears inside me as I stare down at this fuckers lifeless eyes and relish in the sight of the giant hole in the back of his head. For years I wished that my dreams of doling out my revenge would come true and finally having the means and power to make them a reality has warmth spreading through me.

"Look who has the better hole now, you're lucky I don't have a cock or I would be fucking that beautiful hole in your head," I snarl, meaning every word. It would have given me great pleasure to fuck that gaping wound, knowing I am defiling his corpse.

"Waverly." Spinning around with my gun raised I come face to face with Trevante. Unlike Jackson he doesn't seem worried about me pointing a gun at him. "We need to move." Before he can get any closer I push my gun into his chest. He frowns but says nothing.

"There is no *we*, I don't need to be rescued!" I grit out. The bastard smirks as he reaches into his pocket and pulls a key out, my jaw locks at the sight.

"Well, should I just give the key to your collar back to Len?" My nostrils flare in outrage. "Either turn the fuck around now so I can take it off or I'm leaving you behind. Our window to escape is closing, decide now!" The urgency in his tone is the only reason I obey the bastard and turn. The moment I hear the lock click I gasp. When he removes the collar I feel... bare, naked, wrong but so... free at the same time. "Let's move!" His words snap me out of my stupor and I follow after him until he attempts to turn right instead of left.

"Wrong way," I clip out as I go the opposite way and dash through the kitchen toward the back door that is already open. I attempt to take a step outside but he shoves me behind him and takes the lead.

"Stay close," he barks as he dashes outside. I bristle but say nothing as I follow after him until I spot Lionel trying to make a run for a car near the front of the property. Without thought, I break away from Trevante and go after one of my tormentors. Lionel doesn't hear me approaching until the last second. He spins around and at the sight of me, his eyes widen like he's seen a ghost. I raise the gun and push it against his forehead.

"Doxy—"

"Sleep tight, bitch!" I snarl as I pull the trigger, loving that I got to use his words against him like I did with Jackson. My arm's yanked and I fight to get free until Trevante barks for me to shut up and pushes me into the back seat of the car Lionel was trying to escape in. I remain silent as Trevante climbs behind the wheel and guns the engine. The car skids and slides but I don't make a sound until we round the front of the house and I see Karl, Nolan, Mike, Len and Ron standing there, shooting at cars in the distance. The moment they see us they open fire. I roll my window down and fire back.

"You crazy bitch, you're gonna get shot!" I ignore Trevante as I continue to fire until my mag is empty.

"I'm coming for you, motherfuckers!" I scream, then slouch back against the seat once we hit the main road. It's surreal to see the outside world after so many years. Many things have changed, I feel so exposed and suddenly out of sorts. The adrenaline I was running on slowly flees my body. I don't dare relax or even allow myself to think I am safe. I have no idea who this man is and the fact he is my tormentor's son, means he isn't someone I can trust.

"We have a long drive ahead of us." His voice does nothing to soothe my worries.

"Where are you taking me?" The hardened tone of my voice isn't missed by him.

"Somewhere safe."

I scoff. "There is nowhere safe for me until each of those cunts are buried beneath the earth."

"I'm giving you a choice here, Waverly—"

"That's not my name!" I shout. He doesn't react.

"I'm not calling you Doxy."

"That's my name."

"No, it isn't."

"You don't fucking know me!" I clamp my mouth closed as reality slams into me. Here I am arguing back, and it feels natural but also so strange. I haven't spoken back to anyone in years and in the space of mere minutes this man has me arguing.

"You're right, I don't know you but I am trying to help you and I can't help you by calling you that fucking dreadful name."

"It's the only name I have," I mutter as I stare out the open window, loving how the wind feels against my face.

"What happened to Waverly?" he asks after a few moments.

I stiffen and try to control the anger rising inside me as I answer him. "She died fourteen years ago. She was weak and prayed for some man to save her. She died the night Doxy was born. Doxy is strong, independent and doesn't need a fucking man to save her. Doxy doesn't feel, she doesn't pine for anyone, she is the nightmare all those bastards will come to fear as she plucks them off one by one until she reaches the head of the demon."

"I'm guessing the demon is Karl?"

I snort. "No." I meet his shocked gaze in the rearview mirror.

"Who's the demon... Doxy?"

Pride fills me hearing him call me by my chosen name. "My twin, the demon is my brother and once I finish killing these Irish cunts, I'm going after him and all he holds dear to his heart. I'll kill him for having a hand in killing Waverly."

35

By the time we finally stop the sun is peeking over the horizon and exhaustion is weighing heavily on me. I follow after Trevante feeling out of sorts and defenseless with no gun. Before we reach the house, he stops and turns to face me. He runs his gaze over me. It normally irks me and has dread pooling inside me but he doesn't look at me like the others, he's looking past the exterior and trying to see inside me, to understand me.

"Here," he says as he pulls his gun from his waistband and hands it to me. I take it without argument.

"Why?" I ask.

He shrugs and runs a hand through his hair tiredly before answering. "You've survived something no person should and I know you feeling safe is going to be a big thing we need to work on, but the best way I can think of is to let you be the one with the only weapon in the house." I study him for a long moment trying to get a read on what exactly it is that he wants from me.

"Why are you helping me?"

"Because I can." Is all he says before turning and heading toward the small home. It's made out of brick and nestled in the middle of woodlands. It's the perfect house to bring a victim and kill them where no one would be able to find their body. With that thought in my mind, I flick the safety off and follow after him. The house smells stuffy like it hasn't been used in a long time, white sheets covering the furniture. From the doorway I can see the living room, kitchen and dining room. "Down that hall are the two bedrooms and a bathroom, we have to share the one I'm afraid."

"I can shower?" He stops pulling the sheets off the sofa and turns to face me, his gaze searches mine for a second before he sighs and averts his eyes trying to hide the anger in them.

"You can do whatever you like, sleep, walk outside, run, make a mess, look me in the eye and eat whenever the fuck you want." I roll my lips over my teeth and digest his words for a second before moving further into the house. "There's a tub, go take a bath and I'll gather some firewood before I head back into town to grab some supplies."

That shocks the fucking hell out of me. "You're leaving me here... alone?" He eyes me skeptically for a moment before nodding.

"Yes. If you're here when I get back, I'll make us dinner. If you're not, then I wish you well, Doxy Da Luca, and hope our paths will cross again one day."

His words have me scrunching my face. "Why the fuck would you want to meet me again?"

"Because you got out, she didn't and that is something to admire. You may not believe me but I am on your side and I will help you however I can."

"If you mean that, then you will get me a laptop so I can reroute Karl's shipment of girls and set them free." He reels back, his brows draw in as he studies me.

"You know how to do that?" The surprise is clear in his tone.

"Believe it or not I can do other things that don't involve sucking dick."

"That's not what I meant—"

"I don't care." I sneer as I stalk off down the hallway. If he returns with what I asked for then great but if not, I know where his loyalty lies. I shut myself in the far room and wait for him to leave. The moment he does, I rush out of the house and run deep into the woods finding a position where I can see anyone entering the drive as well as keep an eye on the small house.

Chapter Three

Xander

"Reid, he should have called by now, it's been ten fucking days. What the fuck is the hold up?" I growl.

"He would have gone to the safe house, I'll send you the coordinates. I know my grandson, Grayson. If he had heat on him he would never meet with me. Go to those coordinates and he will be there." I pull the phone away from my ear and sure enough there is a message from Reid sitting there.

"What if he isn't there?"

The old bastard sighs. "I'm afraid that means my son finally got his wish and killed my grandson."

"I'll call you once I get there," I grit out.

"No, you won't. There is no cell service out there unless you hike out into the woods." I grind my teeth as I end the call. If I didn't need to earn Knox's forgiveness so badly I wouldn't be here helping the former Irish Captain. I hope that returning home with Karl's head will earn me some favor with my best friend. I miss home. Being out here alone without Knox or Tay watching my six is hard. I hate being on my own, it gives me too much time to think and my mind always drifts back to *her*. The way she would smile at me or the way she flicked her hair, even the way she stuck her tongue out when she was concentrating. I push away those thoughts, knowing all thinking about her will do is send me into a dark spiral and I can't have that. It's been fourteen years and I still can't let her go.

I plug the coordinates into the car's GPS and sigh when it tells me it's going to take a few hours to reach Trevante. Why the dumbass didn't just leave with us is beyond me. I need to find this fucker. Reid said as long as I help him put his grandson on the throne of this family I can have Karl's body to take back to Knox. It was surprisingly easy to strike a deal with the former Captain. When I told him what his son had been up to behind his back and all the shady as fuck deals he had made, he asked me for proof. Andreas and Ian were both all too willing to back me up. Karl has stolen money from his family to fund his activities. I don't know why he has a hard-on for Knox but it can't just be over Lakeland marrying him and not Gio putting an end to their plan of taking over Canada.

Ian is still peddling in the skin trade but is slowly pulling out since the rest of the heads of the families are making it hard for him, which leaves Karl all alone. No one will come to his aid and help him back on his feet. He burned all his fucking bridges and it's a beautiful sight to see. The dumb fuck even tried to recruit Artemis, the Godfather of the Greeks who happens to be engaged to Bishop Murdoch's Granddaughter. There was no way her father, Royal, would have stood by and allowed his future son-in-law to enter into that deal.

The drive is long and filled with nothing but stone fences and mountains. Sheep and cows litter the hillsides and after a while, I find myself envious of those fucking animals. They don't have a care in the world and have no idea they are only allowed to roam free so they can get fat enough to fetch a good price at auction so they can be someone's dinner. My phone rings, pulling me from my thoughts. The sight of the caller brings a ghost of a smile to my face but also has longing hitting me right in the chest.

"Taylan, what's going on, brother?"

His chuckle fills the car. "You may have been able to fool Knox with that bullshit cheery tone but not me. What's going on, Xan?" A whoosh of air escapes me.

"Nothing, just hustling and pushing on."

"I call bullshit. This time of year is fucking hard for everyone, Xander, don't act like you are heartless."

"I don't have a heart," I clap back.

"You do, it's just fractured." The reminder that my heart is broken has me clutching the steering wheel tightly until my knuckles turn white.

"I'm not talking about this—"

"It's the anniversary of her death, Xan. This year is harder than the others because Rave is old enough to understand." My shoulders deflate. Rave is Knox and Lakeland's son, he's seven now and named after Riverland and Waverly. They have another son, Axlyn who is five. I thought the fucking name was so stupid until Taylan told me that it was a mix of mine and his together. For the past five years, I have been fighting harder than I have before to find a way home. I miss my brothers and I know I fucked up fourteen years ago doing what I did to Lakeland. I hate myself for that shit and I don't expect her or Knox to ever forget it but I just hope that they can find it within themselves to forgive me enough so I can return home and be with my family. "I'm trying to get him to let you back for the celebration—"

"Don't," I cut in and say.

"Why not?" His annoyance is clear in his tone.

"Because I have a plan and if this shit works I will be home for good. Trust me, Taylan."

"I do trust you, dumbass, why do you think I never cut you off? Between you and Knox you both need to grow the fuck up. I'm sick of being the middle man." Guilt churns inside me. Tay feeds me information about Knox so I know he is okay and I know he does the same for Knox about me. It isn't fair to him but it's the only way we can know the other is alright without Knox breaking his vow to banish me and act like I never existed.

"I know, but I have to go. I'll check in when I can. Hug those boys for me, and tell them I'll see them real soon." I don't wait for a reply before ending the call, talking to Tay is hard and it always makes me homesick. I spend the rest of the drive lost in my thoughts, it's probably a good thing because the hours fly by and I don't even notice it until I pull off the road onto a dirt track that looks abandoned, the weeds that line either side are taller than my car. I slow the car down and lean forward, peering out of the windshield as I creep ahead. The road is long and if it wasn't for the directions from Reid, I would have missed the driveway. It takes me five minutes to finally clear the brush and for the house to come into view. It's fucking small and looks unlived in except for the car that has bullet holes on the side parked out front.

I come to a stop and skirt my gaze, feeling like I'm being watched which sets me on high alert. I reach for my gun discreetly and hold it at my side as I climb out of my car and look around. I spot something moving out of the corner of my eye and spin toward the woods with my gun raised.

"Calm down, Grayson," Trevante calls out as he stalks out of the woods with hands raised. I frown at the sight of him shirtless and wearing basketball shorts.

"What the fuck are you doing in the woods dressed like that?" I snap as I drop my gun to my side not wanting to sheath it in case this is a trap.

He ignores my questions as he answers. "I'm assuming since you found this place my grandfather sent you?"

"You still have to hold up your end of the deal, asshole. I'm not leaving until I have your father's body." A look flickers across his face and I snarl at the fucker. "You renege on this fucking deal and I'll blow a hole in your head," I shout. He stops at the edge of the woodlands but doesn't come any closer. He keeps his arms raised and that's when understanding dawns on me, I snap my gun up and dart my gaze around. "Come out, motherfucker!" I roar.

"You don't want to do that, Grayson," he warns.

"Shut the fuck up, you little rat bitch. Who the fuck is out here with you?" I sneer at the bastard.

He sighs and shakes his head. "She won't come out here, you want to know the answer to that question then you need to follow me but you leave that fucking gun in your car." The warning in his tone is clear, causing me to bristle.

"Why the fuck would I trust you?"

"Because we're both dead if you don't, and from what I have learned, you wouldn't kill *her*."

I jerk in surprise. "Her?"

He nods. "Follow me but leave that fucking gun behind or

you and me will have a problem." His tone is hard and unyielding.

"You're out of your fucking mind if you think—"

"Do as I say and fucking stow the gun away now!" he screams. We stand here glaring at each other for a minute before I relent. I make a show of tossing the gun in the car and slamming the door, then raise my hands, shooting him a dirty look as I round the car. "Ditch the second one, now." I tense, my nostrils flare in anger as I grind my teeth. "I won't allow you to set her back after the progress she has made."

"Who the fuck is this bitch?"

"Someone you won't want to hurt. Now, do as I say, because if you try anything I will kill you." I growl as I turn and toss my second piece through the open window and turn to him.

"Your bitch better have the information I need." I sneer in disgust.

"She isn't mine or yours," he mutters as he turns, leaving me no choice but to follow after him. My senses are on high alert as I keep my head on a swivel and listen for any sign of an ambush. If I wasn't so desperate to kill his father so I could go home, I would never take such a stupid risk like this. Trevante doesn't stop moving until we are in the thick of the forest. I'm about to call him out when he pushes through shrubs that are taller than me. I follow after him and come to a halt at the sight of a... campsite set up in the middle of this tiny clearing.

I look around, two tents, a small fire in the middle, a couple of tables are scattered but it's the sight of the wooden training dummy, bow target and set up of knives on the far side that has the hairs on the back of my neck standing up.

"What the fuck are you doing out here?" I demand. He

slowly turns to face me and the look of regret that flashes in his eyes has me taking a step back and dropping into a fighting stance. "Motherfucker!" I roar as I ready myself to charge the cunt.

"Touch him and die, *Gray.*"

No one calls me Gray, only she did.

I freeze, my body turning to stone. I'm a statue. My eyes track the movement from across the campsite as she slowly comes out from the cover of the trees. My breath hitches, my heart beats over time as she comes closer and everything inside me goes haywire. One second I'm standing and then the next thing I know, I'm on my ass gasping for air as she comes closer and stands next to the fucker in front of me. Her moss colored eyes look haunted and angry. Her hair is short, around chin length and dyed black, she looks like my Wave but... doesn't. I feel like my eyes are playing tricks on me, this can't be real.

"I'll give you two a minute." She shakes her head in response to Trevante.

"No. Him and I have nothing to say to each other, he won't touch you." She looks at me with nothing but hatred in those beautiful eyes. I open my mouth but no words come out. My mind is playing tricks on me, there is no way my sweet Waverly is alive and looking at me like I am nothing to her. She only ever looked at me with love and joy. I run my gaze over her. She wears black yoga pants and a sports bra. I frown at the scar that runs from the center of her breasts and disappears into the waistband of her pants. She shoots me one last glare before spinning on her heel. I make a strangled sound in the back of my throat at the jagged raised lines on her back. Some are fully healed and some aren't, tears fill my eyes at the sight.

What happened to you Wave?

When she tenses and slowly turns back to face me with a deep seated look of hatred in her eyes, I realize I must have said that aloud.

"Waverly died fourteen years ago, Alexander." I flinch at the use of my full name, she only called me Gray or Xander, never my full name unless she was pissed off. "I am nothing to you and you are nothing to me. Run back to my brother and let him know when I am finished with these Irish cunts I'll be coming after him next. Enjoy the time you have left because it isn't long." She doesn't stick around for a response.

"Waverly, wait!" I call out as I climb to my feet ready to go after her but the fucker darts in front of me and blocks my path. "Move, bitch!" I snap as I shove him in the chest, needing to get to my girl.

He shakes his head. "Her name is Doxy, she will never be your Waverly again." I see red and before I know what is happening, I strike out and clock him across his jaw, relishing in the feeling of releasing some of my pent up rage.

Chapter Four

Doxy

Past.

P.A.S.T, four letters that mean nothing until they are grouped together to mean something. Like before, back then, your past is supposed to stay behind you, not crash into your present. Alexander Grayson showing up here was not part of my plan, seeing him again after all these years doesn't stir longing or any type of emotion aside from hatred. The sight of him disgusts me. He has the nerve to look surprised to see me, like I have risen from the fucking dead.

"Doxy?" I turn away from the creek's edge to spot Trevante walking toward me. I raise a brow at the sight of the bruises on his face and the fact he is sporting a split lip lets me know that he and Alexander had a conversation.

"Is he gone?" Trey releases a loud exhale as he comes to stand beside me and shakes his head.

"He refuses to leave. I told him to run back to your brother but he won't go." I purse my lips and nod. I figured the stubborn fuck wouldn't listen, he never did.

"His presence means nothing to me, we stick to the plan," I grit out.

"How the fuck did you learn all of this?" I drop my gaze to the water as I answer.

"I had a lot of time to practice. I shadow boxed in my room." I leave out telling him about watching Knox, Tay and Xander fight for years. Some people learn from doing but I have a talent for seeing something once and then being able to repeat it without issue.

"Why do you want to learn how to throw knives and use a bow? I know you can shoot."

"Because knives and arrows hurt more than a bullet, I want each of them to feel it and writhe in pain before I finally allow them to die. A bullet is a quiet, merciful death and none of these cunts deserve mercy." The thought of those bastards blood coating my hands has me fighting back a moan, it's scary how picturing their deaths turns me on. Because of them, sex means nothing to me, it's a transaction nothing more than that. I turn to Trevante to find his gaze is already on me. "I want to fuck." His eyes widen and he chokes on air as he stumbles back a step.

"I'll die before I let him touch you!" I flick my gaze to the side to see Xander standing there with his fists clenched at his sides and his eyes burning with bloodlust. Anger spurs to life inside me.

"Get ready to burn in hell then," I spit before closing the space between Trey and me. His eyes are wide and he raises his hands as if surrendering.

"Doxy, this isn't a good—" When I grip his cock through his

shorts he sucks in a ragged breath. I smirk when I feel him growing hard in my hand.

"I have a hole, you have something that can fill it—" Before I can push his shorts down he grips my arms and halts my movements. There's a look in his eyes that resembles guilt as he peers down at me.

"You're not a hole, you're not something for anyone to use to get off. You are a person, you have a right to say yes or no, you are in control here, Doxy. If this is something you really want, then let me show you that it can be more than a cock being shoved into the various holes on your body. Let me show that sex can be more than one sided."

The pained sound from the edge of the woods is ignored by both of us. Xander doesn't get to have an opinion on what I do, he isn't the one who came for me, Trey did. He doesn't have the right to know my story and I know without a shadow of a doubt, even though I haven't known him that long, that Trey wouldn't break my trust by telling him what I endured. Trevante shocks me when he releases my arms and cups my cheek tenderly.

"You are so much more, Doxy. You're special and deserve to be treated like the precious treasure that you are." He drops his hold on me and stalks off, leaving me standing here feeling confused and still aroused but when Xander steps in front of me, my pussy shrivels up and quits it's throbbing immediately at the sight of him. Staring at him now, all I see is regret. His brown eyes are filled with remorse and longing, his black hair longer now and strands flop forward onto his forehead. Unlike most girls, I don't have the urge to push the strands back, the only urge I have is to see him suffer and beg me to finally end his miserable life.

"I can't believe you're alive," he whispers as he reaches out to touch me. I step back and shoot him a glare.

"Don't touch me!" I growl. He drops his hand back to his side and stares at me like I'm a puzzle he can piece together. I always see hurt from my rejection. I see it in his eyes how he is trying to find a trace of the person he once knew but he won't find anything. I am no longer her. The person he knew was weak, she was pitiful and longed for the man standing before me to rescue her. She prayed to a God that doesn't exist.

"Wave—"

"Don't call me that!" I snap.

"It's your fucking name," he shouts.

"No it isn't, that weak bitch died over a decade ago." His eyes widen a fraction as his gaze bores into me.

"She wasn't weak, she was strong—"

"She was pathetic and useless. She cried and begged, longed for a savior but guess what, Alexander?" I don't give him a chance to answer. "Her savior never came. He carried on with his life like she meant nothing and accepted the easy answer that she was dead even though they never found a body. He forgot about the promise he made to always come when she needed him. *You* never came because *you* are weak and chose to accept the easy answer that Waverly Bronson was dead." He opens his mouth but I'm not done. "She lived for a couple of years until they killed her."

He darts his tongue out to moisten his lips and swallows audibly before asking, "If she's dead, then who are you, baby?"

I brush off his term of endearment. "I'm Doxy Da Luca and I am going to be the new leader of the SOCG which I will rename the Da Luca Crime Family." His brows raise to his hairline.

"You're taking your father's last name?" The surprise is clear on his face.

"It isn't his, it's mine."

"You're a Bronson!"

My jaw clicks from clenching it. "I will never share the same name as that piece of shit I shared a womb with. Once I take back the Irish I'm going after him. You can run back to him and tell him that he is going to meet his maker soon."

"I'm not leaving you!" he answers without missing a beat and ignoring my threat.

"Suit yourself, your presence means nothing to me."

The next morning I wake to the sound of the birds and smile, another morning means I'm closer to doing what I set out to do. I push the flap of my tent open and step out into the brisk morning air. There's a mist that covers the land, the gloomy sky matching my insides.

"What the fuck!" I snap my head to the side to see Xander stalking toward me. Before he can lay a hand on me, I drop into a crouch and punch him right in the dick. He roars in pain as he drops to the hard ground like a bitch screaming out in pain. I'm panting as I stare down at him.

"Don't you ever fucking come at me like that again," I scream.

"Well done, Doxy, there was no hesitation or pause in your strike. Next time, cock your arm back a half an inch further and you will incapacitate him for longer," Trey says as he comes to stand next to me. I stand and don't offer any aid to Xander as he rolls to his side and rests on his hands and knees panting. It takes him another few minutes before he finally pushes to his feet, the rage in his eyes is clear as he scowls down at me.

"What the fuck was that?" he shouts.

"That was her applying her training, don't ever fucking come at her again like that," Trey warns him. Xander snaps his gaze to him and vibrates with fury.

"She shouldn't be out here dressed like that!" I look down at my white singlet and black panties and frown.

"Why not?" I ask him genuinely curious.

"Your pussy is out for everyone to see and your shirt is see through. I can see your dusty pert nipples." I shrug.

"Everyone *has* seen my pussy, they've fucked it, touched it, ate it, plowed it, ripped it and so much more. I mean come on, Alexander, you've been inside it." His nostrils flare. "Trey hasn't but he has seen it. Sex is nothing but a transaction. Being in clothing is weird for me as I've spent years naked so they had easy access—" He stumbles back a step, shaking his head, a horrified look on his face.

"No. No, stop," he begs.

"Why? Don't you want to know how they fucked me? Want to know how many of them I took in a day?" He clasps his hands over his ears and shoots me a pleading look before he turns and practically runs off. I smirk at the pussy. I turn to Trey expecting to see him laughing but he stands there with a somber look on his face. "What?" He shakes his head and sighs.

"Don't make a joke out of what you endured," he gently scolds before he takes off in the opposite direction of Xander. I don't understand why he cares so fucking much. When I refused to return to the house that first day, he went back into town and returned with all this shit for us to camp outside.

Being in the house where I had walls all around me made me feel trapped, I couldn't breathe. Being out here makes me feel free and in control. Trey never questioned my reasons why, he just set up camp and told me to get a good night's rest because we were going to begin training the next day. Every day since, that is what we have been doing. We train from sunup to sundown. Xander turning up was unexpected and shocked me but I won't allow my past to taint my plans for the future. What he and I shared long ago means nothing to me now, he means nothing to me.

I have five days to work on training and keeping my emotions locked down before we reroute that boat of women and start rescuing my army.

Chapter Five

Trevante

I blew off training with Doxy this morning, hearing her speak about what she went through like that made me sick to my stomach.

Is that what my mother suffered?

I scrub my hand down my face and growl in frustration, Xander's presence here has changed her. It took me over a week to get her to converse with me but the moment he turned up she went from open to closed off and dark. I know there is history there because she has told me a bit about her past and even if she doesn't show it, I can see that he hurt her... badly.

"We need to have a chat." I don't bother to turn or even acknowledge his presence. I'm not in the mood to go another round with this dick because he thinks he has some type of claim over Doxy, he doesn't! He drops down beside me and I can feel the vexation rolling off him in waves, he hates me because she doesn't. "What..." He takes a deep breath and steels his spine. "What happened to her."

I cluck my tongue and slowly turn my head to the side to face him. "That is a question you need to ask her, it isn't my story to tell."

"I see the turmoil in her eyes every time she looks at me. I need you to tell me why." His pleading tone has me wanting to scoff.

"You sit there and act like you have a right to feel wronged when you haven't the slightest fucking clue as to what she had to suffer through for years." His eyes narrow but I'm far from fucking done. "You come here and think you have a right to feel a certain way when you fucking don't. She suffered because you and the rest of her family gave up—"

"I never fucking gave up on her!" he roars.

I push to my feet. He mimics my move and stands before me vibrating with rage but I ignore it as I hold his gaze and speak.

"She doesn't see it that way. I only know very little about what she suffered through. Pushing her to speak only forces her to retreat further inside herself. She feels nothing, her emotions are nonexistent at this point, all she can feel is anger and the thirst for blood."

"I can't allow her to go after Knox," he says ominously.

"Then pack your shit and get the fuck out of here because I'm going after him. The only reason you are still breathing is because it was memories of you that kept my mind occupied while they fucked me." Xander and I both stiffen and slowly turn to face her. She stands there looking like a fallen angel with her hair billowing around her like armor.

"You can't kill your own brother, Wav..." He cuts himself off when she pins him with a hard glare, he sighs as he scrubs a hand down his face before continuing. "Doxy," he whispers. I fight the flinch from breaking free. I hate that she refuses to let go of that vile name but it's her choice. I just wish my mother had her strength.

"I can and I will, you either help me with what we have planned or you can leave. It makes no difference to me, Grayson." He frowns and grits his teeth at her calling him by his last name, it takes him a second to pull himself together before he finally answers.

"What's the plan?"

Twenty minutes later we are all sitting around the campfire. Xander tried to sit next to her but she glared and shoved him off the log before moving to the other side leaving me no choice but to share a log with a brooding Xander who keeps nudging his shoulder into mine. After the third time I finally snap.

"What the fuck is your problem?" His brown eyes swim with malice.

"You are, why the fuck are you even here with her? From what I have gathered it was your father that kept her locked up for years and tortured her—" He doesn't get to finish that, I lurch forward and tackle him off the log swinging at him. He lands a couple hits to my side until I gain the upper hand and pin him beneath me. I cock my arm back ready to break the cunts nose until an arrow pierces the ground by his head forcing us both to still.

"If this shit happens again, I'll bury an arrow in each of your necks and not bat an eye, understand?" I raise my hands above my head and push to my feet. Xander stands beside me and raises his hands as we both face the woman who just handed us our asses and still has her bow raised with another arrow nocked and ready to let loose.

"Sorry."

"Won't happen again," we both say in unison, except we don't mean it because we both push and shove each other, trying to gain the most space on the log as we reclaim our seats. "Move the fuck over," I snarl.

"Close your fucking legs then, you pin-dick motherfucker." I open my mouth to put the fucker in his place but then an arrow lands in the sliver of space between our legs forcing us both to grunt and leap off the side of the log. I roll and stare up at her standing there with a malicious look in her eyes, the fire at her back just adds to the dark look on her face.

"Both of you can sit on the fucking ground. I don't have time for your bullshit. I have a boat to reroute and women to save. I will not allow either of you two pricks to derail the plans I have spent years putting into motion." I can feel Xander's gaze boring into the side of my head but ignore it as I nod.

"I told you I would help—"

She cuts me off before I can finish. "Start by filling this useless sack of shit in on the plan. I'm going to the creek to wash," she spits as she places her bow down against the log and stalks off. The moment she is out of sight, I grab a handful of dirt and toss it at Xander. He curses and climbs to his feet as I laugh at his expense.

"You motherfucker, I'm going to break your neck," he snarls.

"Sit down you dipshit or I'm not telling you anything." He ignores my request and stands there shooting me a death glare.

"What the fuck is in this for you? Why the hell are you

helping her?" All traces of laughter flee me as I claim a seat on the log Doxy vacated and motion for him to sit on the other. He debates my request for a second before he finally obeys and rests his forearms over the top of his thighs and leans forward.

"I don't have a long story or a grand reason as to why I am helping her. I hate my father and want to see an end to his reign." He eyes me skeptically before leaning back rubbing the stubble that coats his chin.

"There's more," he pushes.

"Why are you helping her?" I counter.

"Because I'm still in love with her." His answer is simple and yet it holds so much weight and power to it. "I never gave up on her. Without a body I couldn't accept that she was gone like the others, so I didn't. I never moved on and will never move on from her." I study him closely for a minute. Alexander Grayson doesn't seem like the type of guy who confesses his feelings ever.

"What if she doesn't feel the same?" His shoulders slump and a whoosh of air escapes him.

"She's changed... a lot but I can still see parts of my girl in her eyes. I'm still fucking reeling that she is really here. All I want to do is hold her and chase away the darkness that is clinging to her like a shadow." I nod my agreement.

"I'm helping her because my mother was the original Doxy." Xander can't mask the shock from spreading across his face as he stares at me.

"What does that mean?"

I take a shuddering breath and push away the shame I feel before answering him. "Doxy means... *Slut* in Irish." Xander's features darken at my declaration. "My mother was the first one. Karl only used her until she got pregnant. When the first child was a girl he..." I close my eyes and force the pain away before continuing, "... forced a miscarriage. He beat her until she lost the baby. He got her pregnant again and this time when he found it was a boy he allowed her to carry the baby to term. Once she gave birth, he took the child and never allowed her to even hold her son or heal from birthing before he let his men in to take turns. She survived another five years before she finally lost it, bit her tongue off and choked on it while she was strapped to a bed being raped."

Horror is plastered across his features as he stares at me. "You were the baby." It isn't a question but I nod regardless.

"When I went to Karl's secret cabin the other night, I had no idea that place existed until Grandpa found out about it. When I entered, I found her hunched over a table..." I fight through my anger to get the words out, Xander's face has already morphed into a picture of hatred. "She was being raped. I shot the cunt in the head, another one tried to touch her but stopped when I threatened to kill him. Karl bragged how he had a trump card for years. What I didn't realize was that card was a woman who was locked in that house for over a decade, being abused by Karl and his men every single fucking day. When he told me who she was and what he called her, I knew I had to save her before she suffered through the same fate as my mother."

"They were... fuck!" he roars as he leaps to his feet and stalks off toward the nearest tree and begins beating his fists against it releasing his pent up anger. "Motherfuckers!" he screams so loud birds begin to flee the surrounding trees. "I'll kill every single one of those cunts!" he vows as he turns to face me with blood trickling down his knuckles. I feel the pain wafting off him.

I climb to my feet and close the space between us placing a hand on his shoulder. He flinches but doesn't pull away.

"She wants to be the one to do it, she needs to do it and I am helping her do that. I know my grandfather had other plans but when I tell him about this he will understand." He flicks his gaze between mine for a second before backing up a step and eyeing me warily.

"What do you gain out of this?"

"Nothing. I want Karl gone and that is it."

"With him gone that means you become the leader of the family—"

"It doesn't work like that for the Irish." He frowns so I push on. "Whoever kills the leader claims that spot." His brows leap to his hairline.

"If she kills him..." He lets his sentence trail off and I nod.

"If Doxy kills my father then she becomes the new leader of the Irish that she plans to rename the Da Luca Crime Family and I am going to help her."

"Why?" he pushes.

"Because I've never had any desire to sit on a throne and run things, I like being able to come and go. If she wants it, I'll help her take it from him and gladly kneel before her." His eyes narrow.

"You son of a bitch, you think helping my girl will get you in her pants, don't you?" I scoff and shake my head.

"Was her offer yesterday not sign enough that I don't want her to throw herself at me. I want something more."

He grinds his teeth and forces the words out. "What do you want?"

"I want inside her heart and mind."

Chapter Six

Xander

Sharing a fucking tent with this cocksucker isn't my idea of a good time!

I lull my head to the side and glare at the bastard, he's fast asleep and snores like a bitch. Unable to sleep, I growl in frustration and shove the flap of the tent open as I escape that suffocation chamber. I suck in a calming breath and crack my neck side to side, stretching but freeze when I see a shadow cutting through the tree line. I grit my teeth and race after the bastard snagging a knife from the table as I pass by. When I break the tree line, I come to a halt at the sight of Wave at the creeks edge illuminated by the moon shadow boxing. A smirk tugs at the corner of my lips as I watch her do a right uppercut with a roundhouse combo—that's her brother's signature move.

I sheath the knife in the waistband of my shorts and cross my arms over my chest leaning against a tree as I watch her train. Pride swells inside me when I see her use one of Tay's combos but when she uses mine, pain fills my chest. She knows all our moves but they didn't save her, they didn't stop those cunts from hurting her. Guilt and disgust for myself surges inside me. For years we lived our lives unharmed while she spent years being abused, tortured, treated like shit and thought we had given up on her. None of us ever let her go. I know Lake still refuses to believe her soulmate is gone, she tells Knox all the time she would have felt it if Wave was really gone and maybe there is some truth to that because here she stands before me.

She looks like a warrior queen in her black sports bra and tiny spandex shorts. I didn't take the time to notice before but her body has changed. She's still slim—more toned now—but she has curves. Tired of standing on the sidelines and watching from afar, I make my presence known. She doesn't stop or even acknowledge my presence as I approach. She doesn't miss a beat with her strikes or even her kicks. Without waiting for her permission I move behind her and grip her hips, she tries to pull free but I tighten my hold.

"Let me go before I hurt you, Grayson," she growls.

"Your stance is off, you're losing balance because your feet are too close together."

"Fuck you."

"Right now?" I whisper as my cock twitches in my pants. I will it to remain flaccid, knowing sex is the last thing she would want or need, but the feeling of her pressed against me has my cock ignoring my order and growing hard.

"You want to fuck me?" her reply stuns me for a moment and she uses that to her advantage as she turns in my hold molding herself to my front as I peer down at her. Those eyes, those beautiful eyes used to look at me with love and wonder but now they... look at me with nothing in them. It sucks the air from my lungs, staring at her now is like the soul has been sucked right out of her body. She glides her fingers up my chest sending a shiver down my spine as memories of the past flood my mind.

"This isn't a good idea," I force out through clenched teeth.

"Says who?" she whispers as she rests her hands on top of my shoulders. "Do you have a girlfriend now or something?" The lack of jealousy in her tone pisses me off.

"No."

"Are you sleeping with someone?" I shake my head. I know everyone thinks I was fucking River but I wasn't. Her and I developed some sort of... bond and she just got me. She was fucking Taylan the whole time, even though we all know she was into me and not him. I hated hurting her because I cared about her but I could never bring myself to touch her, it felt like too much of a betrayal to the woman standing in front of me.

"The last person I slept with was... Waverly Bronson." If my revelation surprises her she doesn't show it. She searches my gaze trying to detect a lie but she won't find one. Yes, I have had women blow me but I've never fucked any of them because I didn't want to tarnish the memory of what her and I shared. I'm a cunt but I still have a heart, it just belongs to her.

"Let's rectify that." In a move so bold and unexpected she shifts and grips my cock through my shorts. There's a chill in the wind but right now I feel none of it as heat floods my body and I war within myself to put a stop to this or give in. A moan slips free when she begins to stroke me.

"Are you sure?" I force out and groan.

"I told you," she says as she continues to stroke me. A tremble works its way through me when she cups my balls with her other hand. "Sex is a transaction, you have a cock that can fill my hole and I want it." Her words have me ready to shove her hands away until she releases me and steps back. I eye her skeptically for a moment until she grips her sports bra and peels it over her head exposing her tits. I groan internally at the sight of them. I've jerked off to memories of them many nights over the years. "Touch me."

Like a moth to a flame I do as she says and step forward on autopilot my hands raise and cup her tits, my thumbs flick over her pebbled nipples but she doesn't make a sound. She pushes her shorts down her legs and steps out of my hold once again, the sight of her bare pussy has my mouth watering. She turns away from me and lowers to her hands and knees, my eyes widened. She was never this bold or sure before. She peers back at me over her shoulder and quirks a brow.

"You gonna fuck me?" My mind is reeling but my body isn't. My legs carry me forward and I shove my shorts down my legs freeing my aching cock. Lowering to my knees behind her I grip the globes of her ass in my hands and groan. Before she can do anything I flip her around and lay her flat on her back with my head between her legs. I use the grip I have on her ass to pull her pussy down onto my waiting tongue. Fuck, she tastes just as sweet as I remember. She cries out but quickly clamps her mouth closed and tries to push off me but I tighten my hold and continue to lap at her sweet little cunt. I flick my tongue over her clit and relish in the small whimper that escapes her.

The moment I push my tongue inside her she tenses, rather than stopping and allowing her to get all up in her head I continue to eat her pussy. After a minute or so she begins to loosen up and her body takes control as her hips rock back and forth on my tongue as she chases her release. Now that I know she isn't going to flee, I release her ass and reach around to cup her tits and tweak her nipples—still she makes no sound. The thought is pushed from my mind when her movements become jerky and she starts to stiffen, a second later shudders tear through her and she grunts as she comes all over my face. She pushes off me and I allow it this time. She resumes her position from earlier and rather than asking questions, I shift and grip my cock in my hand lining it up with her entrance, then pause at the sight of the many scars that line her back. I felt them on her ass too. The skin is raised, angry and red. I want to murder whoever the fuck did this to her and skin the cunt alive but all those thoughts flee my mind as I push inside her and groan, still she makes no sound.

What the fuck is going on?

Before I can voice that question aloud she pushes back against me and I'm powerless to stop the hiss from ripping free at the feeling of being balls deep inside her perfect little body again. Gripping her waist I pull almost all the way out before slamming back inside her expecting her to cry out or scream but she makes no sound.

"You think this is a good idea?" I snap my gaze to the side to see Trevante standing there with his arms crossed over his chest and a stern look on his face. I lean forward to shield Wave's nakedness but she pushes against me until her back is flush against my chest, Trey's eyes drink in the sight of her bare skin, I'm about to tell him to fuck off but she cuts me off.

"Put your cock in my mouth while he fucks me." I still behind her, Trey balks.

"He is not touching you!" I snarl. She ignores me as she waves that cunt forward, he stumbles toward her and when he's within arms' reach, she grips his shorts and pulls him closer.

"I don't think this is a good—" His words die in his throat when she yanks his pants down and frees his cock—which is already hard. She says nothing as she wraps her mouth around him. I attempt to move so I can get to my feet and smash his fucking face in but then she begins to bounce on my cock and all thought flees me.

"Fuck!" I grit out as I grasp her hips.

"Doxy, we... should... stop," he forces out but his words lack heat and right now he is just as powerless as I am to stop her. My mind is screaming at me to put an end to this but my cock is loving every minute. I loathe to admit it but watching her suck his cock as she bounces up and down on my own is turning me on. I flick my gaze to him and the lustful look in his eyes is all the indication I need to know he is enjoying this as well. "Fuck, shit, if you keep doing that with your tongue I'm not gonna last," he growls as he fists his hand in her hair and holds her in place as he takes over. She grips his thighs as he thrusts in and out of her mouth.

My turn.

When she rises up on my dick and prepares to lower herself I meet her midway this time and relish in the strangled sound that comes from her. Trey and I find a rhythm as we fuck her. I feel her pussy clenching down on me and groan, fuck I missed feeling that shit.

"She's gonna come," I force out through clenched teeth. Trey quickens his pace and I do the same. A few seconds later she stills and I know she has come because her pussy is clenching the fuck out of my cock, but still she makes no sound. That thought is drowned out when I thrust inside her three more times and throw my head back, roaring out my release. Trey follows behind a second later, calling her name as he comes. Fuck that was intense and amazing but also... not. Something is wrong with her and I hate that it took fucking her to figure out that the scars on her body are not only on the surface, she has bigger scars that run through her veins and we just can't see them.

Chapter Seven

Doxy

I swallow every last drop of cum from Trey. He eases from my mouth and I shift forward without flinching as Grayson's cock slips free of my heat. I say nothing to either of them as I begin to dress. I can feel their gazes on me but I pay them no mind, there is no need for conversation or hugs and kisses. We fucked. Plain and simple. Wearing clothes still feels foreign to me, I have to remind myself daily that it isn't normal to walk around naked. Once I'm dressed I keep my back to them as I continue on with my training. I do a couple of combinations and drop down before flinging my leg to sweep the ground as I spin in a crouch.

"That's it?" I don't stop training as I answer Grayson.

"Yeap." I make sure to pop the '*p*' as I tuck and roll, I don't need them to understand me or what goes on inside my head. I have a goal. I will achieve it and when I do, I will finally be free of all the fucking demons that haunt me.

"Doxy, we should talk about what just happened." I growl

in frustration as I spin around to see them both standing there shoulder to shoulder, eyeing me like I am a caged animal. Alexander looks like he is about to lose his shit while Trevante has guilt written all over his face.

I square my shoulders and meet Trey's gaze as I answer him. "We fucked. You used me and I used you." They both look like I just slapped them.

"That's not what happened!" Grayson snaps.

"I would never use you!" Trey says with such conviction I actually believe him.

I shrug. "Okay, so you didn't use me but I used you both. I'm not gonna stand here and say I'm sorry because I'm not." I dismiss them both as I turn my back to them and continue on with my training. Unlike them, I don't sleep much so I prefer to spend my nights upskilling myself and when the sun finally begins to rise I go to bed. My anger begins to stir inside me when they both cut in front of me, forcing me to halt my movements, so I shoot each of them a glare. "What?"

"You can't tell me you felt nothing?" Trey implores me with his words but I shake my head.

"What don't you get? I don't have to like you or even know you to fuck you. Sex means nothing to me." Trey recoils while Xander stands there with his fists clenched at his sides, vibrating with rage.

"How the fuck can you say that when you have my cum dripping down your thighs?" he snarls. If Alexander Grayson thinks he is going to get one up on me he is out of his mind.

"Because your cum is one of many I have had dripping down my thighs over the years, it means *nothing* to me." He stumbles back with a horrified look on his face. Trevante won't meet my stare and looks down at the grass. "You both need to realize, I am not the girl you spend your life with. I am not going to fall in love and build a family with you... I can't." I clamp my mouth closed, hating that I showed weakness in my tone as speaking about a family and children still sears my insides. Those images are the reason why I don't sleep. Every time I close my eyes, I see what they did to my son and hate myself. They will never understand me, how the fuck could they?

"Why not?" Trey pushes as he slowly lifts his gaze to my face, but before I can tell him to piss off the other dick speaks.

"You will *never* end up with her." Trey shoots Xander a filthy look.

"Why not? She doesn't seem particularly fond of you?" They take a step toward each other, but before they can fight I cut in and end this bullshit.

"I won't end up with either of you because I don't want to. I have no desire to have a home with a white picket fence or a fucking dog and kids running around my yard. I'm not the girl you take home to Mom. I'm the girl your mother warns you to stay the fuck away from." I don't wait for a reply, fucked and needing space, I turn on my heel and get the fuck away from both of them. I have more important shit to worry about than stroking their egos.

Two days later...

Much to mine and Trey's dismay, Xander won't leave. Tonight we leave to head to Belfast so we can intercept Karl's shipment. Thanks to Trey's grandfather and the fact Karl has been robbing his family behind their backs, we have the help of his Clan Chiefs and with Trevante as the Warlord for his organization, he has men on the inside who have sent word that, Mike, Tom, Jones and Aaron will be at the docks tonight. Those four will be crossed off my list tonight. By the end of tonight, I will have crossed seven of the cunts off.

Mike
~~Daniel~~
Jones
~~Lionel~~
~~Jackson~~
Tom
Aaron

"Are you ready, Doxy?" I turn away from the smoldering fire and face Trey. Since living out in the woods he has ditched the suits and wears jeans and plain shirts. The new look actually suits him, but unlike Xander, Trey wears clothing with color.

"Yeah," I answer and stroll past him, ignoring Alexander completely. I can't stomach the sight of him and the way he looks at me with pity. I don't fucking need it. I'm not a victim, I am a fucking survivor and I clawed my way out of that hellhole. I didn't need them to save me, I saved myself!

I refused to ride shotgun, wanting to be in the back so I could keep them both in my sights at all times. Old habits die hard and all that shit I guess. I can feel them sneaking glances at me but ignore them. Tonight is a huge test. Freeing these women is going to be a massive blow to Karl's income. I plan to stop all of his shipments and then burn down each of his clubs that sell these women. Anyone who has purchased from him will die. I will never allow anyone to live as I did, that is a fate worse than death.

"We have to meet with the others before we hit the docks. You okay with that?" Trey asks, breaking the tension-filled silence. I keep my gaze focused out the window, drinking in the sight of the landscape and loving my newfound freedom. So much has changed in the world over the years. They now have scooters that are electric and even some of the cars don't use gas now.

"I'll address them." Their sharp intake of breath has me gritting my teeth. They think because I was tortured and raped for years that men frighten me, they're fucking wrong. Only two men have me doubting myself and that is Ron and Karl. Once I have dealt with them both, only then I will be truly free.

"I don't want to sound like—"

"Shut the fuck up, she said she'll do it and she will." I hate to admit it but I appreciate Grayson backing me up. Knox and Taylan would always treat me like a little girl and worry over shit that would happen but Xander never did. He treated me as an equal and it's nice to know he still views me as that even after knowing what I went through. No one utters another word for the remainder of the drive. I spend that time planning our attack. While being fucked over the desk at Karl's, I spotted the blueprint layout of the ship and the hull where they store the women. I also know the guard schedule and when they change shifts. I plan to make this quick and easy without alerting anyone we are even there.

We pull into the parking lot of a warehouse district. It's dark and looks abandoned but when Trey honks his horn the roller on one of the large warehouses opens and he pulls the car in. My eyes widen at the sight of numerous men milling about with other vehicles parked inside. Before he kills the engine he turns back to me and smiles reassuringly.

"I'll take you to my grandfather first and then you can do your thing." I nod, then step out not waiting for them. I can feel the gazes of all these men on me as I move toward the back of the warehouse without waiting for the guys. If I am to show these men that I am woman enough to lead them, I need to show them that I can do it on my own without needing my hand being held because let me tell you, it doesn't. I feel Xander and Trey at my back. They say nothing as I slow my steps when the men begin to part and I spot an older man sitting in the back on a brown leather sofa with a cigar clasped between his fingers. At the sight of me he releases the smoke he just inhaled and runs his gaze over me, not in a leering way but in appraisal. I stand tall and keep my head held high as I look to either side of him to see five other men seated, they all look to be in their late fifties and carry an air of power with them. Silence stretches for what feels like forever before the older man finally speaks.

"It takes a strong woman with balls of steel to walk in here through all of my men without cowering behind her guards."

I scoff, his brows raise at my blatant disrespect but I push on. "If anyone needs guards it's them." I sneer jabbing my thumb over my shoulder toward Trevante and Alexander.

"One of those guards is my grandson who I am very fond of

and from what I hear, he is fond of you and has given strict instructions that you are not to be harmed." I keep the surprise from my face.

"I don't need his protection," I growl.

"That may be so, but you are in a room filled with men who could easily overpower you." As if to prove his point a guy I spot out of the corner of my eye takes a step toward me. Before he can even blink, I yank the blade from my waistband and have it pressed against his throat. His eyes widen. I take in the sight of him and shake my head.

"You're just a kid," I say quietly. The boy gulps and darts his gaze to the old man waiting for instruction but all he is met with is laughter. Ignoring Trey's grandfather, I focus on the kid in front of me until I feel someone coming from behind me. In a swift move, I grab my other knife with my free hand and press the tip into the stomach of the bastard who tried to rush me. Xander and Trey both begin to shout and fight but they are held back by a half dozen men. Tired of this bullshit I keep both my blades pressed to each of these pricks as I focus back on Reid Solomon. "You want to keep measuring who's cock is bigger or do you want to take out your son?" The carefree look evaporates from his face, then he clicks his fingers and both the guys step back. The boy swallows audibly as he slinks back into the crowd.

The other fucker tries to come at me again but Trey manages to break free and rushes him shoving him backward, then punching him square in the nose. The fucker drops to the ground as Trey whirls on his grandfather.

"She's with me and if any of you try to touch her or even look at her in a way I don't like, I'll slit your throat in front of your mother before I kill your entire family. Fuck around and find out, I dare you." The dominance in his tone has me looking up at him with a brow raised. His chest rises and falls in rapid succession as he tries to calm his anger. Xander breaks free and comes to stand on my other side but unlike Trey, Xander draws his gun and points it at the old man. Chaos erupts and all the men surrounding us draw their weapons and have them trained on us as they shout for both Xander and me to drop our weapons. "Stop this!" Trey shouts at his grandfather but he isn't listening, his gaze laser focused on me.

When he speaks, all the voices around us quiet immediately. "How is a little thing like you going to help rid me of my son without causing a war within my family?"

I don't falter in my response. "Simple. I'm going to take out his operations and then go after each of his inner circle, forcing him to flee and hide. I'll have him thinking that every man he trusts has turned on him, forcing him to run. When he thinks he has run far enough away and is looking over his shoulder constantly without being able to trust anyone, I will take him out and then I will claim his place as the leader of the Irish." Laughter sounds out around us but I pay these fuckers no mind.

"What did my son do to you?" Reid asks. I sheathe my blades in my waistband and grip the hem of my shirt, Xander and Trey try to stop me but I shove them both away as I yank the shirt over my head and turn my back to Reid so he can see all the scars. The sharp intake of breaths around the room is all I need to know that they can all see them. I slowly turn back to Reid and point to the long scar down the middle of my torso.

"Your son gave me all those scars and more on my ass and legs, but this one is my favorite." Reid slowly climbs to his feet with a horrified look on his face, the other five men follow his lead when he comes closer and stops a couple of feet away from me.

"Why is that your favorite?" he says barely above a whisper.

"Because this is the scar I got when they tore everything that makes me a woman out of me when I dared to give birth to a child of their making." Xander and Trey both gasp, I can feel their gazes boring into me but I don't acknowledge them.

"Karl and his men..." Reid can't finish his sentence, so I do it for him.

"They brutalized me, raped me, beat me, treated me like I was nothing but shit under their boots for years. I know everything your son has planned. I'm going to kill him and each of those cunts that took something that wasn't theirs to take." His gaze skirts over my face for a second before he asks.

"Who are you?"

I lift my chin as I answer, "My name is Doxy Da Luca." More gasps and murmurs break out around us. Reid darts his gaze to his grandson for a moment and frowns as he slowly returns his gaze to mine.

"What's your real name? I know that *Doxy* isn't it, I outlawed any type of this shit with women when I found out what Karl had done to Trevante's mother." The anger in his tone is clear and that appeases me.

"Your son has never stopped selling and buying women. He has a shipment of women coming tonight and I plan to set them all free." His gaze hardens.

"What. Is. Your. Name?" he grits out through clenched teeth. Anger spurs to life inside me.

"It doesn't matter who I was before. Your son killed that girl and she isn't coming back."

Chapter Eight

Trevante

The tension throughout the warehouse is tangible, I can taste it on the tip of my tongue. Every person in here is taut and tense, ready to strike in a second. I want to defuse the situation, but in doing so I would make her look weak and the last thing I want to do is undermine her in front of everyone. Call me crazy but a part of me knows that she needs to do this on her own to help her heal. She may not say it but I know being here in a room full of Irish men is fucking hard for her.

"That may be so but if you want my help and the help of my men you will answer my question." She bristles at Grandpa's demand and I can tell from the hard set of her jaw that she isn't going to answer him. In her mind who she was before no longer exists. She views her past self as weak but that's just the anger she is harboring inside herself.

"The girl that died, her name was Waverly Bronson and she was the twin sister to the Don of the Re Della Strada, Knox

Bronson," Xander answers for her. Doxy's shoulders tense when Grandpa's eyes widen as he stares at her.

"Oh sweet fucking Mother Mary," Grandpa grits out as he scrubs a hand down his face and shakes his head. "Lennon, get her brother on the phone—" Before he can finish, Doxy cuts him off.

"No. I am not going back there until I finish this shit here first, then and only then will I go after my brother and claim his empire as my own." Shock ripples through each man in the room at her declaration. It's clear no one expected that shit to come out of her mouth.

"Come again?" Nano asks. He is one of the Captains that has turned against Karl and has dealt with Knox a lot over the years as he tried to keep the peace, but Knox isn't looking for peace now, he wants the blood of every Irish man on his hands.

Doxy slowly tears her gaze from Grandpa to stare at Nano. "If you're too stupid to keep up that's on you. I won't repeat myself when I know you heard me loud and clear. Knox is my next target."

"You want to go after your own kin?" Dexter asks from his place next to Grandpa.

"Yes. He is no kin of mine. He will pay for his sins like every single one of these bastards. I'm tired of explaining myself, I have a ship to meet and four men to kill. Either you will help us and prove you were telling the truth when you said you had no idea what your son was doing or you join the list of names that have to be killed and I save you for last before claiming my position as leader." Grandpa's eyes swim with respect as he stares down at Doxy. I know he meant what he said because I was with him when he began to outlaw the trafficking of women and young girls—what Karl was doing was behind everyone's backs. Most men in this room have daughters, sisters and wives and refused to take part in that shit when it was outlawed years ago. Bishop Murdoch was the one to start putting a stop to the skin trade and over the years many have followed in his footsteps.

"You have a lot to prove to me before you will even be considered as a leader for my people and before you protest, it has nothing to do with you being a woman. It has everything to do with you proving you are worthy of the title over my grandson who doesn't wish to lead." I eye the old man warily, I know how he feels about someone who isn't blood leading our people. He's up to something.

"Even if you don't approve, I'll still take that spot and there isn't a fucking thing you or anyone else can do about it." I can see from the way his eyes crinkle in the corners that he likes her spunk and the way she won't cower to his demands.

"We shall see. Your first test begins now. Explain your plan for the shipment tonight and then I will decide if my men will help you. Fail this test and you won't get another chance." Without missing a beat she begins to explain the plan and I share a surprised look with Xander. As far as the both of us were aware there was no plan, we were going to discuss it when we got here but clearly we underestimated her.

With three hours to kill before we leave for the port, I step outside to get some fresh air. Doxy is with my grandfather and the captains in the back room. To further punish me for not wanting the role as leader he told me to take a walk. The old fucker smiled as he closed the door in my face. The only reason I left her in there is because I know my grandfather won't allow harm to come to her, contrary to what happened earlier. I may not have told him exactly who she is but he knows me well enough to know that I had my reasons for keeping her identity a secret from him.

"I'll kill you if she gets hurt." I lazily turn and spot Xander in the shadows inhaling a blunt. I shake my head.

"You think getting high before a raid is a good idea?" A billow of smoke escapes his lips before he drops the blunt to the ground and stomps it out, then comes toward me, leaving a foot of space between us.

"You think keeping up this nice guy act is going to get you in her pants?" My jaw locks in vexation as I scowl at the fucker.

"You think you know her because you shared a past but you don't, she isn't that person anymore—"

"No, but she will be."

I snort. "You think you're the one to make her see that becoming Waverly Bronson again is the answer to all her problems?" I don't give him a chance to answer. "She will never be her again, if you think for a second that you are the person to make her miss her old life, then you are fucked in the head."

"You think you're that person?" he bites out.

I shake my head. "You and I both know I'm not that person and nor are you. There is someone out there though that will bring her back but until that time comes, I will stand by her side and help her however I can for as long as she will allow me to." Xander presses in until we are chest to chest, his gaze boring into my own as he tries to read me.

"What the fuck are you getting out of this?" he snarls so close to my face I can smell the weed on his breath.

"Nothing–"

"Bullshit. You want something out of this..." He clamps his mouth closed and then narrows his eyes as he presses in closer, pushing his forehead against mine. "You want her." It isn't a question so I don't bother responding because he's right, I do want her and I'm not willing to let her go without a fight. From the moment my gaze collided with hers, I felt something deep inside me come to life. I've never wanted to be tied down or be at the beck and call of another but it seems it didn't matter what I thought I wanted because from that moment of meeting her, I've been willing to change everything about myself and my life to fit in with hers. "I'll never let you take her from me." The conviction he says that with has me believing that he would do anything to make sure he is the one who ends up with her.

"What if she doesn't want you?" I ask.

"She doesn't know what she wants right now," he snarls.

"What if she didn't just want one and wanted both?" He reels back as if I had hit him and looks at me with disgust.

"That shit was a one-time deal, it won't happen again."

I shrug and purse my lips. "Suit yourself, I'm willing to share if it means I get to keep her but if you're not..." I let my sentence trail off.

"You think you can just share—"

Xander is cut off. "No one is sharing anyone!" At the sound of her voice I spin around to find her standing there with Nano, Vaughn and Grandpa, the four of them all stare at us with weird looks, clearly they heard our conversation and I feel like a dick that she overheard us discussing her like a piece of meat we have a right to claim. "Quit thinking with your cocks and get your fucking heads in the game or fuck off." She turns and heads back inside without so much as a backward glance. My shoulders deflate, I just fucked that up.

"So that's why you ordered her to be unharmed." I purse my lips and nod. Grandpa smiles and nods his head. "Very well, the girl will not be harmed but she will be tested,

Trevante, and you will not stop that. She wants to lead, then she has to prove her worth like every other man."

"She isn't a man!" Xander snaps from beside me.

"No, she isn't, which is the only reason why I am open minded about this." I frown at his answer.

"What aren't you telling me, old man?" I ask.

"Time will reveal all, be patient, Grandson, and you may just see the rise of a true queen."

Chapter Nine

Xander

With Knox, I always rode shotgun, that was my spot.

Being reduced to the back seat with Trevante while Wave rides shotgun with that dick Nano grates on my nerves. She shouldn't be here. I keep warring within myself to send her ass back to the warehouse and do this without her but I know she will fight me. For fourteen years I dreamed of her being alive and well and one day seeing her again, but I didn't expect that dream to come true except, she isn't really back. She's still a prisoner of her own mind and a slave to her vengeance.

I know what that feels like, being a prisoner of your own mind is the worst.

I was freed of that burden eight years ago when the truth came out about what I had done the night of Wave and Lake's accident. I was freed but at the same time I lost everything, my family, my home and worst of all, I lost my best friend.

"Stop here," Wave instructs Nano. He does as ordered and

pulls off to the side of the road with the others following behind doing the same thing.

"The ship is already here, we're too late," Nano says with a slight hint of anger in his tone but it isn't directed at the woman sitting beside him.

"No, they won't unload the women until all the cargo has been removed. Karl doesn't have enough pull at the ports since Ian stopped backing him. Once all the workers leave, then the others will come to claim the girls but we'll have already freed them before then." I'll admit, I am in fucking awe of her and my cock is twitching in my pants. Her leading is something I never thought I would see, she used to follow and do whatever Lake did but now, she seems to have come into her own.

"How long before we move?" The hint of respect in Nano's tone has pride bolstering inside me, she earned that shit on her own. I cut a glance to Trey to see the fucker is sitting there with a satisfied smirk on his face.

"As soon as the crane operator removes the last container from the ship we move, the room the girls will be in is in the engine room of the boat."

My face contorts. "Why there? The heat would be suffocating!" I growl. She swivels in her seat and meets my gaze head on with a cold look in her eyes.

"You won't hear them scream over the engines. If they die from the heat then they weren't cut out for this life." The way in which she says that shit like it's just a matter of fact is fucking worrisome, she is more detached from her feelings than I thought. I'm a cold, heartless fucker and I don't care for many people, but she is coming across like she cares for nothing, no emotion.

After ten minutes, the crane finally stops and the final

container is loaded onto the back of a truck. We wait another five minutes before getting out. I frown when I watch her head to the back of the car and pop the trunk. When she returns, she has her bow slung over her shoulder with arrows strapped to her back and a knife on each hip, she looks like a fucking badass. She ties her hair in a messy bun atop her head, then cracks her neck side to side.

"She looks like a wet dream." I grit my teeth at the fucker's comment and try to ignore him as I listen to her relaying orders to the ten guys that came with us. She refused to allow more, saying they would draw too much attention. "She was born for this shit." I hate to fucking agree with the dick, but watching her and seeing her command a group of men without an ounce of fear shows he's right.

"She should never have had to suffer to end up here," I spit out.

"No, she shouldn't have, but going through that shit shaped her to be the woman that now stands before us. She needs us both, Xander." I turn and glower at the bastard but he keeps his gaze ahead. "You may not like it or even want to admit it to yourself but you know I'm right." I don't bother answering because fuck him! When I move to take the lead I attempt to reach for her but she shoots me a scathing look.

"You try that shit again and I will put a knife between your fucking eyes. You follow *me*." My nostrils flare in anger but she doesn't stick around for a response, she takes off down the steep bank with the others trailing after her. Gritting my teeth, I fall into step beside Trey and follow after her.

We're all hiding behind a large container as we wait for the two scouts Wave sent out to return. When they do, they go straight to her, not Nano. She nods to the two guys, then looks at all of us.

"We move quickly and silently, I want these women gone before Karl's men arrive," she says.

"How are we getting them out of here?" the guy to my left asks.

"Peta is bringing a truck, he'll be here in ten minutes," Nano answers. Done with the discussion, Wave takes off with all of us trailing after her, all our heads on a swivel as we cross the open space. As we board the ship, Wave draws both her blades and it takes every ounce of self-control I have not to dart in front of her and take the lead.

"Protect her but stop trying to hold her back." I snarl at Trevante over my shoulder before darting through the metal door after Wave. She doesn't falter in her steps. She's sure and moves with poise like she has done this a million times. How she knows where to go is beyond me. When we finally get to the engine room, I look around but see nothing, she continues on until she reaches the back wall where there is a set of lockers.

"Move this," she demands. Two men brush past Trey and me and shift the lockers out of the way to expose a door with a padlock on it. Wave doesn't ask, she just snags the gun from the guy closest to her holster, turns and shoots the lock, causing all our ears to ring. She hands the gun back to the guy without a word and kicks the door open. The moment she does, we are assaulted by the stench of piss and... fuck, that's definitely shit I smell. Screams sound out but that doesn't deter Wave as she raises her hands in the air, showing she isn't a threat. "We are here to help you and set you free but in order for us to do that, I need you to be quiet and trust me because the man that brought you here has men coming to collect you very soon and believe me, you won't like what happens."

"Why should we trust you?" one of the girls calls out.

She doesn't falter in her response. "Because two weeks ago I was you and now I am standing before all of you trying to save your lives so you don't suffer the same fate I did." Her words seem to be enough for them to trust in her. She steps aside as the girls slowly start trickling out. My eyes widen at the sight of them, they look malnourished and filthy, some of them look deathly ill.

"Follow me but be quiet," the guy behind Trey says. He leads the girls out of the room and they all shakily follow after him. Bile rises in my throat and disgust churns my stomach, how the fuck could someone do this?

"Eight of the girls didn't make it," I hear Wave say to the two guys beside her. "Put the locker back and let's go." Her tone is hard and unyielding, she brushes past us without a glance and races after the girls. Once we make it back to the dock, the truck is already there and the girls are being loaded inside. At the sight of a girl no older than ten I freeze. She's a fucking child and here she is about to be sold to some sick cunt that will rape her all because he has a kiddy fetish.

"Peta will take them back and hold them at the warehouse until we return," Nano says to Wave as she stands back with her arms crossed over her chest, watching the girls with anger in her eyes.

"Once the truck is gone I want this area surrounded. Mike, Tom, Jones and Aaron will be the ones to board the boat. The moment they are inside your men will move in on the drivers," she says.

"What about the four on the boat?" he queries.

"They are going to burn alive for what they did to me. As soon as the men take out the drivers, pull them back because that boat will go up in seconds." I frown at her words but she continues to explain to Nano. "I may have caused a gas leak in the engine room."

"Holy fuck, while we were standing there with our dicks in our hands she was already onto phase two," Trey mutters from beside me. Too stunned to say anything, I just nod.

The moment the truck leaves the dock we all scatter and hide in the shadows or behind containers as we wait. Twenty minutes later a truck and four SUVs pull up. I spy Wave from the corner of my eye, she tenses as men begin to exit the cars and her jaw works side to side. I know without a doubt some of those cunts out there are the ones who hurt her. My blood boils in my veins with the need to skin each of the cocksuckers alive for touching her. I shift but she clamps her hand down on my shoulder. I meet her dark gaze.

"They are mine, you don't get to play hero. You lost that right when you didn't try to find me. I will save myself and kill each of those sons of bitches for killing a part of me until there is nothing left!"

Chapter Ten

Doxy

The moment Mike, Aaron, Jones and Tom enter the boat like I knew they would, they always do the collections because they like to try out the *merchandise* to make sure they are good enough for sale before delivering them to Karl. I nock an arrow and peer around the container, lining up one of the bald-headed fucks with the long beard in my sight. I take a deep breath, then let the arrow go. Warmth spreads through me when I see the arrow pierce the side of his neck. Before a commotion can start my guys rush out of their hiding places and take out the rest of the six. One shot rings out and I curse beneath my breath before racing toward the boat, knowing those fuckers would have heard the shot.

I feel Xander and Trey hot on my ass but they don't try to stop me as I jump onto the boat. I make it to the door in time to see Mike and Tom at the end of the small hallway inside the boat, their eyes widen at the sight of me.

"Doxy?" Mike breathes. I harden my gaze as I look at them.

"Come fight me, baby, you know how much I love it when you fight." I throw their words back in their faces. Before I can say anything else, Xander hauls me backward as Trey steps in front and tosses something inside.

"Rot in hell, motherfuckers," he snarls before slamming the door closed and turning the wheel to lock it.

"Move, now!" Xander screams at me. The three of us run and leap back onto the dock, each of the guys grabbing my arms and dragging me after them. When I hear an explosion behind me and the force of the blast sends the three of us sailing through the air, I know now that Trey threw a grenade inside the boat. I slam against the hard ground with a grunt, only for the air to be knocked out of me a fraction of a second later when those two fucking idiots land on top of me. I grit my teeth and struggle beneath their fucking weight until they shift off me, my body aching as I push to sit up and hiss when a stabbing makes itself known in my side. "You okay?" I nod and grit my teeth as I push to my feet. I've endured worse than this.

The heat from the flames can be felt all the way back here, the three of us were lucky to escape with our lives and have no life threatening injuries. I glance back to see Trey offering his hand to Xander, who stares at it for a second before accepting his help to his feet.

Mike

Daniel

Jones

Lionel

Jackson

Tom

Aaron

With four more names crossed off my list, I turn away from the fire and stalk past both the guys without uttering a single word. I feel like I can breathe a bit easier with seven names marked off my list. Eleven more of the cunts to go and I will be free to return to Canada and start the real war. The guys follow me up the incline where we meet Nano and the rest of the guys, each of them nods their head in a show of respect and for the first time in a long ass time I feel a flicker of... pride.

I push that feeling aside as I slip inside the car and keep my gaze focused out the window. Nano, Xander and Trey climb inside and for the first ten minutes of the drive no one speaks. I'm caught up in my own thoughts and planning my next attack. I vowed to destroy each of these fuckers and their families but I don't know if I can do that after seeing those girls tonight. Ron has two daughters, I doubt they are aware of what their father has been up to in his spare time. If I were to kill each of their families, that makes me no better than them and I am nothing like those fucking cockroaches!

"Those girls you saved tonight." I pull my gaze from the window and look over at Nano, he's chewing on his bottom lip and gripping the steering wheel tight. Unlike Trevante, his accent is thick and I actually enjoy listening to him speak. "What you did for them... you saved them."

I shake my head. "They each would have found a way to save themselves, I just spared them the pain of having to do it."

He cuts a glance to me for a second and I see the argument swirling in his eyes. "No. You saved them, kid, not only did you do that but you also earned the respect of my men and... me." I won't deny it, hearing him say that means a fucking lot considering I have been treated as if I am nothing but a hole to fuck for years. This is the high I have dreamed of feeling for years and it's exhilarating.

I say nothing and focus my gaze out the window. I feel the two guys in the back staring at me like they are waiting for some type of revelation, they'll be waiting until hell freezes over for that shit. I may have felt a flicker of something at Nano's words but that's all it was, a flicker and nothing more. I used to feel everything, constantly worrying about what others thought of me but now, I care for nothing. I was stripped of human emotion. I was made to feel nothing and forced to be a doll who wants for nothing and feels nothing aside from what I was told to.

The scenery passes by in a blur as I'm sucked into my own thoughts, memories playing on a reel as pictures flash through my mind of what Aaron and the others did to me. I remember when Jones, Mike and Tom came to find me when Master was out of the house. Mike and Tom beat me with such brutality that I felt nothing when the guys, Tom and Jones, ran a train on me until Master came home and found them in my room. I thought the pain of the beatings would end there but I was wrong. They were ordered to take me to the basement where I was chained to the wall and whipped.

I tried to remain silent but I failed, I was being punished for allowing the three of them to touch me when Master wasn't home. Those were the rules—they could have me whenever they wanted as long as Master was home. I shudder. I can still hear the sound of the whip sailing through the air, I can feel it tearing through the skin on my back, opening old scars. When I passed out, he stopped and waited until I came to again, then he continued. He never allowed me the reprieve of passing out, he wanted me awake and alert so he knew I would feel everything.

I would take being whipped and beaten over watching what they did to my son. I feel my breathing growing erratic and quickly pull myself from those thoughts. Whenever I get sucked into that black hole I always spiral and right now I don't have time for that, I need to remain strong.

I'm not just doing this for myself, I'm doing it for my son.

As Nano brings the car to a stop inside the warehouse, I see Reid and the other Captains standing in front of us. I don't wait for the others as I climb out and make my way toward the former leader who also happens to be the father of the man that ruined my life. At my approach, a wicked glint enters his eyes. I come to a stop before him with a blank look on my face, I don't need to explain shit. My actions tonight showed what I am capable of and the fact the truck carrying the girls is already here proves I am more than competent.

Reid runs his gaze over me as he strokes the stubble on his chin. I don't fidget under the pressure of his gaze or even when I feel Xander and Trey come to stand behind me, offering their support that I don't need.

"It's not often I'm proven wrong, kid." I refuse to bristle at him calling me kid.

"I enjoy being underestimated, it makes proving you wrong all that much sweeter." A smile tugs at the corner of his lips but I'm not done. "You have my terms and know what I am planning here, either you agree and offer to help or you stay the fuck out of my way because I will not spare you or your men." His brows raise but I don't wait for a response as I cross the warehouse floor. This time the men don't leer at me or say a single word aside from giving a slight nod of their heads in a show of respect.

I find the girls all huddled into the far corner with blankets wrapped around them, their odor gag inducing, but I lived with that same stench for years so it no longer bothers me. All their frightened gazes are on me and I hate that I can see myself in each of them. I know what it's like to be taken and worried you may never see the people you love most again. I would rather be dead than feel how they are feeling right now.

"You all have a choice," I say in a firm tone, I won't coddle these women and treat them like victims because they aren't, they are fucking survivors! "You may return home to your families or wherever it is that you came from." I run my gaze over each of them noting the shock on some of their faces at my words. "Or you can stay here with me and fight to help me end the men that stole you from your homes and planned to sell you to some sick fuck that would have used your body for his own pleasure and tried to destroy your mind in the process." They begin to murmur among themselves for a moment until the girl that spoke to me in the boat stands up. She raises her chin and tries to hide the fear from showing in her features but I see the way her hands tighten around the blanket that covers her body.

"You said you were us two weeks ago, how did you go from this," she says motioning her hands around herself and the others, "to where you are now in such a short amount of time?"

I shrug my shoulders. "I saw an opportunity to escape and I took it, I won't lie. I had some help from... a friend." I can hear

Trey bristling behind me but I ignore him as I push on. "You don't ever get over something like you have been through but you learn to deal with it and move on. For those of you that want to leave, you can, no one will stop you." I peer over my shoulder at Xander and Trevante who both look rigid and pissed off, not at me or the girls but at the situation in general.

"You have our word, no harm will come to any of you," Trey vows.

"You are under our protection now," Xander adds and I can see from the way the girls shoulders lose some of the stiffness that their words have brought them some form of comfort.

"I want my mommy." I cut my gaze to the left where a young girl stands with silent tears trekking down her cheeks—my heart breaks for her. She can't be any older than nine. I crouch down to appear less intimidating and smile at her.

"Do you know where your mommy is?" She sniffles and nods so I push on. "Where is your mommy?" A sob tears out of her, the woman who spoke earlier shifts and wraps the wee child in her arms trying to calm her down as I watch on in horror. How the fuck could any person do this to a fucking child?

"Her mother was one of the ones that didn't make it," a timid voice calls out. I look to the center of the pack and see a frail young teenage girl who has fire in her eyes, that look is one I know well. "I'll care for her," she adds.

I shake my head ready to offer another solution but Trey cuts in before I can. "All of you who are underage will be taken to one of our safehouses where you can recover and we can formulate a plan for what comes next. The rest of you can call your families—"

"Our families are the ones that sold us, none of us wish to

return to them," one of the girls calls out. I grind my teeth so fucking hard they begin to ache, I fucking hate people!

"Then you all may remain here with us where you will receive help and be safe." Hearing that from Xander shocks me enough that I stand and turn to face him. The serious look on his face and the conviction in his tone tells me he means every word.

"What if we want justice against the bastard that brought us here?" I face the teenage girl with fire in her eyes and smile wickedly.

"Then you join me in my hunt to kill each of the cunts that tried to take something from each of us that was never theirs to begin with. I will teach you everything you need to know to survive," I declare.

"I'll teach each of you to fight," Xander adds.

"I'll show you all how to shoot," Trey tacks on.

"And we will all fight alongside you." I spin around to see Nano, Reid and the other Captains standing there with firm looks on their faces. Nano cuts his gaze to me and nods his head. "You earned the respect of my men tonight like I told you, kid. You have my word that we will stand beside you and help you put an end to this skin trade and keep each of these girls safe from harm."

I hear the truth in his words. "Prove to me that you mean what you say by helping me raid his sex clubs and freeing the women there." Nano's eyes burn with an intensity. I see Trey and Xan both smirking at me in awe.

"We take the clubs down as soon as you have a plan, kid." A funny feeling blooms inside me when each of the Captains tip their heads in my direction. I close my emotions down and focus back on the girls and getting them to safety.

Chapter Eleven

Xander

For the past two days I have stood back and watched the woman I thought I knew command men twice her size and not even flinch under the intensity of their hardened stares. Trey and I have both been beside her this whole time, neither of us are willing to allow her out of our sight. She has spent a lot of time with Nano who seems taken by her. I wanted to skin the cunt for getting close to my girl but Trey held me back and told me to watch, so I did.

Nano made formal introductions to each of the Captains and told each of those men that she single handedly freed the girls and blew up the boat. The respect he feels toward her can be heard in his tone. Wave—Doxy doesn't show an ounce of emotion when the men commend her on what she did. She thanks them in a monotone type of way, then goes back to planning with Nano's three head guys—Calvin, William and Brett. Trey and I stay close by and listen in, whenever Trey adds something she will nod and acknowledge he spoke, but if I say something, she shoots me a filthy look and ignores what I have said.

I'm growing fucking tired of this game she is playing and it grates on my fucking nerves each time she speaks to Trevante but blows me off when I say a single word. Since the night we rescued the girls we have been staying at one of Reid's safe houses. The place is perfect. It's an old campground with cabins for each of the girls to stay in and even has room for some of the men. Reid didn't come with us and took all the Captains except for Nano, who remains with Doxy. He's going to England to speak with Ian. I hate that I'm not there to be a part of this talk but given that I have been stripped of all my titles, I am nothing but a glorified pet at this stage.

"We move in on Prime tomorrow night. Donald will be there and I want him alive," Doxy announces to the three guys.

"You have our word," Brett says with a nod.

"No one moves in until I give the order. I want all the girls out safely, no harm is to come to them." Again they all nod their agreement. The conversation stops when Anna enters the makeshift office. Doxy shoots her a hard stare but the girl ignores her, she is only seventeen and seems to have the weight of the world on her shoulders.

"I'm coming with you," she states. Doxy shakes her head and sighs. She may not show any emotion to me or any of the guys but it seems Anna is the only one who can force her to feel something aside from emptiness without even trying.

"You're not ready, you'll remain here—"

Anna cuts Doxy off before she can finish. "Why do you get to call the shots?" Something in Doxy shifts, I see it in the way her eyes glaze over and her left eye twitches.

"Because I know all of them better than anyone else. I call

the fucking shots because I earned it and fought for the right to. You don't know me, Anna. You have no idea what the fuck I had to go through in order to stand where I am. You are not coming with us." The girl opens her mouth to argue but Doxy pushes on. "You want to prove yourself? Then you remain here. We'll return with a prisoner and I will unleash my wrath on that cunt. If you can stomach the sight of what I am about to do, then on the next mission you get to come." The girl's face lights up as she nods happily.

"You got it," Anna says before she quickly exits the room. That girl has the same look of bloodlust in her eyes as Doxy.

"That's it for tonight. Get some rest and I'll brief the others in the morning." Brett, William and Calvin all tip their heads to her before exiting through the same door as Anna. The moment Trey, Doxy and I are alone she turns her back to us and starts rolling up the blueprints of the club—Prime—that we are hitting tomorrow night.

I've had enough of being ignored and can't bite my tongue any longer. "Why the fuck do they get a say in planning this shit but I don't?" I snarl. She drops the stack of papers in her hands and slowly turns to face me with a dark look in her eyes.

"Because none of them have a link to my past but you do." Her words are like a bucket of ice water.

"You think I'm reporting everything back to Knox?" Her eyes narrow at the mention of her brother's name.

"Aren't you?" she counters. Trey the bitch shifts away from me.

"Your brother hasn't spoken to me in eight years."

"Why?" The air whooshes out of me at her question, it's a simple question but one I can't answer truthfully, yet.

"I did something that broke his trust."

"That doesn't explain why you are really here."

I grit my teeth, how the fuck can she not see it? "I was here for Karl's head." Her features slacken at my declaration. "I was going to take his body back to Knox in the hopes of earning his forgiveness."

"What changed?"

Is she fucking dense?

I throw my hands in the air as I close the space between us, forcing her to crane her head back in order to meet my gaze. "You. You changed everything!" The sign that my words have any effect on her is the slight furrow in her brow. "I don't care about your brother forgiving me anymore. I don't give a shit about anything aside from *you!* Can't you see that?"

She purses her lips and studies me for a second before she speaks. "No. I can't see past the need for my vengeance. I can't think about anything aside from killing those cunts. All I want is to watch them suffer before I go after Knox and everyone from my past."

My eyes widen as her words sink in. "I'm from your past."

"Exactly," she sneers without an ounce of remorse. I reach out and grip the back of her neck hauling her flush against me.

"You plan to kill me too, baby?" I say in a husky tone, her eyes fill with lust and my cock twitches in my pants.

"Yes."

I smirk. "Your mouth says yes but your eyes are telling me you want me to fuck you. Which is it?"

"You can fuck me now, take me right here in front of Trey and I promise you it will not sway me from my decision." I hear the truth in her words but I can't allow myself to believe what she says. If I do that then that means I've lost her and I just got her back.

"Is that what you want? You want me to fuck you in front of that little bitch so he knows who you belong to?"

Her eyes burn with indignation. She grips the front of my shirt and pulls me down until we are at eye level. "Fuck me but it changes nothing. I told you, Grayson, sex is a transaction. I feel nothing but the reprieve of some of my pent up frustrations easing after I come. It means nothing to me." I can read between the lines, what she really means is, *I* mean nothing to her.

Fuck this.

I smash my lips against hers, she can say whatever the fuck she wants but I know deep down inside of her that she feels something for me too. No woman can go through what she did and hand their body over to another without trusting them to take care of her and respect her boundaries. She let me fuck her by that lake because she knew I would never hurt her, she only allowed Trey to join in because she wanted to prove to herself that she wasn't in over her head.

Before I can deepen the kiss further she breaks it and steps back. I'm about to protest but when she grips the hem of her shirt and pulls it over her head I snap my mouth closed. The black sports bra she wears looks like it's suffocating her tits. I attempt to step forward but freeze when that fucker plasters himself against her back. He doesn't skip a beat as she peers at him over her shoulder, he captures her lips in a kiss and my first reaction is to break his face but my cock hardens at the sight of her kissing him.

Do I like this?

My train of thought is cut off when he grips her bra and pulls it over her head, breaking their kiss as her gaze remains on him. That pisses me off more than him kissing her. He flicks his gaze to me and I see the want he has for her in his eyes.

"Kiss her." As if my body has a mind of its own I step forward. She swings her head to me and I don't wait for her to refuse me, I seal my lips to hers and moan the moment her tongue invades my mouth. Unlike last time, this isn't hurried or rushed, we're taking our time exploring each other. I feel Trey cupping her tits from behind. I swallow the moan that tumbles from her lips when he tweaks her nipples. "Pull his cock out, baby." I tense at his words not liking him being in control but that thought flees me when she pops the button of my jeans and peels the zipper down.

The moment my jeans hit the floor she pushes my boxers down my legs and I feel my hard cock slap against my shirt. Her dainty fingers wrap around me and I hiss, breaking the kiss. Her eyes are glazed and filled with lust as she strokes me. My mouth waters when she drops her head back to rest against Trey's shoulder as he nips at her neck and continues to tweak her nipples. Before I can get lost in the feeling of her stroking my dick, she drops her hold and turns to face Trey.

He smirks and opens his arms wide allowing her control over what happens next. She grips the waistband of his sweats and pushes them down his legs, dropping to her knees in front of him. He strokes her cheek with the backs of his fingers and moans when she grips his cock.

"Suck both our cocks, baby," he growls. She reaches and grabs my cock. Using her hold on my dick, she pulls me forward so Trey and I stand opposite each other, his eyes slam closed and he flings his head back, groaning when she wraps her lips around him. "Fuck, all the way, baby. I want you to swallow me as far as you can." She obeys him without complaint, her hand continuing to work my dick and I bite down on my lip to keep from groaning but the moment she releases him with a wet pop and takes me into her mouth, I lose the battle and groan.

"Fuck your mouth feels so good," I praise as she continues to bob her head up and down on my dick while stroking Trey with her hand. I cut a glance to him and see he's watching her and the way his eyes darken at the sight of her gagging on my cock gets him off. Before I can get too lost in the feeling of her hot wet mouth, Trey grips her hair and pulls her off my dick, her gaze swinging to him immediately.

"Stand." She does as he commands and it pisses me off. "Lose your pants." She quickly rids herself of her yoga pants and panties, the sight of her bare pussy has me nibbling on my bottom lip. "You're going to bend over the desk, sit on my face so I can eat that perfect little cunt while my boy fucks it." I stare at him in... I don't know, awe I guess because the way Doxy's eyes light up changes everything. She's getting off on him commanding her. Trey releases her and sits down, resting his back against the desk. She comes forward and folds herself over the edge of the desk, he grips her legs and places them over his shoulders then grips the globes of her ass pulling her onto his mouth. She cries out and fuck it's the most beautiful sound I have ever heard.

I plant my feet either side of Trey's legs and line my cock up with her entrance. I jerk back when I feel his tongue accidentally lick the tip of my cock. He pauses his movements but before I can dwell on that shit, I push inside her, loving the cries that tear from her as I slowly push inside her inch by inch.

Fuck this feels like home!

Chapter Twelve

Trevante

I suck her clit into my mouth as Xander slams the remainder of the way inside her, she throws her head back and screams out. I look up to see him wrapping his hand around her throat and forcing her back against his chest where he meshes his lips against hers. The sight of him pulling pleasure from her gets me fucking hard, my cock is aching to be balls deep inside her tight little body but I don't think she is ready for both of us yet. She breaks the kiss with Xander and turns to peer down at me with a wanton look in her beautiful eyes.

"I want you inside me." I feel Xander begin to pull out but she pushes back against him holding him there as she peers over her shoulder at him. "I want *both* of you inside me." Xander's brows raise in surprise as he looks down at me.

"Got any lube?" he asks.

"Top draw on the left," she answers. I free myself from my position and locate the lube in record time while Xander continues to fuck her. I pause and watch the way he grips her hips and growls every time he slams deep inside her tight little cunt. "Fuck," she grits out, I can see from the strain on her face that she is close to coming. I open my mouth to tell him to stop but he pulls free of her and turns her to face me.

"Toss me the lube." I do as he says, then stalk toward Doxy. Her eyes drink in the sight of me and I relish in the way she licks her lips at the sight of my cock. Without hesitation I grip her waist and lift her, her arms and legs locking around my neck and waist. She reaches between our bodies and lines my cock up with her pussy. I hold her stare as I inch inside her, loving the way her breaths quicken. The moment I am fully sheathed inside her tight wet heat we both moan, fuck she fits me like a glove. "Open her ass for me."

I do as Xander says and grip her ass, parting it for him. This is all new to me but truthfully, I would be willing to try anything for her. The first experience I ever had with a threesome was in the woods with them both. He presses against her back. I've done anal before and I know it takes women a long time to adjust and prepare for a cock in their ass so I ease my thrusts and wait for her to give the okay.

"Fuck!"

"Doxy!" Xander and I both roar in unison when she slams down onto both our cocks. She moans while the both of us try to regain some semblance of control over our bodies. I've never seen a woman take a dick in the ass like that and fuck me if it isn't the hottest goddamn thing I have ever seen.

"Fuck me!" she orders. Xander and I lock eyes and I get what he is saying without words, he wants us to fuck her into submission and force her to feel something. I nod my understanding as I lean back and kiss her. Xander hooks his arms under her knees and forces her legs open, fuck, he's opened that pussy right up for me and it feels fucking amazing. It takes us a minute to find a rhythm and when we do, euphoria overtakes us. She alternates between kissing me and him. Xander and I watch as she kisses each of us because the sight of her touching the other turns us both on and gets us off. "Keep going, don't fucking stop or I'll kill you both." A fine sheen of sweat dots my brow as I fight off my orgasm needing her to come, I see Xander gritting his teeth trying to do the same. Fuck, I won't last. I reach between us and place my thumb flat against her clit as she continues to bounce up and down on both of our cocks. The moment I press harder against her, she throws her head back against Xander's shoulder and screams both our names as she comes. I follow her over the edge a fraction of second later, then Xander comes just after I do.

That was the most intense fucking sex I have ever had!

I place a chaste kiss to her lips and smile reassuringly before slowly pulling out of her. I grip her waist and hold her steady as Xan slowly eases out of her. She doesn't flinch or show a speck of emotion but I gave Xander my word, she will feel something tonight, I'll make sure of it. She attempts to get free of my hold but I don't allow it.

"Come on, no one is in the house," I say as I lead her from the room with Xander on our heels. The three of us are naked but I don't care. I drag her down the hallway after me and enter the Master bedroom she has been sleeping in, but frown at the sight of the bed with the bouquet of flowers I placed there still in the middle. I purse my lips but say nothing as I lead her into the adjoining bathroom. Xan brushes past and steps into the shower. Doxy looks from him to me in question. "Get in the shower, I'll be back soon."

"Where are you going?" I smile as I cup her cheek and place a kiss on her forehead.

"That shower isn't big enough for three, baby, I'll use the one across the hall." I leave her standing there with her mouth slightly agape. I know Xander needs this time with her and if this *thing* is to work between the three of us, then they need to get on the same page. I interfere with their shit but if I can offer them some time alone to work through whatever *it* is, then so be it.

I make sure to take my time in the shower, giving them as long as I can before I return because make no mistake, I will fucking return. There is something about her that calls to me and I know Grandpa thinks it's because she was in the same situation as my mom but that isn't the case. I can't even explain it really, I feel drawn to her almost like a rope is pulling me toward her and the further away she is the tauter the rope becomes and I won't allow it to snap. I've hidden myself away from the world for too long. I buried myself in work and trying to find ways to take out Karl so we would all be free of his reign, but I've never truly lived. I've never really felt alive until meeting her.

Stepping out of the shower, I dry off and find a clean pair of sweats from my bag and pull them on before exiting the bathroom. The moment I enter the hallway I freeze at the sound of their shouts.

"You know nothing, Alexander!" Doxy screams, I can hear the anger in her voice and that seems to be a default setting for her when he is around.

"Then tell me! How can we go from fucking fifteen minutes ago to you hating me?" Xander shouts back. I shake my head. Him pushing her to feel something for him and not allowing her time to process through her own feelings is going to backfire. Yes, we want her to feel something but not for us, I just want her to feel in general.

"I've already told you, sex means nothing to me! You want to go outside and fuck me in front of all of those guys, then do it. Them seeing me getting dicked changes nothing. Do you know how many men have fucked me while others watched?" I clench my fists at my sides and try to reign in my temper, hearing about her past kills a piece of my soul. Fourteen years she was my father's pet and I never fucking knew. If I had pushed harder or followed him one night I could have saved her from years of pain!

"No one will ever get to see you in that position again aside from me *and* Trey." Being included by Xan means a lot. I know this is new and weird for the both of us considering I licked his dick unintentionally but hey, I'm not mad about it.

"Being in that position isn't something I fear, I stopped caring about who saw me fucked a long time ago. It was around the time I stopped praying that you, Knox and Taylan would rescue me." She pauses for a second before pushing on. "Actually, I think it was around the time that I got pregnant and gave birth." At this revelation I storm down the hallway and kick the door open. They both swing their gazes to me. Doxy stands there wearing only Xander's shirt while he wears a pair of low-cut jeans and nothing else.

"Where is the baby?" I snap. Her eyes harden and a black aura begins to surround her as she starts to shut down in front of me. My breath hitches as her eyes take on a faraway look like she is reliving a memory, a dark fucking memory.

God, I would give anything to take away that look from her face.

WARNING!!!!
YOU WILL NOT MISS ANYTHING SIGNIFICANT
ABOUT THE STORY IN THIS CHAPTER.

TRIGGERS

Infant loss
Maiming of an infant's body
Death of an infant
Forced to watch as the infant is maimed

This chapter is not crucial to the story but it is
highly detailed in explaining the traumatic birth
and brutalization of the infant.

Chapter Thirteen

Doxy

Trevante stands there, staring at me with a pain filled look in his eyes and it triggers my anger to flare to new heights. Who the fuck do they think they are to stand there and judge me or demand answers about what I have lived through!

"Dead." I answer in a tone void of all emotion, they will never understand the scars that mar my insides after the loss I suffered. There is no coming back from that and I will fucking destroy each of those bastards that had a hand in taking my innocent child from me.

"What happened?" Xan asks. I scoff as I face him.

"What? You want to know the story about how I had so many men ravish my body like they had the fucking right, only for one of them to get me pregnant and kill my baby?" His eyes darken and his nostrils flare as he locks his jaw.

"Yes. We want to know everything," he answers.

I laugh but there is no humor to it. "Buckle up, boys, this is going to fuck you up and make you squeamish," I announce. I close my eyes and force my emotions to remain locked in the cage I have kept them in all these years. I've never had a single soul to tell or confide in about what happened to my sweet little boy.

I feel the pain radiating all over my body and grind my teeth to keep from crying out as I cover my swollen belly—internally I'm screaming for them to stop and take out their anger on me and not blame my child. They say that they will never allow me to sully their DNA by creating a child with me. I'm nothing but white trash, American scum, they are Irish royalty and I'm beneath them. That all may be true but my baby is none of those things.

I'm terrified to give birth here and I have spent months worrying about what will happen once I do give birth. I made sure to keep Master happy and not anger him or risk facing his wrath since learning I was pregnant. None of these fools realized I was with child but I did when I missed my period. I hate each of these disgusting pieces of shit but this baby is a gift and I will not allow whoever its father is to tarnish my baby.

"That cunt will die, I'll never allow you to give birth to my heir," Fin spits out as he stomps on my ankle. I scream out when I feel the bone break but I refuse to move from my fetal position knowing that the second I do, they will hurt my belly.

"Fuck, we need to move. We have another shipment of bitches to bring in," Donald says.

"We'll be back, you fucking bitch, and when we do, that

mutt will die," Nolan sneers. I remain silent as they leave and don't breathe until I hear the lock click.

"Argh," I whimper when I stretch out, pain radiating through my body but I compartmentalize it. I've gotten so good at that since being here. I run my hands over my belly in worry, I push and prod trying to rouse the baby to move. Normally it takes a few minutes for bub to reboot after I take a beating, then the baby goes back to kick boxing inside me.

Hope of my baby being okay flees when I feel wetness between my thighs, I grit my teeth and ignore the pain in my ankle as I open my thighs.

"No," I whimper when I see blood, frantically beginning to push on my stomach. "Come on, please, please, please. God, please don't do this," I beg. "You're okay, Momma is here and you're going to be okay. Fuck, please be okay!" Tears trek down my cheeks and I don't care. I know there are cameras in here and Master will be able to see me being weak but fuck him, because I know where the blind spots are now and use them to my advantage.

I cry out when a stabbing pain makes itself known in my lower back. I arch forward trying to alleviate the pain but it does nothing. I breathe through it as best I can but when the next wave of pain shoots down my spine, another stabbing pain hits me in the gut, tearing a scream from me. Sweat begins to coat my skin and I know what's happening but I refuse to admit to myself that those cunts caused me to miscarry and now I am being forced into preterm labor.

"Please... not my baby," I grit out through clenched teeth as I push myself back to lean against the cold concrete wall. The pain in my ankle is nothing compared to the pain ricocheting through my battered body.

The agony is never ending, I'm so tired and exhausted. I'm only aware that a significant amount of time has passed because I can hear the sound of footfalls above me indicating that they are back and will no doubt come down here to let off steam. When another pain in my back hits me, I bite down on my lip to keep quiet but this one is different, I feel pressure and the urge to push overtakes me. I grunt as I bear down and push with all my strength. I do this four times before I cry out in panic when I see a head between my legs. Another contraction hits and I push with everything I have, reaching down and grabbing my baby gently before they hit the ground.

I shakily turn their little face to me and cry out, it's a boy!

He's so tiny, too tiny to be born.

My heart fractures inside my chest as I rub my fingers over his chest and try to blow into his mouth, praying to anyone who will listen to save my beautiful baby.

"Come on, mommy's here, come on, baby, breathe," I beg of my son as I press two fingers against his chest and blow into his mouth trying to revive him. His tiny body is limp in my arms but I don't stop until I feel another burst of pain but this one isn't as bad as the others. I push and stare in horror when the placenta expels itself from inside me. More time passes and I finally face the fact that my sweet sleeping boy was too good for this world, God clearly needed more angels and he took the best one from me.

I hold my little boy close to my chest and place a kiss on his tiny head. Tears flow freely down my cheeks.Tthere is a lump so large in my throat but I know if I allow the sounds I'm fighting to keep inside me out, they won't stop.

"Take momma with you, I don't want to be here without you," I whisper. I close my eyes and lean my head back against

the wall, smacking it against the wall a couple times as I bite down on my lip to quieten my cries. "Take me, please, don't leave me here without my baby," I beg, plead, fuck, I even pray to the fucking Devil to drag me to hell if it means I don't have to live in a world where my son doesn't exist.

My blood turns to ice when I hear the lock on the door click. When the door swings out to reveal Master, Nolan, Fin and Donald, I keep my son clutched against my chest as I use the wall and my good foot to help push me to stand. The pain in my ankle is nothing compared to the pain in my heart. I run my gaze over each of them when disgust, hatred, and the need for their blood to coat my hands overcomes me. All four of their gazes are trained on the small innocent child in my arms. I snarl. They have no fucking right to look upon my son.

"I'm going to kill the four of you last, the others are pathetic and will die quickly but you four, I will drag it out. The only other to join you sorry sacks of shit will be Ron. I'll kill each of your children and end your family line. You will feel the pain I feel, I swear it."

The four of them exchange a look before laughing at me like my threat means nothing. I swear to Christ almighty that I will kill them all before I leave this fucking wretched world!

"Take the mutt and chain her up, she will be taught a lesson," Master snaps. I tighten my hold on my son as Nolan, Fin and Donald come toward me.

"Don't you fucking touch him!" I scream. When they are within reach, Donald cocks his arm back and punches me in the face. I fall to the side dazed and seeing spots. Before I can register what is happening, Fin kicks my son out of my arms. I scream out and try to crawl to my baby but Nolan holds me back by my hair as I watch in horror as Donald picks my son by his foot, smirks at me, then swings my baby's tiny body against the wall. I scream so loud. They all stand there laughing as I watch them hit him against the wall again and again until his body is practically mutilated. I remain on my knees numb and fucking empty unable to do anything aside from watch them defile my son. The worst is when they finish and toss his body on the small wooden table in the center of the room. Master steps forward and turns his head to face me as he pulls his gun from his waistband.

I sway back and forth, exhausted and just fucking defeated. I wish he would turn that gun on me and end all of this.

"You will be punished for this act of defiance, Doxy," Master growls.

"Kill me, please just fucking kill me," I plead. Laughter sounds out around the room but it cuts off when he pulls the trigger and I watch my little boy's body jolt from the impact of the bullet.

Chapter Fourteen

Xander

I stand here feeling broken, devastated, angry and... I can't even explain how I feel after hearing that.

"You want to know the worst part, they tied me to that table and raped me beside my son's lifeless body. They didn't care I had just given birth, they took me harder than they ever had but the worst was Karl, rather coming inside me he pulled out and jerked himself off and came all over my innocent baby's corpse. For three days I was chained to that table forced to stare at the decomposing body of my baby boy. I can still smell his rotting flesh and every time I close my fucking eyes I relive that night."

"Doxy–"

She cuts Trey off before he can finish. "The other's families will not be harmed but I will kill Donald, Fin and Nolan's sons," she vows. Trey closes the space between us and comes to stand beside me.

"And what about Karl's only living heir, will you kill me too, Doxy?" he asks.

She doesn't miss a beat. "No, unlike the other three's sons, you don't appear to rape women but make no mistake, if I have to use you to get to your father, then I will. I feel nothing because I have lost everything."

I run my gaze over her and take in the way she is looking and then it hits me. "You haven't complained once since we have fucked you about us not using a condom because they did more then take your son from you, didn't they?"

Her eyes burn with a look I can't decipher. "Yes, the day they came and removed my son's body from the room they had a team of doctors and nurses. They had a surgery performed and removed all my reproductive organs. I can never have children." I stumble back a step as Trey gasps and attempts to reach for her but she bats his hand away. "I don't need your fucking pity!" she roars.

"What do you need then?" he asks her.

"Revenge," she snarls before she storms out of the room, slamming the door behind her. Trey tries to go after her but I hold him back.

"Let her sort through what's in her head alone for a minute," I say as I release him and drop down onto the edge of the bed, covering my face with my hands. I'm man enough to admit I'm fighting back fucking tears. I wanted all these Irish fucks dead for fucking with the Re Della Strada but after hearing what Wave has gone through, I want to drag it out. I want to play with them and make them scream!

"She stopped being Waverly Bronson after her son died." I snap my head up and look at Trey. He looks dazed out and caught up in his own thoughts as he stares at the wall.

"What?"

He slowly turns his head to me with the same dazed look in

his eyes. "She became Doxy Da Luca because in her mind, Waverly Bronson died the night her son did." I stare at him in shock, is that the real reason she has stopped being Wave?

"How do you know?" I mutter. He shakes his head as if to clear his thoughts and focuses back on me.

"If you had to witness what she did would you not be wishing that God would kill you too?"

"I don't believe in heaven and hell, once we're dead that's it"

"Don't ever say that shit in front of her!" he scolds.

I glare at the fucker. "She knows how I feel about that shit."

"Yeah, well start changing how you feel about that shit because she had a kid, Xander, a fucking baby that was murdered. She thinks if she dies now she will get to be with her son. You are not going to take away that hope of being reunited with her son from her, do you hear me?" I mull over his words for a minute and nod my head stiffly. If she needs to cling to the hope of an afterlife to get her through then so be it. "We should go find her."

I follow after him but remain lost in my own head, unable to think of anything else aside from what she disclosed. What she went through would break most men, fuck that shit would break highly trained soldiers. How the fuck she still finds the will to live is beyond me.

Trey and I search for her for nearly an hour, returning to our cabin tired and pissed off, Trey follows me down the hallway and when I push her room door open I pause in the threshold, the bedside light is on but no one is in the bed. I creep further into the room with Trey right on my ass and the both of us still at the sight of her asleep on the ground in the corner of the room with no blanket or pillow and only wearing my shirt.

Fuck!

I turn to Trey to find a horrified look on his face. He came to the same conclusion as I did. She's mentioned bits and pieces about her time with that cunt and one of the things was never being allowed to sleep in a bed. Ever since we arrived, I could tell the bed was untouched but never paid it much thought until now.

"I'm gonna kill them all," he grits out through clenched teeth. I grunt my agreement, they will all die painfully and slowly for what they did to her and her child.

"If you harbor any feelings toward your father or have an issue with what is going to happen to him, you need to leave now because he won't make it out of this alive. I give you my fucking word on that."

He's quiet for a moment as he moves around the room and snags a throw blanket from the end of the bed and gently lays it over her. I motion for him to follow me out of the room and lead him into the kitchen where I grab two beers from the fridge and offer him one. He nods his thanks before taking a long pull. I do the same and down half the fucking thing, if there was anything stronger I would be shotting that shit. I place my bottle down on the counter and level Trey with a look. He sighs and runs a hand down his face.

"I have no reservations about Karl dying or the end of the SOCG."

"Then why take so long to answer?"

"I may be okay with him dying but if I'm being honest I have always hated my father, which is why I don't legally have his last name."

I whirl around and level him with a stern look. "What the fuck is your name?"

"Solomon? Trevante Kane. I changed my name when I was old enough to do so, I refused to have his last name and took my mother's as a way to honor her and also, it was my way of saying fuck you to Karl and letting him know that his name and legacy will end with him and not me." I take a long look at him and honestly, I respect the hell out of him for being honest with me.

I decide to share something with him in return. "Knox never knew I was dating his sister until eight years ago." Trey snaps his head back and stares at me.

"Why?"

I shoot him a dry look. "She's his baby sister and in his eyes, no one would ever be good enough for her."

"Why risk your friendship with him?"

I smile sadly. "You've met her! She is worth risking everything for. I love Knox and Taylan, they are my brothers and always will be..."

"But you love her more," he finishes for me.

"Yeah."

"He found out, didn't he?"

I nod. "Yeah, eight years ago."

Trey frowns. "But she's been gone for longer than that."

"I know. I never told Knox about me and Wave because I knew it would push him over the edge. The night we thought she died she called me. I went to help her and her best friend but she wouldn't get in the fucking car. I begged her to come with me and promised I would send Knox back for Lake but she's so fucking stubborn just like him. By the time I got to her it was too late, the car was hanging over the side of the bridge and..." I clamp my mouth closed as memories of that night play out like a movie in my mind. I lost it when the car went over and I heard her screams. I ran Lake down like she was nothing and then jumped in after Wave.

"Are you going to tell him she's alive?" His question pulls me from my thoughts.

"I won't lie, I've thought about calling him numerous times."

"What stopped you?"

I exhale loudly and take another swig of my beer before answering. "Her. If I go to her brother and tell him she's alive, he'll come for her and right now I'm hoping that her taking out Karl and the others will help lessen her anger toward her twin."

"Go to Knox." Trey and I both turn toward the entryway to see Wave standing there in a pair of jeans and a form-fitting tank top. The angry glint in her eyes tells me she has heard most of our conversation.

"No. I won't do that."

She cuts me off before I can finish. "It wasn't a request. I know rumors are circulating and after we take out his club, those rumors will reach him. I want him to know it's me coming after each of these cunts so he can be prepared for when I come for *him*..."

"I'm not leaving you," I say firmly.

She shrugs. "I'm taking this club and then going after the others before taking Karl. You have three weeks to warn him or I take him out blind. I'll be the ghost of his past that he never saw coming."

"You want to fuck around with someone's head, fuck with mine not his," I bark.

"It's not your head I want to fuck with, Grayson, it's your cock." I stand here stunned as she saunters into the room, and stands before me with her gaze locked onto mine. I see the lust swirling in the depths of her gaze. Sex is a coping mechanism for her, I see it plain as day now. She uses her body to distract us and herself.

"You want me to fuck you right here, baby, on this counter?" My words have her eyes growing hooded.

"No, you're going to stand there and watch as Trey fucks me on this counter so you learn that I don't care what you do. Run back to my brother or don't, what you do means nothing to me."

Chapter Fifteen

Trevante

If Xander thinks for a second that I am strong enough to deny her request, he's a fucking fool. My cock is already hard at the prospect of fucking her while he watches.

When she rounds the counter and stands before me I don't falter in my actions, I grip her waist and hoist her up until her ass is perched on the edge of the counter. I push my way between her thighs, grip the back of her neck and pull her to me so I can claim her lips in a kiss filled with raw passion and need. She moans into my mouth. I growl my approval before breaking the kiss and ridding her of her pants. She spreads her legs for me and the sight of her perfect pink pussy has my mouth watering.

"You get to call the shots out there, baby, but in here, we rule." Her pupils dilate at my decree, I flick my gaze to Xan and see him standing there with a stiff jaw and clenched fists at his sides. I would love nothing more than to fuck her alone and I will one day but not now, I need to make this work with him in order for the three of us to see if whatever this is will work out. "Get on your knees and taste her dripping cunt." His eyes narrow at my order but the small mewl that comes from her has him obeying.

Xan lowers to his knees in front of her, she has her gaze locked on to his but I'm not having that. "Eyes on me as he eats that cunt, baby." She snaps her gaze to mine and I relish in the sight of her need reflecting my own.

"Fuck!" she cries out before clamping her mouth closed and swallowing her own moans. I know why she doesn't make a sound when we have sex. I hate that she thinks she will be punished for making a noise.

"I want to hear every sound, baby, you stay quiet and he stops. Do you want to be left on edge all day?" Xander pulls back and winks up at her, her mouth is slightly agape as she looks between the both of us.

"You know there are a lot of willing cocks just outside that door, right?" she snaps back. Xander growls and I laugh.

"If you really wanted their cocks inside you, you would have done it already. Lie to everyone else, baby, and even your-self but Xander and I both know the only cocks you want inside that tight perfect little pussy are ours." Fire swirls in her eyes and I see her nipples hardening through her shirt. "You keep quiet, he stops and then you suck both our cocks so we can get off, then if you're a good girl, we might fuck you tonight just to ease that ache between those perfect thighs." She darts her gaze from me to Xander a couple of times before finally settling on me. I see the triumphant look on her face and sigh. Xan and I may not agree on much but when it comes to fucking her, we're both on the same page.

"You gonna let him make the rules or you gonna be a man

and fuck me like one?" Her taunt has Xan rising to his feet and staring down at her. I move in until I'm standing shoulder to shoulder with the fucker.

"That's cute. You're trying to play us against each other but it's not gonna work. Now lose the fucking top, I want to see those tits." Her nostrils flare and her anger spikes but she's too turned on to deny us. She peels her shirt off over her head and fuck the sight of her tits has me licking my lips. Xander pops the button on his jeans and frees his cock then wraps his arm around her waist pulling her forward until her ass dances on the edge of the counter. "I'm going to fuck you and then he's going to fuck you. You gonna be a good girl, baby, and take our cocks?"

Xan grips himself and runs it through her slick folds, she throws her head back and moans. "Yes, I'll take them, now fuck me."

She doesn't need to tell him twice, he slams inside her, drawing a loud scream out of her that has me pushing my own pants down and stroking my dick. Doxy wraps her arms around his shoulders and locks her legs around him, pulling him in closer so she can take him deeper. Xander's thrusts are punishing as he fucks her, this isn't about pleasure this is a fucking reminder, he's showing her with his body that she belongs to him.

The sight of his cock disappearing inside her cunt has me moaning. Fuck, watching her milk him and cry out each time he hits that sweet spot inside her has pre-cum practically dripping out of me. I force myself to release my dick and stand here and watch this like a man. I want nothing more than to come with them but I refuse to do that by my own hand.

"Grayson." She looks horrified that she spoke his name and

it fucking destroys me that even during the peak of her emotions where her body and mind should only be focused on the pleasure she is getting, she's still thinking she's done something wrong based on the trauma she has endured.

"Scream my fucking name as you come all over my cock, baby, I want everyone to know who can make you scream." As if his words are her undoing she comes screaming his name, fuck. Seeing her come was hot but hearing her scream has my cock aching painfully to be inside her just to hear what she sounds like screaming my name. Xander comes a second after her, roaring out her name.

"Wave!" She tenses but before she can get lost in her own head, I shove the fucker out of the way, ignoring his protests as I push a finger inside her. She arches her chest into me and moans. I pull my finger free and bring it to her lips. Her eyes widen a fraction but she obeys without having to be told. She sucks my cum-covered finger and moans.

"Kiss me, I want to suck him off your tongue." She lurches forward and smashes her lips to mine. Fuck, tasting him and her together has me groaning. I inch forward and line my cock up with her pussy and push inside her. I shudder loving the feeling of his cum inside her tight little cunt. She breaks the kiss and stares into my eyes as she moans.

"That feels so good," she whispers.

"You like my cum inside you while he fucks you?" She flicks her head to the side to look at Xander and nods. "Take all of him like a good girl and he may just let you come again." I pull almost all the way out of her before slamming back in, the sound of her cries are like a balm to a battered soul. I can't take my eyes off her, she is perfection. She's never looked more beautiful then she does now, naked and clinging to me. Her eyes beg me to give her the euphoric bliss that her mouth refuses to ask for. I feel her pussy clamping down on my dick and know she is on the edge of another orgasm. Reaching between us I pinch her clit between my fingers as I stare deep into her eyes.

"Come for me, baby," I whisper.

"Trey!" she screams out as she detonates and comes on my cock like the perfect thing that she is. This time there is no horrified look on her face. I seal my lips to hers as I slam inside her three more times. I try to break the kiss but she holds me in place, swallowing my roar as I come inside her perfect little cunt that is still milking me for all I am worth.

It takes me a minute to calm down enough to ask. "Are you okay?" She frowns and purses her lips.

"Yeah?" She sounds troubled that I would even ask such a thing. I gently ease out of her and already hate not being inside her. Xander the mother fucker shoulders me out of the way like I did him, and before I can utter a single word, he pushes two fingers inside her drawing a shocked gasp from Doxy.

"You got to taste me, now I want you to taste both of us." My eyes widen as he pulls his fingers free and holds them to her lips. She opens without needing to be prompted and sucks them, flicking her gaze between us both and moans. "You like that, baby?" he asks as he slips his fingers out of her mouth.

"Yes," she answers without hesitation. "I was planning on going to work out but now, I think sexercise is the best work-out." Xan and I share a look before focusing back on her. "You both got to fuck me, now I'm going to fuck you and this time, I'm calling the shots, boys."

My cock is rock fucking hard again already!

After going another three rounds with Doxy and the sun rising we all decided we needed carbs before continuing the marathon. The room is trashed, we destroyed pretty much everything.

"The mattress is on the ground, so technically it isn't a bed," Xan tries to reason with her as I cook breakfast.

"Leave it alone, Grayson."

"No. If you won't listen then Trey and I will be sharing the room with you and your ass will be in the middle so we know you are on a fucking bed of sorts. Don't argue with me over this!" She grinds her teeth and shoots him a look that would have a lesser man bowing their heads in submission. She huffs out her annoyance and stamps across the kitchen toward me. I raise my hands in surrender about to tell her I had nothing to do with whatever that was but she grips my shirt, yanks me down to her and kisses me! "Real fucking mature, we can both play this game."

She breaks the kiss and turns to face Xander with an evil glint in her eyes. "You said I can't touch anyone else but the both of you so same rules apply—touch another female and I'll slit your fucking throat." Xander gapes at her and honestly, if the two of them arguing means she takes out her anger on my dick then I'm not opposed to it at all.

Doxy refuses to sit next to Xander so I'm forced to sit between the pair of them and if the hostility wafting off each of them is anything to go by, this raid tonight is going to be bloody. I can barely swallow over the tension that is choking me. My elbows are plastered to my sides not wanting to touch either of them in case it sparks another round of fighting. Xander got over her kissing me but when she tried to blow me as I stacked the plates, he lost his shit and even accused me of loving this. I'm man enough to admit that I shot him a smirk and leaned back against the counter ready for her to suck me off until the fucker shoulder checked me out of the way and dragged her to the other side of the room.

"Doxy?" The three of us snap our gazes toward the doorway to see Calvin standing there.

"What is it?" she asks as she pushes back from the counter. I can tell from a glance at Xander that not being the one in charge is new for him as well and taking a significant amount of strength from the both of us to remain seated and allow her to conduct herself.

"We got word that Ron will be there tonight." I see the muscles in her back tense up and that is the only indication she gives that she is affected by his words, her face is a picture of rage.

"Donald and Ron are to be taken alive, the rest can die," she says in a cold tone. Calvin reaches back and rubs his neck shooting her a sheepish look. "What?"

"The men won't listen to me, I have no rank so I think it may be best if they hear that from you directly." The way in which he speaks and looks at her with respect goes a long fucking way in my book.

"Let's go," she clips out as she leads him from the room. Xan and I sit here and watch her leave. I can't help but smile, the day we fled Karl's house she was a mess of nerves and I could see the anxious energy swirling in the depths of her eyes but now, all you see when you look at her is fierce determination.

"I'm gonna make her need us," he vows from beside me.

"She doesn't need anyone, all she needs is herself."

"No." I face him and quirk a brow. "She does need us, she doesn't want to admit it to herself."

"So, you do agree there is an us?" I say, trying to lighten the mood. Xander pins me with a deadpan look.

"The fact you licked my dick should be enough clarification for you." Laughter booms out of me as he shakes his head and mutters about me being an asshole.

Chapter Sixteen

Doxy

Breaching the club was easy, no man ever pays a woman any mind or thinks she is plotting mass murder. All these pigs see is a sexy woman in skimpy clothes who they hope to fuck by the end of the night. Ignoring all of their stares, I head straight to the back, making sure to keep my head down so I'm not spotted on the cameras. Once I hit the back of the club, I tap the earpiece twice so it activates.

"I'm in, heading to the girls now," I say. Trey, Xan and the other men are all surrounding the building, I refused to rush in here guns blazing and risk one of the girls being caught in the crossfire.

"Keep your head on a swivel, they would have marked you from the second you entered that building," Xander says through the coms.

"You have three minutes tops before they come looking for you, cameras or not. It is unusual for a woman to enter those clubs freely, move your sexy ass now," Trey adds. I ignore the idiots as I maneuver my way down the dimly lit hallway. There are no guards which doesn't surprise me. They have beaten all of these women into submission and rule them by fear, and there is no escape from this part of the building, only the front door and the fire exit behind the bar.

I hear soft murmurs behind the second to last door on the left. I pause and listen closely and when I hear only female voices, I push the door open only to be greeted by a horrific sight. I draw my gun without hesitation and raise it, his surprised gaze is latched onto mine.

"I have Donald and the girls, move in now and secure their exit." Donald grips the girl's hair who is on her knees with his cock in her mouth and shoves her aside. He doesn't even bother to put his pathetic cock away before taking a step toward me. I flick the safety off in warning.

"I wondered where you got to, Doxy," he purrs, making me feel sick.

"Take another step and I'll put you down," I snarl, the cunt just smirks and wags his eyebrows as if he thinks I'm joking. That is the only warning he'll get from me. The second he lifts his foot, I fire the first shot. The girls all scream and rush to the back of the room where they huddle together as I close the space between me and Donald, loving the sight of him on his knees and clutching his shoulder where I shot him.

"You fucking bitch—" He doesn't get a chance to finish. "Argh!" he roars so fucking loud as I fire a second shot.

"Keep it down, Donald, you're going to alert everyone to the fact I just shot your little dick off." He tips his head back and stares up at me with tears in his eyes. He looks like a pathetic little bitch, whimpering because I shot his baby dick.

"Why?" That one fucking word has every ounce of anger I

have buried inside me rushing to the surface. A haze overcomes me and I guess I must have blacked out because when I return to my senses Trey and Xan are there, pulling me off Donald. His face is unrecognizable and covered in blood. I see patches of blood covering his arms, chest and legs and frown. Looking down to my hands that are covered in blood I spot the knife clutched in my grasp and frown.

When did I pull my knife?

Darting my gaze back to Donald, I notice that his cheek is sliced and his eyeball on the left side hangs loosely against his cheek by the muscles. When Xander and Trevante release their hold on me to go and check on the girls, I crawl forward until I'm kneeling beside his lifeless body. His one eye that is open is bloodshot and filled with terror. That look sends a delicious shiver down my spine, his mutilated body brings a dark smile to my face. The stab wounds that litter his body fill me with a sense of strength I didn't know I possessed. I close my eyes and take a deep breath savoring this moment.

I waited years for this feeling.

"Waverly!" I snap my eyes and pin Xander with a glare for using that fucking name, he knows better but the longer I look at him I frown. He looks... worried. "Don't look at me like that, I've been calling your name for ages and you were zoned out. We need to move now. Calvin and the others have rigged this place to blow in five minutes."

I nod and tear my gaze from his to look down at Donald again, for years he terrorized me and enjoyed every moment. "That was for my son, you piece of shit. May you rot in fucking hell until I get there, we'll meet again motherfucker but next time, you won't die quickly." I sneer in disgust then spit right in his face. Xander grabs my arm and drags me to my feet before pulling me after him. I spot Trey waiting for us at the end of the hall with a concerned look on his face.

"Later, we need to move now," Xander snaps. Trey nods and then falls into step behind me as we rush through the club. I look around in surprise at the bodies that are scattered around the floor. Blood coats every surface, the sight of the carnage brings a warmth to my body that feels euphoric.

Once we arrived back at the cabin, Trey and Xander tried to get me to shower but I brushed them off and went in search of the girls that are currently congregated in the makeshift hall in the center of camp. Men scramble to get out of my way and bow their heads in respect, I earned that shit! For so many years I wasn't seen, if someone did notice me I was seen as an object, something for them to play with. I was nothing, meant nothing and no one respected or gave a shit about me.

William sees me approaching and nods his head with a smile and opens the door for me. I don't stop until I stand in the middle of the hall. All the women from the boat stand around the room looking at the new lot of girls. There are eighteen of them total that we saved tonight but it's not enough! There are so many of them left trapped out there forced to surrender their basic human rights, they are no better than fucking stray dogs!

Not anymore!

"Stop looking at them with pity!" I shout. All the girls from the boat drop their gazes to the floor. I notice that the newcomers keep darting their gazes to the back of the room and that's when I spot the guards. "All of you, get the fuck out now."

I keep the shock from displaying on my face when all of them leave without question. It still shocks me that my word is valued and respected here, that is going to take a long time to get used to.

"Did you just flex your lady dick, D?" I scowl at Anna, the girl is a pain in my ass. She laughs and comes to stand beside me leaning in slightly to stage a whisper. "You have two shadows behind you." I sigh, I may be able to get the others to leave but something tells me that I can't shoo Trey and Xander away that easily. I slowly turn to face both guys, both their gazes are trained on me and the fact they each have their arms crossed over their chests and a *try to fucking get rid of me* look on their faces tells me they aren't going anywhere.

"Don't make us refuse your order in front of your girls." My brows draw in at Xander's words, they aren't my girls, they are free women and should be able to choose for themselves.

Turning back to the girls, I run my gaze over all of them. The boat girls seem less edgy than the club girls but they all still hold that skeptical look in their eyes like they are waiting for me to turn on them and call all the guys in here to take turns on each of them.

"They need you to guide them, D." I stare at Anna out of the corner of my eye, she has a hard look on her face. She reminds me so much of me in the way, she shields her emotions and doesn't allow you to see past what she wants you too.

"I'm not their keeper," I grit out.

"No. But you are their savior, Doxy. Our own families sold us to pay a debt. We didn't have a loved one coming to our rescue, we had *you*!" Her words wash over me like a balm. I never set out to save these girls so I could become their hero. I never had that type of complex, that was Riverland's thing to save people, not me.

I push away the memories of my past and lock down all my emotions as I address the girls.

"You're all getting a choice, you can either wallow in your self-pity and allow it to eat you from the inside out or, you can rise above the injustice of what you have suffered and claim your vengeance. A lot of you have been through hell—"

"You have no idea!" I snap my gaze toward the club girls to find a raven haired beauty with piercing green eyes glaring at me. I watch as she slowly climbs to her feet, her hands are clenched at her sides. "You think you can relate to us because you have a pussy?"

A chuckle escapes me. Anna whistles between her teeth knowing I'm about to put this girl in her place.

"Every hole on my body was used a lot more than yours ever will be, trust me on that one, little girl. I can relate to each of you because I was their toy for over a decade. I was beaten, raped, treated worse than an animal and still managed to get free of them and stand here before you all. I didn't have a loved one to come to my rescue, my family all believe I died and for that, they will pay once I dethrone this Irish piece of shit." The anger that laces my words can be heard. "I'm offering you all a chance to help me save other women like us, help me give them the same freedom you have all been given. I want to break the fucking chains these cunts have placed on us. I know we will never truly be free of our demons and I for damn fucking sure have a first class ticket to hell when my time is up but I won't cry about that shit. I'll smile as I look the fucking Devil in the eyes and tell him how I killed every motherfucker that thought they had the right to touch me."

"You're not gonna... put us to work?"

I shake my head at the blonde girl who is crouched down next to the raven-haired girl who is still glaring at me. "No. If you want to work then you can train with my men each morning, learning how to defend yourself. No man here will lay a finger on you unless *you* want him to. You have my word that if any of them harm you, I'll have the fucker walk the line and each of you will be able to claim a piece of his flesh for a trophy. If you wish to leave and return to your families then you can. All I ask is that you keep this location quiet and hidden so the rest of us may put an end to this tyrant once and for all."

"I want to learn. I want Callahan to pay for hurting me. I want to do what you did to that man tonight," one of the club girls called out. I keep my face blank and take a breath trying to control myself. I feel Trevante and Xander creep in closer, the warmth from their bodies seeps into my back and I fucking hate to admit it but knowing that they are here and have my back helps soothe something inside me.

"What Doxy did tonight is something we cannot teach you," Trey announces to the girls.

"But, we can teach you how to channel your pain, aggression and hatred for these men so you can use it against them," Xander adds.

"Why the fuck would we ever take you at your word?" This raven haired bitch is starting to work my last fucking nerve.

"Because we're here for *her*, we will do whatever it takes for her to get her revenge. Unlike those fuckers that wanted to hurt you, Trey and I don't want that. We will remain here with all of you because we care and because I love Doxy." Xander admitting that shit aloud doesn't make my stomach flutter with butterflies or make me giggle like a schoolgirl, they are just three meaningless little words.

"You have a choice, a choice I'm sure no one else will grant you. You can return home to the people that sold you like you were cattle or you can remain here with us and fight. Like Xander said, he and I are no threat to any of you, we only see one woman and she is the badass you are all currently glaring at and judging. You think because she stands before you, strong, brave and ready to fight for what she believes is right that she hasn't suffered. Let me tell you all something, no one's trauma will ever be the same and that is okay but do not diminish hers because you can't see her scars or bruises. Put your trust in her and I swear on my life you will be thanking her for freeing you from the cage you have all placed yourselves in. Now, be brave like her and break free." Trevante's words hit home with each of the girls, I see it in the way their features change as they regard him.

He's even inspired some type of hopeful feeling inside me.

Chapter Seventeen

Xander

"Anna!" I boom across the training yard. The little shit turns to me and glares before releasing her hold on Kimber, the raven-haired girl that still refuses to speak to Doxy even after being here for two weeks.

"What?" the little shit snaps as she pushes the strands of her brown hair from her face, murky brown eyes spitting fire. We found out she is only sixteen and her father was the one to sell her. She is Italian and her father owed a debt to the Irish he couldn't repay so that is why he sold her.

"No fucking weapons! This is sparring and you've already maimed three of our fucking men!" I snarl as I close the space between us and offer Johnson a hand up from the ground. The poor fucker releases my hand once he's on his feet and clutches his side where she stabbed him. "Go get that shit cleaned up." He nods and stalks away but not before shooting Anna a filthy look. The little shit just smiles and wiggles her fingers at him.

"Stop bringing a knife to training. You do it again and the next time you spar you'll be fighting me," I warn her.

"Seriously?" The gleeful tone of her voice has me fighting not to groan.

"No." I spin around to see Doxy and Trey standing there. Ever since the night we brought the girls back from the club, she has shut me out. She speaks to Trey but in single word responses. She even ditched us for a whole day to go and get tattooed. None of the men would help us go after her and it was then we knew for sure that these fuckers are loyal to her alone. Nano was the fucking one to drive her there. Her arms, back, sternum and the back of her thighs, fuck, even her ass is tatted. She tried to play off their importance but Trey and I know, she got them in those places to hide her scars. We may fuck every night and morning but there are no emotions involved, she literally uses mine and Trey's cocks to get off and then that's it. Most guys would be okay with a chick that doesn't do attachments but not me. I can see it is starting to get to Trey as well. "You bring a knife to a spar again and you will be fighting me, Xander has a flight to catch." I jerk back in shock and dart my gaze to Trey. He and I are kind of friends now so he shoots me a look that tells me I won't like where she is sending me.

"I'm not going anywhere—"

She cuts me off before I can finish. "Your plane leaves in four hours, your bags are packed and loaded into the car. Tell my brother I'll see him real soon." I stand here like a fucking idiot as I watch her stalk off without so much as a backward glance.

"I tried to talk her out of it but she wouldn't listen to me." I roll my lips over my teeth and nod. "If it helps, I booked you a return flight?" I shoot him a side eye that has him smiling. "Look, I know we aren't exactly besties or anything—"

I snort. "What gave it away?" I deadpan.

"The fact you're such a cuddly teddy bear that likes to share his toys." I shake my head and smile at the asshole's comment as we make our way toward the cars. "I'll watch out for her. I'll call you tonight after the raid. I swear I won't let anything happen to her." I must be a fucking idiot because I believe him. I come to a stop beside the car and face Trey, holding my hand out to him. He flicks his gaze from my hand to me, then knocks it out of the way as he hugs me. I stand here stiff and feeling fucking weird, I may see his cock as often as Wave's pussy but that doesn't mean I want to touch the fucker. I push him back and shoot him a warning glare that has him laughing. "I licked your dick once and you're acting like I want to do it again."

"Do you?" I blurt out.

"It has crossed my mind." I balk at the fucker, it takes a second before laughter bursts out of him and I grit my teeth.

"Watch out for her and call me," I clip out as I climb into the back seat, leaving the bastard standing there laughing at my expense. I rest my head back and close my eyes. I haven't been home in eight years. Knox was clear, if I was to return home he would kill me and somehow I don't think Wave would shed a tear over my loss. I hate that she is pushing me away. She has no fucking trouble talking to Trey but when it comes to me, she detaches herself and turns fucking cold.

I lull my head to the side and gaze out the window, I hate that I have to fucking leave her. The fact I have to put my trust in Trey to keep an eye on her and keep her safe grates on my nerves. I just got her back and now I'm leaving her behind, again.

"Turn the car around!" I shout.

"What?" Paul says.

"Turn the fucking car around and take me back to her, now!" I roar. I can see him debating my request so I pull my gun and press the barrel into his temple. "Do it now." He growls his displeasure but does as I say. The second we get back I don't wait for him to come to a full stop. I leap out and race inside our cabin, following the sound of voices and storm into the kitchen. The moment I enter they all go silent and face me.

"Xander?" Wave looks shocked at the sight of me. I cross the room, grab her face and kiss her not caring that all her men can see it. I break the kiss and rest my forehead against hers, we're both gasping for air.

"You want your brother to know you're coming, then you call him or text him but I'm not leaving your side, do you hear me? I'm not fucking leaving you again." A flicker of emotion passes through her eyes briefly before she snuffs it out. Fuck, I hate when she hides how she is feeling.

"You disobeyed an order, Grayson," she grits out.

"Then punish me but I'm not leaving you," I vow.

"We need him for the raid tonight, Doxy. He's got a skillset none of the others have. He is an asset to this mission and with him here I can guarantee that we will get in and out without any casualties." Pulling back I look to Trey, slightly awed by the fact he isn't pissed I'm back. He looks happy to have me here... that reaction is fucking unexpected.

"Fine," she clips out before turning away from me to face the others. "We raid the two clubs tonight, I want all the girls out alive and safe."

"Some of the girls want to come tonight," Brett announces.

She shakes her head. "No. They aren't ready for this. All the men are named that I want alive and brought back here. They can get their revenge on them," she declares.

"Karl won't be there tonight," Nano says from his perch on the arm of the sofa.

"I know. Once we raid these two clubs he's going to go underground and stay hidden." She turns to face Trey and me and an uneasy feeling begins to churn in my stomach. "The both of you will go after Karl while we—"

"No!"

"We do this together!" Trey and I both say in unison.

Her eyes darken. "You will do as you're fucking told. Bring me Karl alive. If he goes underground it will be months before we find him and we don't have that time."

I cut a glance to Trey who looks just as confused as me. "Why don't we have time?" I ask.

She lifts her chin and meets my gaze. "The Murdochs, *Memento Mori* and Godfathers have aligned themselves with my brother. The Re Della Strada is planning on invading Ireland and I won't allow Knox to step foot inside my turf."

I reel back. "Why the fuck are they coming after us?" I snap.

"Calvin managed to get word from one of his guys inside Karl's circle. Karl placed a call to the Don of the US and told him he was under attack. The dumb fuck thinks that they will come to his aide, they aren't coming to help, they are coming to overthrow Karl and take Ireland." That is not what I expected to come out of her mouth.

"You want Karl and his operation to shut down quickly so you can go to Canada." I think out loud but then it clicks, I scowl down at her. "You were never sending me back to Knox, you were testing me to see if I would run to your brother or prove my loyalty to you!" I grit out through clenched teeth.

She shrugs her shoulders, not caring that her test hurt me. "I had to know if you were loyal to him or me, turns out I was wrong and you aren't as attached to my brother's side as I thought." My mouth parts but no words come out.

"I told you he wouldn't betray you, Doxy, he is loyal to you, not your brother." I cut a glance to Trey and grind my teeth.

"You knew?" I growl. He at least has the decency to look sheepish.

"I told her it was a bad idea but she wouldn't listen. I'm sorry."

I tear my gaze from him to look at her. "When will you see that I am fucking here!" I roar. "I never left you, Waverley, I never gave up on you."

"Yes, you did!" she screams.

"Leave, now!" Trey barks at the men who quickly obey him.

"No, I didn't. I tried to find you for years, I never gave up hope."

"You found me by pure luck because you and Knox had a little fight and he kicked you out," she taunts.

"No. He banished me because I ran his wife down the night your car went over the bridge which resulted in her losing her memories and miscarrying their kid," I spit before I turn on my heel and flee.

Chapter Eighteen

Trevante

I could feel the tension radiating off of her in waves, she hasn't been able to calm down at all since Xander dropped that bomb on her about her brother's wife. I hated having to leave her to go on the raid without us but she won't even speak to me now either so I had no choice. Xander hasn't spoken a word since we got in the car and headed in the opposite direction as Doxy and the others. William got a tip that Karl is hiding out in one of his downtown apartments.

It's clear Xander pissed her off because she has only allowed us to take three men with us, who follow close behind our vehicle. I need to clear my head but it's fucking hard, I know Karl needs to suffer and die but as much as I hate him he's still my father at the end of the day. I've spoken to Doxy and told her I wouldn't stand in her way but I also couldn't be a part of her torturing my father. Grandpa has also agreed not to intervene as long as when she is finished with him she would hand over his body so he may be buried in our family cemetery.

No one has any idea what she has planned for the men that she is bringing back but I can imagine that they will be suffering for a long time.

"You should call her brother," I say, breaking the tension filled silence.

"Why the fuck would I do that?" he bites back.

"Killing my father is one thing but killing her twin, her own blood, that is something she can never recover from."

"You want to warn him, go ahead but I'm not." The bastard even hands me his phone as if taunting me and trying to call my bluff. I shoot him a dirty look, then snatch it from his hand and scroll through his contacts. I'm about to hit dial on Knox's name until a thought hits me. Before I can talk myself out of it, I scroll up and click the name before bringing it to my ear.

"Who the hell is this?" she answers after the fourth ring.

"My name is Trevante Kane." I can feel Xander's eyes on me but ignore him.

"Is that name supposed to mean something to me?" I smirk, this girl is ballsy and I like that.

"No, I guess not but believe me when I tell you this, Mrs. Bronson..." Xander snaps his head toward me and I hold up a finger and shoot him a look to remain silent. His jaw locks and he grips the steering wheel tighter but remains silent. "There is a purpose for my call and you won't believe me—"

"Spit it the fuck out, asshole."

"Your best friend is alive, Lakeland." I end the call just in time to see the headlights shining through my window. "Watch out!" I shout but it's too late, the car ploughs into us and sends us spinning, the airbag smacks me in the face and has me seeing stars. My head is throbbing and feels like it has a drummer playing to the beat of a Slipknot song.

146

"Trevante?" Xander calls out, then coughs, I can hear from the tone of his voice he's hurt. I open my mouth to answer but snap it closed when I hear gunfire. "Fuck, can you get out?"

I clear my throat. "Yeah."

"Good. Get the fuck out and run." I push the airbag out of my face and turn to face him, my eyes widen at the sight. We crashed into a power pole and the steering wheel is pinning him in place. I dart my gaze to his.

"I'm not leaving you." He grits his teeth and fights through the pain.

"Fucking go, Trey. This was an ambush and if they get both of us then she is alone, again. Fucking leave me and go!"

"She told me about that night on the bridge, I feel like we are reliving her deja vu." His eyes harden and his nostrils flare.

"Just go."

I nod my head and shove his phone in his pocket before reaching and pulling his head to mine. He grunts in pain. "I'll come for you, Xander. I swear to God, I won't let her lose you again. I'll come for you without her if I have to, brother." His eyes fill an emotion I can't decipher.

"Tell her I love her—"

"Tell her yourself when I get you back," I snap as I shove my door open and grunt in pain. I quickly pull my gun and begin shooting at the fuckers as I run. I feel like a fucking pussy for leaving Xander behind but the thought of Doxy thinking we both left her kills me. I can't allow her to think someone else abandoned her when the both of us are fighting for her, we're fighting with her to rid herself of those demons in the hopes she will finally be able to let us in. "Fuck!" I grit out as I round a corner and duck down behind a dumpster. I can see them at the end of the alley. I pop the mag out of Xander's gun and praise fucking Jesus for him being an anal bastard and reloading before we left.

"I know you're around here, Solomon!" I slam my eyes closed and grit my teeth at the sound of his fucking voice, he's baiting me. "I'll tell ya what, Son, I'll let you go so you can rush back to scrape what's left of your whore off my club floor." Panic flares to life inside me. "Yeah, I know about the raids, boy. I hope the explosions tore her apart!" Dread spurs to life inside me, he knew.

We have a fucking rat!

"I'll keep Xander safe. When that whore is ready to return home and come to heel like the Doxy I raised her to be, then you know where to find me, boy."

"Boss, we need to move. We just heard over the scanner that the cops are coming." I hear one of Karl's guys say to him.

"See you soon, boy," Karl calls out. I should have come out and shot him but I knew it was a trap. He had more men than us—fuck! I push to my feet and wait another couple of minutes before checking to make sure they have all gone before running back to the car in the hopes they didn't get Xander. I run around to Xander's side and punch the roof of the car.

"Fuck!" I roar just as Xan's phone begins to ring. I pull it out of my pocket without checking who is calling and answer it. "What?"

"You listen to me, you little cunt, you ever call my fucking wife again and spit some bullshit—" My brows hit my hairline.

"Knox?"

"Who the fuck are you?" he snaps.

"Xander was just taken by Karl, he is going to use him to lure your sister—"

"You keep my sisters name out of your fucking mouth, you

cocksucker, or I'll fucking kill you! You tell Karl I'll see him real fucking soon." He ends the call.

"She'll see you sooner, dumbass," I mutter as I race back to the car that was tailing us. When I only spot two bodies I grit my teeth, we definitely had a fucking rat!

I break every speed limit known to man as I drive like a madman through the city. I can see the smoke over the old buildings and hear the sirens. My blood is pumping so loud in my ears as I panic, I can't lose her. I just fucking found her and I won't allow Karl to take another woman I love from me. He murdered my mother and I refuse to allow him to hurt Doxy any more than he already has. The car screeches as I round the corner and slam on the brakes. I jump out, ignoring the cops and firefighters yelling at me to get back. When I try to cross the barrier I'm grabbed and hauled backwards.

"My girl is in there!" I scream.

"Calm down, you need to stay back," one of the cops yells.

"My girl is in there!" I shout again.

"Sir, we can't let you go in there, it's not safe." I deflate in their hold and after a while they release me. I drop to my ass and stare at the burning building. I look across the street to see Karl's other club has gone up in smoke and in turn taken out the buildings on either side of it. He knew we were coming, he fucking knew! Who betrayed us?

The sound of ringing pulls me from my thoughts, I realize it's Xander's phone and fish it out of my pocket and hit answer.

"Yeah?" I say in a dejected tone.

"Come back to the palace where you first took me and ditch the phone." At the sound of her voice I leap to my feet as relief washes over me.

"You're alive," I breathe out.

"Thanks to Nano, we all are but you won't like what you will learn when you get here."

"I have something to tell you as well—"

"Not over the phone. Come here and then we can talk," she says before ending the call. I toss the phone as I rush back to the car and head toward the safe house I first took Doxy to when I found her. The drive is long but my need to see her and hold her keeps me from crashing after the adrenaline flees my body. I pull off the road and continue down the long driveway, men have their guns drawn and aimed at me until I step out of the car.

"Where's Xander?" Calvin asks.

I shake my head. "Where's Doxy?"

"Right here." I spin around to see her coming out of the forest, I should have known she wouldn't stay inside the house. I smile at the sight of Anna and Kimber following behind her, she got all the girls out but did they save the ones from the club? "Where is he?" she asks when she comes to a stop a few feet away from me. She may not show it but I can hear the worry in her voice.

"We were ambushed." Her features harden. "Xander was trapped in the car and told me to run, to come back to you."

She remains silent for a long time as she tries to calm her anger, her shoulders rise and fall in quick succession. "We find him, we find your father."

"Yeah," I breathe out.

"Then I'm killing your grandfather." I reel back and smack into the side of the car.

"W-what?" I stutter out.

"Your grandfather set us up." I shake my head denying what she says.

"It's true, contrary to what your grandfather said he would never allow a woman to lead the Irish much less an American woman." I pull my gaze from Doxy to stare at Nano.

"How do you know?" I whisper.

"I had William tap his phone. He placed a call to Karl warning him that we were raiding his clubs and you and Alexander were going after him tonight. He had a rat in our midst." I scrub a hand down my face as I try to come to terms with what they have said.

"Are you sure—"

Doxy cuts me off. "We nearly died tonight!" she screams.

"I know!" I shout back. "I have to be sure. He fucking raised me, Doxy, he is a good man—"

"No, he isn't! All those girls inside those clubs are dead. Innocent fucking girls paid the price for his betrayal and I will not let that shit go. Reid will die." She doesn't wait around for a reply as she turns and heads back toward the forest, leaving me standing to digest what she has just said.

"I'm sorry, Trevante. I wish it wasn't true and I had hoped that Reid would come around to the idea of that girl taking over but he is set in his ways."

I narrow my eyes at Nano. "Why are you so accepting of her? I see Monroe and Fred are here with you but the other Captains aren't, am I to assume they have the same beliefs as my grandfather?"

"Yes, Monroe and Fred have the same belief as I do. It

doesn't matter if she doesn't have a cock swinging between her legs. Do I wish she was Irish? Yes, I do, but given the fact she has been here for over a decade makes her Irish enough for me. She wants what is best for the men *and* the women and that is all we can hope for in a leader."

"She doesn't want to lead!" I snap. He purses his lips and I study him for a minute only to scoff. "You already know that though, because she has promised to hand everything over to you once she takes Ireland back and ends her brother. She is going to name you as the head."

"She has told me that yes, but I refused. I am not the man for the job, Trevante. I put your name forward, it's your birthright and if you want my opinion, it's about time you take what is owed to you."

Chapter Nineteen

Doxy

Sitting here by the creek I look at my reflection in the still water. I don't see the girl I used to be anymore. I don't see the innocence in her eyes or the joy of life and what the future holds for her, all I see is the empty shell staring back at me. I had my story tattooed all over my body. The three tattooists that worked on me at once thought I would tap out and not be able to handle the pain but I proved them wrong. I liked that they never asked questions about my scars. I think they knew how I got them because when I went to pay they gave me fifty percent off and said it was their pleasure to help me cover up my past.

"Can I ask you something?" I peer over my shoulder to see Kimber standing there with her hands stuffed into her pockets. She looks nervous and that is a look I have never seen on her before.

"Yeah."

She slowly lifts her head and meets my gaze. "How do you sleep at night?" I snort out a laugh.

"Look at where I am, Kimber, what makes you think I sleep?" She nods her head and comes to sit beside me but keeps enough space between us so we don't accidentally touch. I have also noticed she doesn't spar with any of the others and trains on her own, she doesn't like being touched and I respect that.

"Every time I close my eyes, I see them." I keep my gaze ahead and not look at her, knowing that the second I do she will clam up.

"I see them too," I whisper.

"I hate that I have gotten free of them but I'm not really free. I'm still a fucking prisoner and I've been sentenced to life without parole. I can't escape them, I can't outrun them—"

"You'll escape them. You will out run them but not until you are truly ready to let go," I say. "I preach about wanting to kill them and make them pay but the truth is, every fucking day I wake up I pay the price. I feel the ghosts of their hands on me. I fuck Xander and Trey as a way to show myself I have the power. I control when I want to be fucked, I control how I get fucked. My body has become my weapon and I hate it, I fucking hate myself for using sex as a way to feel strong."

"Why do you only fuck them?"

"Because in a sense I trust them not to hurt me. I may boss them around and feel nothing toward each of them but I do trust them not to cause me harm. I know they are both dominant in bed and want to call the shots, they take the control from me knowing that is what I need. I don't know if I will ever be able to have sex without feeling used or use it as a way to make myself feel strong."

"The thought of having a man's hands on me..." I peer over at her and see her shiver in revulsion.

"Everyone deals with trauma differently. I find strength in using my guys to get off. You find strength in training so you won't ever be at the mercy of another man again."

"Your guys, huh?" I frown and purse my lips as I turn away from her. "I see you with them. I know you like them but you don't let it show, why?"

I answer without hesitation. "Feelings are a weakness. The moment you allow yourself to care for someone they hold power over you. I have been stripped of power for years and I refuse to allow anyone to have that hold over me again. I cared for my family once, they chose to believe I was dead and gave up on me. Love is what makes you falter, rethink yourself and I won't do it."

"How did you end up here?"

"I honestly don't know. After I pushed my best friend out of the car, it went into the water and when I woke up, I was strapped to a table."

"Fourteen years is a long time," she whispers.

"You have no idea."

"I do actually." I snap my head toward her.

"What does that mean?" I ask.

"I'm twenty-one, Doxy. I was sold when I was nine." My brows raise and I jerk back.

"You were with them for twelve years," I whisper. Anguish roars to life inside me. She was a fucking child, innocent and pure and they... they fucking defiled her. "I'm sorry." Her features harden.

"Don't fucking pity me. I got out, you said we can be

victims or survivors and I am a survivor. I will get my revenge and then I will find where the fuck my daughter is."

"You have a kid?" I rasp out past the lump in my throat. Her eyes turn glassy and fill with unshed tears that she quickly blinks away.

"I've never told anyone about her," she says brokenly.

"What happened to her?" I hear the pain in my own voice.

"I don't know." The bitterness that laces her words can be felt.

"How long ago did you have her?"

"I was thirteen." My face slackens and I gasp. "She would be about eight now." I slam my eyes closed and try to breathe through the sharp pain in my chest, I know what she is thinking. Her daughter is eight and she's imagining all the ways those cunts have hurt her.

"I had a son," I say quietly. I feel her gaze on me as I stare ahead at the water.

"Had?"

I smile sadly and nod. "He was perfect, so pure, so handsome and born sleeping." I hear her sharp intake of breath but push on. "They stole him from me—Karl, Nolan, Fin, Ron and Donald all hurt my baby boy and will fucking pay for what they did to my son. I will make their deaths slow and painful."

"He used to visit me, you know."

I frown. "Who?"

"Karl." My face slackens. "He stopped coming to see me when I turned seventeen, he was over me then because I was no longer a child."

Disgust rolls through me, I fight back the bile from rushing up my throat. "I'd rather shit in my hand and clap than ever think about the vile things he has done to women over the years." Her laughter booms out around us and I can't help but smile. When she snorts I lose the battle and begin to laugh with her. Our laughter cuts off the moment we hear someone approaching. We both jump to our feet and turn to see Trey coming toward us.

"Catch you later, shit clapper." I smirk at Kimber as she heads back to the others. Trey stops a few feet away from me, I can feel the dread rolling off him in waves.

"I've never heard you laugh before."

I scoff. "It's hard to find things to make you laugh when your life is a clusterfuck of events that are out of your control."

"I promised him I would find him, Doxy. I'm going after him tomorrow."

"You really give a fuck about Xander?" I ask in disbelief.

His gaze meets mine and I can see the resolution in his gaze. "Yeah. I do give a shit about him and I know you do as well. He's your family, he's closer to you than a blood relative."

"My tampon has blood on it and I still throw that shit away." His face morphs into a picture of disgust at my metaphor. I groan and tilt my head back to stare up at the night sky but the moment his hands grip my waist, I snap my gaze back to him. I see the lust in his gaze lurking just beneath the surface and heat begins to pool inside my belly.

"I love you, Doxy, and it's because I love you I am going to give you what you want. You can use my body to take the edge off but come tomorrow, I'm going after him because you may not admit it but I know you need him just as much as you need me." I search his gaze looking for a sign of deceit or anger but I see nothing but understanding. He slowly trails his hands up my sides as he bends down and ghosts his lips over mine. "If you want me to stop, say the word."

"Don't stop," I breathe out. He slants his lips over mine and I open for him without complaint. I moan when the taste of him ravishes my system. I'm not the type of girl to go slow, not anymore. I grip the hem of his shirt and pull it off, breaking the kiss. I reach for mine but he grips my hands, halting my movements.

"No way, I am not taking the chance of one of those fuckers walking out here and seeing you naked." I gape up at him.

"You do—"

"I don't give a fuck who has seen you naked before or how many, you're our girl now and I will kill any fucker who sees you bare, got it?" My jaw unhinges at the same time my pussy clenches on air. "Lose the fucking pants, baby." I shove my yoga pants down my legs and kick them to the side, hearing him so in control and aggressive is turning me on. "Lay down." I do as he instructs and spread my legs. "Fuck baby, that pussy is perfect."

"Taste it."

His eyes blaze with need. "Not yet. I want you to touch yourself, can you do that for me?" I falter for a second, I've never actually done that before.

"I don't know how." His brows raise in surprise. Before I have a chance to feel nervous or embarrassed, he drops to his knees and runs his hands up my thighs sending a shiver down my spine.

"Pinch your nipples for me, baby." I lift my hands and do as he says arching my back off the ground, that feels... good. "Now run your hands down your body." I follow his instructions. "Now, circle your clit with your index finger." I lick my lips and do as he says, a moan tumbling from me without consent. "Now, I want you to push your finger inside that perfect little cunt and finger fuck yourself while I watch." His words have me growing slick with need. I circle my entrance, loving the way his eyes track my movements. He pushes his pants down and frees his cock. The moment I push a finger inside my pussy, he begins to stroke his cock.

"Hm," I whimper before biting down on my lip to remain silent.

"Fuck no, I want to hear everything," he snarls. I release my bottom lip and begin to pant as I work myself up. I circle my clit with my other hand as I continue to finger fuck myself. "Fuck, baby, you look so fucking hot playing with that beautiful pussy. Make yourself come, then I'm going to fuck you so hard you black out."

"Oh fuck, Trey," I cry out as I feel my orgasm cresting. He groans and drops his hold on his cock before smacking my hands away and slamming inside me in one swift move, causing us both to cry out.

"Fuck, baby, your pussy is so tight." .

"Fuck me," I plead. He does as he is told and thrusts inside me at a relentless pace. He lifts me and grips my waist.

"*Fuck me*," he demands. I bounce up and down on his glorious cock, loving how deep he feels inside me.

"I'm gonna come," I whimper, then his hold on me turns punishing as he meets me thrust for thrust. The orgasm rips through me without warning. I toss my head back and scream.

"Take it, baby, take it all," he orders a second before he comes with my name on his lips. We're both panting and trying to regain control of our bodies. "I love you, Doxy."

The air rushes out of me as I stare down at him and shake my head. "Don't waste your love on me. I'm not worth it and I will never love you back," I say before climbing off his lap and pulling my pants on before heading back to camp.

I'll never be weak, I'll never give anyone that power again.

Chapter Twenty

Xander

I grunt when another blow lands to my ribs. Karl stands at the back of the room smiling like he won the fucking lottery. I'm in the center of the room with my hands chained above my head, suspended slightly so only the tips of my boots touch the concrete floor, forcing my arms to bear the majority of my weight. They've worked me over pretty good, my face aching and I'm sure they have cracked a few of my ribs. I'm not dumb, I see the knives and tools that line the metal cart against the wall, they are just getting warmed up before the real fun begins.

"All you have to do is make a call, bring her here and return all those whores, then this will end. I'll ship what remains of you back to that little prick. I'm not unreasonable, Alexander," Karl taunts like he's doing me a favor. Rather than answering, I look at the cunt who has been working me over and spit right in his face.

"Motherfucker!" he snarls, then lands a combo of jabs,

kicks and even uppercuts me. I hang here limply, feeling every ounce of pain they have inflicted upon my body but still, none of this hurts worse than thinking about never seeing Waverly again. I hope Lakeland believes Trey and tells Knox she is alive. I know Wave hates him but Knox would come for her and give her the army she needs to take over Ireland.

"I think you hurt Fin's feelings." At the mention of the cocksucker's name anger swirls inside me. Karl laughs when he sees me shooting Fin a death glare, he's one of the cunts that hurt Wave's son. "He wasn't the only one who got to play with your girlfriend, we all enjoyed her." I look around the room, ten of the bastards are in here grinning. These are the last ones on her list. I know it without needing to hear their names, these cunts hurt my girl and for that, they will all fucking die, slowly. I will peel the fucking skin from their bones and have them begging for death.

"I'm going to give you all a chance. You can let me go now and I will end your miserable excuse of a life quickly or, don't heed my warning and I'll drag your end out slowly." They all look around at each other, it takes a solid minute before laughter breaks out and I grit my teeth as all these mother-fuckers brush off my threat.

"You think you're getting out of here?" the cunt to the right of Karl asks. I keep my face blank of all the pain I'm feeling and put my gladiator mask in place. If they think they can beat me, torture me or break me, then they are out of their fucking minds, I have nothing left to break. The only thing they could break me with isn't here, she's safe and I know Trey will keep her away from here. I would never forgive myself if she was stupid enough to stage a breakout for me and she was captured.

God, I would die a painful fucking death before I ever let these cocksuckers lay a single finger on her again.

"Clearly Fin knocked him too many times in the head," Karl jibes, the rest of his followers cackle like a pack of hyenas. I remain stoic, still trying to give myself some time to figure a way out of here. I know I've been chained up for hours so it has to be close to dusk and surely these cunts have other shit they need to do. They must at least have damage control to do since Wave took out two more of their clubs. "Nolan, take Ed, Stephen and George and deal with the damage at Prime. Fin, take Frank, Len and Thomas and go check out the two clubs from last night. Ron and I will keep an eye on this leech." They do as instructed but before they can leave Ron blocks the doorway and shakes his head.

"Don't be rude, say goodbye to our guest," he jeers. The men stand around and laugh for a second before focusing their attention on me. I brace myself for the pain that is about to unfold. The fuckers make a line and each take their turns inflicting as much pain as possible in the five second window they have given themselves before they leave the room. By the time the last one leaves the room I am nothing but limp weight in my chains and panting, barely hanging on to consciousness but I will not give them the satisfaction of passing out.

I'll admit, they have worked me over pretty fucking well but I see from the glint in Karl and Ron's eyes that the both have something in store for me. I frown when Ron walks across the room and retrieves a metal bucket. I begin to think that they are going to strap me to a table and place a rat beneath the bucket on my stomach and then heat it so it claws its way through my insides. He holds my attention with rapt interest when he positions the bucket in front of me and gets right up in my face.

"You'll get special treatment because I know how much she likes you." My brows raise as my face clears of all emotion. "Hmmmm, she tasted so good." I jerk forward and headbutt the cunt. He stumbles back cursing and holding his nose as it gushes out with blood.

"You'll pay for that!" Karl roars before stalking across the room to the metal cart and grabbing a whip. I stare the cunt down. I've seen the scars on her body, I know *he* did that to her and if he thinks I will shrink away and cower in fear he's fucking wrong. He comes to stand behind me and tears the back of my shirt open, exposing my naked flesh.

"You're going to fucking wish I killed you slowly," Ron promises as he steps aside just as Karl cracks the whip, taunting me. I brace and try to prepare myself for what is to come. Their laughter ricochets around the room, building to the anticipation of what is about to happen. I close my eyes and force my mind to quieten and lock away all my emotions.

He can't hurt me, she isn't here.

I keep repeating that over and over in my head, reminding myself that no physical pain can harm me, the only person that can hurt me is nowhere near here. I hear the whip crack again and ready myself for the inevitable lashing that is coming my way.

"Twenty should be enough to get us started before Ron gets to play with you. Same rules apply, your whore knew them well. You count them aloud, the moment you stop we begin again." Shock, shame, anger and guilt war inside me at the knowledge of how she had to live through this shit for years. "You scream out or pass out, we begin again."

"I'm going to flay you alive, peel the skin from your fucking bones while—" The whip sails through the air and the burning pain that rips through me is a feeling I can't even put into words. I gasp and draw in a sharp intake of breath as I breathe through the searing pain.

"He didn't count it out loud, boss," Ron says with humor in his tone.

"No, he didn't. We'll class that as a warm up strike, shall we?" Karl answers. I hear the tip of the whip drag along the ground and tense in anticipation of the pain that is coming but then a phone ringing breaks the tension in the room. "I don't like interruptions when I am teaching!" Karl scolds. Ron quickly fishes out his phone and hits answer.

"Darling, daddy is—" Ron clamps his mouth closed and darts a fearful look to Karl before placing the call on speaker.

"Do I have your attention?" My eyes widen at the sound of Waverly's voice.

"If you hurt a single hair on their—"

She cuts Ron off before he can finish. "Shut the fuck up. You don't call the shots here, you do as I say and I won't let thirty men take turns on your wife Meg. When they tire of her, your daughters Christine and Zoe can take their mother's spot and entertain my men. Now, do I have your attention?" Karl moves toward Ron with the whip still clasped in his hand, they share a loaded look before Ron swallows and answers.

"You have my attention," he sneers. I wipe the shock from my face and play it cool.

"Now, I assume by the big boy tone of your voice that you're with that dead man walking." Karl beams like a proud father.

"Are you ready to come home, Doxy?"

"Say another fucking word you cock sucking son of a cunt and I'll slit his daughter's throats." Ron stumbles back a couple steps and shoots Karl a pleading look, he was untouchable a minute ago but with the threat of his daughters lives on the line he's been reduced to a fucking puppet.

My girl did that shit!

"What are your terms, Doxy?" Karl asks, Ron's eyes widen with a pleading look asking him to shut the fuck up but Karl ignores him. He doesn't give a fuck about Ron's daughters, he just wants to taunt Doxy.

"You have something that belongs to me." Karl snaps his gaze to me and sneers while I smirk. "I want him back." She sounds like a fucking queen.

"I am the leader of this family, you are nothing but a common whore that can be replaced in a—"

"You have three hours to bring him to me unharmed or I start with the wife then move on to the daughters. Don't be late." The second she ends the call, Ron is shouting and pleading for Karl to release me and save the lives of his family. I bite back the snort from breaking free. Ten minutes ago he had the biggest dick energy and now he is a pleading pussy.

"I will not meet the demands of some fucking whore!" Karl roars, silencing Ron. "He is going nowhere, she's a stupid cunt."

"How so?" Ron asks.

"She's at your house. Get the men, we're going to get that bitch back. She needs to be taught a lesson and I am dying to give it to her in front of this soon to be dead bastard." Both of them stroll out of the room and slam the door closed behind themselves. I hear the lock click into place and smirk.

Their greatest mistake is underestimating her. I bet my life on the fact she isn't at Ron's house and is staking out this joint.

Chapter Twenty-One

Doxy

I toss the phone back to Trey and recline in my seat as we wait for Karl and Ron to make their move. I know Karl better than he knows himself. He's going to call the men he has on his payroll and bring them all here to his safe house in the hills where they will hatch a plan to come after me at Ron's house. Idiot. Trey and the other Captains were able to pinpoint three locations where he could be hiding and sure enough, we found them at the second location.

"You're not really going to hurt them... are you?" I lull my head to the side and stare out the window as I answer Brett.

"I would never harm an innocent woman and I would never harm a child. I only said that to incite Ron's wrath so he wouldn't be thinking clearly and make mistakes. Him worrying over his family will distract Karl and the others."

"How do you know?" Trey questions.

"Because I know all of them like the back of my fucking hand. Karl thinks he's smarter than me because he has a dick.

That is going to be his biggest downfall." Trey drives us back to the house we have taken over a couple miles down the road. I stand by the window watching cars speed past but none of them ever head back down the mountain. I have allowed Anna and Kimber to come with us on this mission but they are not to engage anyone unless their life is in danger. "Calvin, get everyone into position, I want to move now before they flee to Ron's house." He marches off to do as he's told while Trey slides up beside me. I close my eyes and run through my list, it's nearly complete.

Karl
Nolan
Fin
~~Donald~~
Ed
Stephen
~~Mike~~
George
~~Daniel~~
Frank
Len
~~Lionel~~
~~Jackson~~
~~Tom~~
Thomas
~~Jones~~
~~Aaron~~
Ron

"Are you ready to end this?" he asks quietly.

"Yes. I want Karl, Nolan, Fin, Ron, Ed, Stephen, George, Frank, Len and Thomas alive."

"What are you going to do to them?" I slowly lift my gaze to his and smile, his features harden at the look in my eyes.

"Karma is going to be so fucking generous to them." Before he can answer, William enters the room and alerts me that the men are ready and getting into position. "No one is to move until I give the signal."

"Yes, Ma'am," he says before leaving.

"Your grandfather is next, Trey. I won't allow him to get away with outing us." His face falls.

He takes a deep breath and nods. "I know. But I need you to know that I can't be a part of... a part of whatever you have planned for him." I search his eyes trying to decipher his feelings and I see it, the guilt, love and confusion over why his grandfather betrayed him.

"Because of what he meant to you, I will do you this favor. I'll end him quickly and not make him suffer like the others, but I cannot and will not offer that courtesy to your father." I walk away without waiting for a reply, his agreement or disagreement means nothing to me.

"Doxy?" I pause but don't turn to face him. "I'm sorry." I spin around and gape at him.

"For what?"

Sadness fills his gaze. "I'm sorry for everything my family has done to you. I'm so fucking sorry for everything that you have suffered through and had to live through. How you can stand to be near me, let me touch you, allow me to be inside you and listen to the sound of my voice is beyond me. I don't deserve to stand in your presence." The anguish with which he says this can be felt. I hear the self-hatred in his tone and I loathe that he feels this way about himself.

"I hate your father. I didn't mind your grandfather until he crossed me but you are innocent, Trevante. I am cold, heartless and feel nothing but I will never harm an innocent person."

"I'm not innocent, I share their blood!" he shouts.

"I share the same blood as Knox but that doesn't mean he and I are the same. You didn't ask to be born to that piece of shit. You are not him, Trey. Don't even put yourself in the same category as him or I'll beat the shit out of you."

"Why did you let me touch you?"

I answer without hesitation. "Because I saw the pain in your eyes, your demons spoke to mine."

Nano isn't happy with my plan but he doesn't call the shots, I do. I have men scattered around the house and we've had scouts scoping out the area. They were able to count at least twenty inside but none of them have laid eyes on Xander. I knew they wouldn't, Karl would have him locked up in the basement.

"This is fucking risky, I don't like it," Nano grits out from beside me. I turn and glare at the asshole. I like him but I will not have him underestimating me in front of all the men.

"I don't care what you think, there is no other way to draw them all out. I'm doing this," I snap.

"Doxy, I don't know if you are aware but as the new glorified leader that means it is our job to make sure you are safe and not in danger. You walking out there *alone* is fucking dangerous! What are you not understanding about that?" I appreciate his concern but this is not up for debate.

"I'm not understanding the part where you said I am the leader and then questioning me instead of obeying my fucking instructions?" Nano purses his lips but wisely remains silent and takes a step back, nodding his head.

"Understood, my apologies," he mutters as he walks away to join the others.

"If he tries anything, I won't obey your orders." Sighing, I look at Trey.

"He won't kill me," I answer.

He darts forward and cups my face between his hands as he bends down so we are eye level. "I get that you are a badass and call the shots but I am also a man who has fallen in love with you, and I can't just stand by and do nothing as you risk your life."

I can see he means every word he says but I can't bring myself to feel anything. I try but all I feel is numb.

"The risk is worth the reward," I say before pulling free of his hold and stalking out of the cover of the surrounding trees. The moment I hit the gravel driveway I know they would have seen me so I wait in the center for Karl to make a show of sending all his men out to surround me before he makes his appearance thinking he is the one in control.

Like clockwork, the front door swings open and men dash out of the modest size house with rifles aimed at me as they form a large circle, thinking they have me trapped. That's the thing with men, they naturally assume because we don't have balls that we are weak—newsflash, vaginas are stronger because we can take a fucking pounding. I force myself to remain calm and complacent when I see Frank, Len, Thomas, Stephen, Fin,

Ed, Nolan and Ron exit the house. They all wear masks of hatred and the look in each of their eyes promises pain. No one utters a word as Karl strolls out. The moment his gaze meets mine he smiles wickedly and moves away from his men stopping halfway toward me and then claps.

"What a show you have put on." I fight the urge to bristle because all these weeks of feeling angry, jaded and hungry for vengeance only for him to stand before me, which forces my nightmares to play on a reel through my mind. I feel my hands growing clammy and breaths coming in short pants. I hate my reaction to him and loathe that he still has this type of power over me. I never feared the boogeyman or monsters under my bed, but I feared him for years! "You've grown brave in our time apart." His tone is laced with a hard edge. "You will be punished for making eye contact, drop to your knees and beg my forgiveness and I will make your punishment swift."

I straighten my spine and take a deep breath, I am not that broken doll anymore. They may have killed Waverly Bronson but Doxy Da Luca was born that night, she rose like a phoenix from the ashes. She is stronger, smarter and more cunning than Waverly ever was. I am here and I am fucking fierce, they can't hurt me anymore.

"Drop to *your* knees and beg my forgiveness and I will shorten your punishment by two years. Continue to think you are in charge and calling the shots, then I will add a year to each minute you make me wait." Karl looks at his men and then they all begin to laugh. I gasp at the audacity of them and hate that some of my bravado waivers. I fucking despise how the sound of his voice or the sight of him can reduce me to the scared, fearful broken doll he made me to be. I clench my hands at my sides so he doesn't see them trembling.

You are strong.

You are brave.

You can do this.

I take a shuddering breath and lift my chin. When I hear the guns around me begin cocking I grit my teeth. "Shoot me then you spineless bastard," I sneer.

"Not before you tell me where the fuck my family is!" Ron bellows. I open my mouth to tell him to fuck off but I snap it closed when I feel someone slide up beside me. I know who it is the moment the tension eases and I manage to take a full breath since I walked out here.

"They will be seeing you in hell if you don't shut the fuck up, you sick piece of shit. No pun intended." He says the end part sarcastically. Ron's eyes widen in indignation but he wisely keeps his mouth shut. Trey flicks his gaze to his father and looks him up and down with disdain. Karl crosses his arms over his chest and smiles.

"The prodigal son returns," Karl says with such distaste.

Trey scoffs. "I am nothing to you. You are sadistic and breathing on borrowed time. Hand Xander over and your men won't have to suffer."

Karl's answering laughter grates on my nerves. "You stupid fucking boy, did you really think I got to where I am by being dumb?" He doesn't give us a chance to answer. "I know Nano has his men surrounding us right now but what you didn't account for was me learning from Gio and Percy's mistakes and making sure that I was the one sneaking up on your men." I can't keep the shock from displaying on my face when Kimber, Nano and Anna appear from around the side of the house with their hands cuffed in front of them and men dragging them toward us.

I failed, I failed them all.

Chapter Twenty-Two

Trevante

I look at her and see the devastated look in her eyes, she is shutting down and preparing herself for what is to come.

Fuck this!

I grip her face and force her to turn to me, lifting her head so her gaze can meet mine. "He thinks I don't know him, you think you know him best but what you both didn't account for was the fact you both know each other better than the other so you didn't see each other's blind spots."

"I rescued those girls, gave them hope and it was for nothing," she says brokenly, this is the first time I have heard emotion in her tone aside from when she told us about her son.

"Don't hate me, Doxy. When trust is broken, sorry means nothing but I swear I never meant to break your trust." Her eyes narrow as she studies me.

"What did you do?" she asks with apprehension clear in her tone.

"Pick which one dies first?" I snap my head toward my

father, sadness fills me when I see my grandfather, the man who raised me to be better appear from inside the house. Karl had the manpower to surround us because he had Reid's men at his disposal. "I think the whores should die first," Karl taunts. Doxy breaks free of my hold and stills at the sight of Nano and the girls on their knees in front of Karl with his gun pressed against Kimber's forehead.

"Enough, Trey. You will stop this now and return to my side where I will continue to teach you how to take over and rule better than *him*," my grandfather says. His hatred for Karl is clear but the fact he can't stand to see a woman lead us is the only reason he is prepared to work alongside his son who he hates. "You're surrounded, son. You have my word the girl will meet a swift end and no one will touch her—"

"I'll kill anyone who tries to fucking touch her!" I scream as I spin around in a circle, eyeing each of these cunts, daring them to try and make a move.

"Trevante, you are making a fool of yourself, we have won!" I face my grandfather and shake my head.

"I always knew Karl was a worthless piece of shit but I expected more of you." His face falls but Karl's is a bright shade of red.

"She dies first for that, you cunt!" Karl cocks his gun, Doxy moves to step forward but freezes at the sound of my voice first.

"He won't like you upsetting her," I taunt as I cross my arms over my chest and stare at the bastard who gave me life.

"He's chained up in my basement, you little prick!" he roars.

I purse my lips and make a show of appearing confused. "What makes you think I was talking about Xander?" Karl looks to my grandfather who is just as perplexed as him but it's

Doxy's burning gaze that has me turning to her. I see it in her eyes, she knows what I did.

"I hate you," she forces out through clenched teeth.

"But I love you and I couldn't watch all your hard work not pay off." I tear my gaze from her to face the bastards I share blood with. "You see while you were all out here measuring who has the bigger dick you didn't factor in the fact that there was a fourth player on the board." Both Reid and Karl frown. "You were so focused on outdoing Doxy that you didn't realize I was staging a coup of my own."

"What the fuck did you do, Trevante?" Reid bellows.

"I gave you a choice!" I shout. "I begged you to choose me and help me so she could rule but you betrayed me. Doxy may know Karl but I know you too and I knew you would double cross me so I brought in back up."

"You have no men, they are all on their knees waiting for my order to shoot to kill," Karl snaps. "You have nothing, boy!" He sounds like a smug son of a bitch and thinks he has won this battle before it has even begun.

"I have the Re Della Strada, motherfucker!" On cue, red lasers appear as if out of thin air, every man having at least three or four dots on them. Two of the guards standing behind us try to run but are gunned down within a split second. Karl begins to bark orders at them to take out the shooters but none of them move an inch. "Your move, Doxy," I say low enough for only her to hear. When she looks at me I see the hatred in her gaze. I did the one thing she never wanted me to do, I sent Knox a picture of her and asked for his help. He wasn't able to deny me when I showed him proof his twin was alive and needed his help even if she didn't know it. "The wrong man will teach you that you can do it all by yourself but the right man will show

177

that you can but won't let you. I couldn't let you do this on your own."

"All units, shoot to kill!" Reid orders, but before a shot can ring out, I tackle Doxy to the ground and use my body as a shield as bullets begin to whizz past us. She throws me off her and rushes toward Kimber, Nano and Anna, keeping low and managing to not get shot.

"Do not shoot my sister!" Knox's voice comes through the earpiece in my ear. "Tay, get Xander out and everyone else, move in now and kill every one of these—" Before he can finish I cut in.

"No one is to touch Karl or his inner circle, she wants them alive. That was the deal, Knox!" I growl before pushing to my feet and chasing after Doxy. She's locked into a hand to hand fight with one of Reid's guys, the second she lands a jab to his throat he drops to his knees gasping for air. She snatches his gun from his side and drops down into a crouch spinning around in time to shoot Ed right in the center of his forehead. His blood sprays all over her but she doesn't miss a beat as she moves onto her next target. She yanks the blade from its sheath on her thigh and runs toward Stephen who has his back turned and leaps into the air. She plunges the knife into his back. He roars out in pain but it turns to a strangled gargle when she yanks the blade out and slits his throat from behind.

I tear my gaze from her as I rush toward the guard she killed and snag the keys to the cuffs from his pocket, then make quick work of uncuffing the girls and Nano.

"Give me a gun," Anna snaps.

I shake my head. "You need to get out of here—"

"How the fuck do we do that?" Kimber screams at me.

"We need to move now!" Nano barks. We all stay low as we

move to the edge of the house for some cover but before we can make it the two girls break away and rush back into the fray.

"Fuck," I bark out as I chase after them. I was trying to get them to safety before helping Doxy, she is pissed enough at me without these two getting themselves killed and making getting back into her good graces ten times fucking harder. I pull my gun out and shoot a masked fucker who was sneaking up behind Kimber before making my way toward Doxy, who is locked into a knife fight with Frank.

"Fucking kill the bitch!" George screams. Without thought I raise my gun and fire two shots, hitting George in the chest and side of the neck. The sound of his body hitting the hard earth brings warmth to my blood. I spy men rushing out of the surrounding trees, some of them are ours but I also recognize some of them as Reid's men.

Doxy doesn't take her eyes off Frank as she shouts for me to go after Xander. I want to argue with her but when I see Karl and Reid race into the house I'm left with no choice but to obey her order or risk them killing Xander. She may not want to admit it but Xander dying would destroy her and I won't allow that to happen, she has lost enough already.

Chapter Twenty-Three

Xander

I can hear shouting and gunfire, but can't tell from the sounds of the shouts who is winning. I fight against my restraints, trying to get free, needing to get the fuck out of here and make sure Wave is safe and unharmed. I can't fucking lose her, not now when I just got her back in my arms. If she is hurt in any way I'm going to fucking kill Trevante! I hear pounding footsteps above me and the shouts begin to grow louder, but I can't decipher a word they are saying and it's starting to fray my fucking nerves.

When I hear the lock on the door click open, I wipe my face of emotion and keep my head held high, these cunts will not break me. The moment the door opens and I see who is standing in the entryway my jaw unhinges—there is no fucking way he could be here, I'm certain I'm seeing shit now.

"Well, look at you just hanging around while the rest of us work." I snort at the pun and crack a smile.

"What the fuck are you doing here, Taylan?" My best

friend scoffs and shakes his head as he makes his way over to me.

"Saving your ass, obviously," he says as he gets to work on undoing the chains around my wrists, but at the sound of footfalls coming toward us, he shoots me a look to remain silent and darts back across the room to close the door quietly and stands flush against the wall so when the door opens he will be concealed. Rather than using his rifle that is strapped to his back he pulls his two sidearms, ready to take out whoever comes through that door. I'll be honest, seeing him again after all this time has my chest aching at the sight of him. I fucked up but when my back was against the wall and needed a way out, they came for me!

The door bursts open to reveal Karl and Reid, the former darts his gaze from the door handle then to me, shit! I keep my face blank but he isn't stupid, he knows he locked that door when he left. He shoves his father out of the way, lifts his gun and then leaps to the side as he yanks the door closed. Taylan and Karl both stand there with their guns aimed at each other.

"Taylan, on your right!" I shout. He lifts his other gun and points it at Reid who already has his gun pointed at Tay. Panic unfurls inside me, it's two against one and I don't like my best friend's odds. He is well fucking trained but I know they are too, they may be old but they didn't rise to where they are by being weak, as much as I hate to admit that shit even to myself.

Karl spits on the ground. "Taylan Carter, Knox Bronson's pet bitch," he sneers. Tay being the cocky fucker that he is grins and nods his head like an idiot. He may appear like the jokester and easy going one out of him, Knox and me but his thirst for blood and his temper rivals mine and Knox's like no other.

"Oh, you've heard of me, good because that would have

been really awkward, Karl, if you forgot all about little old me." If I could roll my eyes I would, Taylan can get under anyone's skin without much effort at all.

"Drop your guns kid and I might let you live," Reid cuts in to say, Tay pushes his lips to the side like he is debating his request but I know he isn't.

"I really can't do that because Knox said I have to save Xander and if I fail he will never let me live it down and that is a fucking tragedy for me because that fucker loves to throw my fuck ups in my face and I can't—"

"Shut the fuck up!" Karl shouts. In a fraction of a second, Taylan's facial features change from playful to downright murderous, Karl just flipped the switch inside him without realizing it.

"Basement, both of the Solomon's, Xander is chained, two on one, all units to my location," Taylan says with pure dominance in his voice. Karl and Reid share a loaded look.

"You dumb fucks, he just put the Re Della Strada into motion and they are coming to kill you!" Karl curses beneath his breath at my outburst and tries to shift toward the exit but Reid shoots him in the knee, then tries to flee. Tay sighs dramatically then fires a shot that hits him in the temple killing him instantly. Karl is groaning in pain and clutching his knee. Tay quickly disarms him and shoves his gun into his waistband, then comes to me.

The second he frees my arms I flop forward unable to hold myself up. He wraps his arms around my waist and holds me against him. "I got you brother, *always*." I close my eyes and let his words wash over me as I hear the others storm into the room. Karl's painful cries go silent in an instant. I know it isn't because of the RDS guys, it's because *he* just entered the room.

"Face him, own your shit so you can come home, brother," Tay whispers in my ear, then shifts to my side, allowing me to lean into him so he can bear the brunt of my weight. I slowly lift my head and lock eyes with my other best friend, his green eyes remind me so much of his twin's but unlike hers, I see emotion in his eyes.

We stand here staring at each other for a long time. He's aged since the last time I saw him but he still looks like Knox but harder, he has more of an edge to himself now. He looks me up and down and I expect to see hatred in his gaze when he meets my stare but all I see is shame and guilt.

"Okay, so you're not going to kill him obviously so can we get the fuck out of here and deal with this later?" Tay's voice breaks the trance Knox and I were in.

"Cuff and take him upstairs, I want him alive," Knox orders Marco and the others. Tay helps me from the room and it's fucking painful but I bite back the grunts of pain that want to escape me. I can feel Knox's gaze boring into the back of my head as we make our way toward the front door. I see bodies littering the ground and hate that I missed the action, I just hope that Wave is okay.

When we finally make our way outside, Tay slams to a halt at the sight in front of us. Trey is standing there with a broken look on his face. Ice fills my veins as worry begins to churn inside me.

"Where is she?" I shout. He jolts as if I shocked him and focuses his gaze on me.

"She's gone," he mutters.

"What the fuck do you mean?" I snap.

"Where is my sister?" Knox demands as he comes to stand beside me.

"She took Len, Thomas, Nolan, Fin and Ron with the girls and what remains of her men. I tried to stop her but she pulled a gun on me."

"What did she say?" I force out as I try to tamper my anger.

"She said she will see us where her life ended and Knox's began."

"She also tasked me with taking Karl to her." I dart my gaze to the side to see Nano, Brett and William standing there. Knox's guys lift their guns ready to take them out.

"Don't shoot them, if you do you will just piss her off!" I say.

"I am not handing this cocksucker over, if she wants him she can come to me and get him," Knox replies.

"It doesn't work like that, the boss gave an order and we follow it... no exceptions," William speaks for the first time and I have to admit hearing how loyal he is to Wave has my respect for him growing.

"She doesn't command me—"

Taylan cuts Knox off before he can continue to scream like a bitch. "She has three weeks to meet us back at the bridge or we will come after her." The three men bristle at his threat but say nothing.

"What the fuck do you think you are doing?" Knox demands as he comes to stand in front of Taylan and me, breathing hard. I can see he's pissed the fuck off.

"Giving your sister the bastard that stole her fucking life from her, he is hers to kill not yours! Pull your fucking head out of your ass, Knoxville, and realize that Waverly isn't a child anymore. She is a woman and has an army of her own. She doesn't need us or *you*." Knox stumbles back a step, shaking his head, trying to deny what Tay says but he can't because deep down inside he knows as well as I do that we all failed her. Taylan motions for Marco to hand Karl over to Nano. Everyone ignores his cries of pain as he is dragged toward their waiting car. Trey tries to follow after them but Brett turns and holds him at gunpoint.

"Our orders were to return with Karl only, you are not accompanying us, Trey."

"Fuck you, Brett, she needs me and she needs Xander even if she won't admit it," he volleys back.

"Why the fuck does Wave need him *and* you?" Knox growls, Trey spins around to face us but his moment of distraction costs him. Brett jumps into the car and they burn rubber out of here.

"Fuck! We need to go after them!" Trey shouts as he jogs back to me.

I shake my head and flinch in pain. "You and I both know she will be long gone, our only choice is to listen to what she says and wait until she comes to us." Trevante stares at me like I have lost my fucking mind and maybe I have, but I also know pushing her doesn't work. She showed us how she felt without uttering a single word, she came for me and she saved Trey. She cares about us, she just refuses to admit that to herself.

"One of you cunts better start explaining to me what the fuck is going on between you and my sister, now!" Trey and I both look at Knox, who has his fists clenched at his sides, nostrils flaring with each deep breath he takes. He looks like a bull ready to charge.

"We saw the beauty in her darkness and she saw the darkness in ours, we are in love with your sister."

3...2...1

I still know Knox better than he knows himself, three

seconds is all it took for Trey's words to sink in, then Knox is flying off the handle and beating the shit out of him. The dumbass should have kept his mouth shut and let me deal with him but no, fucking Romeo thinks his stupid ass poetic lines will make everyone fall for him. That shit may have worked on his sister but Knox is nothing like Waverly. He has a heart and it beats for his wife and sons, Wave has one but it beats for nothing and no one right now.

I'm going to thaw that frozen block of ice around her heart and force her to see me... to choose me and Trey.

Chapter Twenty-Four

Doxy

"Dede?" I turn away from the sight of William fucking Ron and face Kimber who scrunches her face in disgust. I get her and Anna not being able to stomach the sight of William, Brett, and Calvin raping Karl and the others that I brought here but I live for it. I relish watching the three guys taking turns on all of them. It brings me great joy to see them cry or scream out so I can punish them with my whip like they used to do to me.

"What is it?" Kimber nibbles on her bottom lip looking uneasy, which has me narrowing my eyes. In the past two weeks since we captured these fuckers and moved off the grid I have gotten to know Kimber and Anna a lot better and I would even go as far as to say we are... frenemies of sorts.

"Xander and Trey are trying to track us again." I growl out my annoyance as I brush past her and head out of the shack, leaving the three guys to have their fun while I deal with this shit. I cross the yard and enter the barn where we have set up our operation HQ. When we raided another club, we found a woman in the midst that is amazing with computers and is a dark web hacker.

"Josie, what have you got?" I ask as I come to a halt beside the woman as she types furiously.

"She's in the middle of sending a mass shutdown virus so she can block them from hacking into the CCTV through Ireland so we can move freely." My brows raise in surprise at Anna's response, it appears Josie is worth her weight in gold.

"Boo ya, bitches!" Josie shouts, shocking the fuck out of me and earning a glare from everyone in the barn. She looks around at all of us and ducks her head sheepishly. "My bad," she mutters.

"Where are they?" I clip out.

She flicks her gaze to me and beams, Anna says she has some type of hero complex about me and it grates on my fucking nerves. I am no one's hero.

"They thought they were slick and rerouted their IP addresses to show them being in Dublin but I hacked through their firewalls and rerouted the servers—"

"English, Josie!" Kimber snaps, earning a scowl from the hacker before she answers.

"They tried to make it look like they were in Dublin but they aren't, they're in Canada."

"They are growing restless, Doxy," Nano states as he slinks out of the shadows across from us.

"I don't care what they are doing, they can fuck off if they think I am going back there."

Nano cuts me off earning a filthy look. "As the leader of the Da Luca family, you are bound to your word and gave the Re Della Strada your word you would meet them in two weeks. You can't go back on that."

"Says who? You?" I counter.

"Says everyone. Your word is your bond, and breaking it makes you untrustworthy. If you want to fight the RDS, then let's go to war because hiding out in the middle of the fucking sticks is not my idea of fun. The men are restless and want to return to their families, they can't do that when you have the whole camp on lockdown." I can hear the stress in his tone. I know the men are growing tired of being cooped up here, we are running out of space for everyone since we have taken down Karl's clubs. We have even taken in Reid's men but I refused to take the other Captains back, they were given a swift death for their betrayal. Nano proved his loyalty to me by taking them out. I needed to know he would kill his own friend if I ordered it, which is why I have named him as my second.

I mull over his words as I dart my gaze around the room and take in the many faces of the women and men who have joined my cause to fight for freedom. Anyone caught trafficking women or children will be taken out, I will not offer second chances to anyone who dares to deal in that fucking trade.

"Leaving your past behind was an option, not giving up on your future is your choice, Doxy." I crunch my face in confusion.

"What the hell does that mean, Anna?"

"It means that you need to get your ass on a plane and get the closure you need from your past so it can stop holding you back from your future." Anna and Kimber are the only ones who seem to get away with speaking to me like this, the other women treat me with respect but not these two. They have even given me the stupid fucking nickname *Dede*.

"Before you judge me, Anna, make sure you're perfect," I snarl as I turn and stalk toward the exit.

"So, I'll have the men ready to fly out in the morning?" Nano calls after me, earning a grunt. I grind my teeth when I hear him and the bitches laughing at my expense.

I can't run from my past any longer, it's time to go home...

I wake gasping for air, covered in a fine sheen of sweat. I look around the small tent and sigh. I'm not back there with them, they are my prisoners now. I am in control. I hate myself for even admitting it but since I haven't been the meat to the Xander and Trey sandwich my nightmares have returned. I may not have slept much before, but now I can't even manage to get an hour of sleep without being woken up by a memory covered in sweat or waking with tremors.

I get up, leave my tent and head for the shack, needing to see for my own eyes that they are still chained. Karl, Nolan, Fin, Ron, Len and Thomas are the only survivors from my list. Unlike their pals, they won't be as lucky to die quickly, they will be tortured and raped by anyone who wants a turn. I've even let some of the girls in here to have a turn at whipping them. My only rule is they are not allowed to shoot or stab them because I won't risk them getting an infection and dying.

I push the door open and smile at the sight of Calvin thrusting into Karl's ass. All of them are naked and chained to tables exactly like I was. Ron spots me first and begins to thrash and tries to speak but can't thanks to the gag in his mouth. He has no idea what I did with his family and I never plan to tell him. Turns out, his wife has been trying to leave him for years but he beat her into submission. She agreed to allow her daughter to record the clip I played over the phone to Ron, in return I would make sure Ron could never come after her or their daughters. It brings me great pleasure to know he is conjuring up all the worst possible scenarios of what could be happening to his family, it is going to break his mind.

"Doxy, did you want me to stop?" I shake my head and motion for Calvin to continue as I lean against the wall and smile at the sight. For years I wished, prayed and even offered my soul to the Devil if he would grant me this dream of seeing the men who broke me in the same position as I was and here they are, bloodied, bruised, used and slowly breaking. See, a woman can be raped and slowly heal over time because we are warriors, we will never forget or truly get over the trauma, but we will force ourselves to survive because we aren't weak. Men, they are different, especially ones like these bastards. They were so drunk on power and thought they were untouchable, above everyone around them so breaking their minds is easy, all you have to do is break their bodies and take away their free will and they will be nothing but a shell.

"No is a full sentence." I lull my head to the side to see Kimber standing there with a haunted look in her eyes.

"Another nightmare?" She nods, much like me she doesn't sleep much either.

"This one was the worst. I finally got my little girl back only for them to take her from me again," she whispers.

"I have Josie searching for her and combing through all Karl's correspondence." She turns to me with wide eyes. "I may not have a heart, Kimber, but that doesn't mean I can't relate to you. I'll deal with this shit in Canada and then you have my word that all my efforts will be put into finding all these girls and your daughter who were sold to homes as slaves. We will bring your little girl home." Tears fill her eyes.

"Why?" she rasps out.

"I may not be able to bring my little boy back but I can bring your daughter back to you and I will. You have my *word*." In a move that shocks the fucking hell out of me she... hugs me! I stand here, still and unsure what the hell to do until she steps back and sniffs a couple of times.

"I will always be loyal to you, Doxy. Whatever you need from me I will do it. I swear it on the life of my daughter."

"I know."

"How?"

"I saw it in your eyes that night by the creek. You let me in and you didn't even know it. You have my loyalty as well. Never break my trust, Kimber, because you will *never* earn it back again." She nods.

"Calvin?" He grunts out his release and turns to face me while his cock is still buried in Karl's ass.

"Yeah, Doxy?"

"We leave in the morning. Find ten guys to remain behind so our guests don't get lonely. I want them all worked every hour on the hour while we are gone." Karl's eyes widen, bringing a smile to my face. "Do you need a reminder about looking at me?" He quickly darts his gaze away earning a chuckle from me, how the mighty have fallen.

"I'll hand pick them myself, Doxy. Are they allowed to embrace their darker desires?"

"The darker the better, they have free reign so long as they don't kill them," I say firmly. I refuse to allow them to die after only two weeks, they will suffer for as long as I say.

"Yes, Doxy."

Chapter Twenty-Five

Trevante

Being here in Knox's house is not how I pictured spending the past two weeks. Oh, we are not guests. Xander and I have been strapped to chairs in the basement and treated as if we are traitors. We haven't been tortured but Knox has come down here and knocked us around a few times but never utter a word. Xander says he is just working out his frustrations with us because we have both fallen for her. If the bastard would ungag me, then I would give him a piece of my fucking mind!

"You're here." I snap my head to see a woman standing in the corner of the room shrouded in the shadows. She steps forward and I immediately know who she is. Lakeland Bronson. Her brown hair is loose and flows around her shoulders, her green eyes are locked onto Xander who stares straight back at her with a guilt-ridden look which has me frowning. She moves with purpose as she comes toward us, stopping in the middle of him and I. She looks between Xander and me and purses her lips for a second before reaching out and yanking the cloths from our mouths.

I suck in a long pull of air. "Thanks," I rasp out.

"What he said," Xander mutters bitterly, turning away from Lakeland who doesn't seem bothered by his reaction.

She purses her lips and turns back to me, offering a kind smile which I return. "You're the one who called?"

"Yes," I answer.

"Why?" Her question stumps me.

"Because I knew you would come," Xander answers for me, still not looking our way.

"What made you think that?" she counters. He slowly turns his head and lifts his gaze to hers.

"You said you would know if she was dead, you would have felt it. I knew you would send him because it was the only lead you have had since she went missing." Lakeland's eyes fill with sadness but I also see hope lurking in the depths of them.

"Xander, is she really..." She clamps her mouth closed, unable to finish her sentence.

"Yeah. She's alive, Lake." A whimper escapes her before a smile graces her beautiful face.

"I knew it. I told him for years that *I* would have felt it if she was gone. I knew my soul didn't shatter for a reason because she is still alive." She moves briskly toward the wall and grabs a box cutter. I tense in anticipation and begin to worry that she may share a crazy streak like Doxy until she begins cutting away the duct tape and freeing us from our confines.

"He's going to be pissed, Lake," Xander warns. Lakeland's features harden as she stares up at my friend.

"I'll deal with my husband how I see fit, now you take him

and clean up. I won't have you meeting your nephews looking like you crawled out of a donkey's ass." I choke on my own spit. "I have clothes and everything else laid out in the guest room for him, you know where your room is." Xander recoils.

"I still have a room?" he mumbles.

Her eyes soften as she reaches out and grabs his hand giving it a squeeze. "You and I may have a fucked-up past, Xander, but that is where it will stay because my best friend loves you and I will not allow anything to come between her and me when she comes home. I've had years to process and come to terms with that night, I'm at peace with it." Xander eyes her with a look of awe.

"What about Knox?" She scrunches her face at his question.

"He's uh, working on it." Xander's face falls so she quickly rushes to add. "Give him time, Xan, he needs you as much as I need Wave. If he really hated you he would never have named his son after you." With those parting words, she leaves us standing here in Knox's torture basement, slightly battered and slightly bruised but nothing serious. At least Xander's eye is open now and he is starting to heal.

"Let's go, Knox will be back soon."

"How do you know he isn't here?" I ask as I follow after him.

"There is no way in hell he would have let Lake come down here if he was home, she is playing him at his own game and winning."

"What game?" I ask confused and exasperated.

"The game where he comes home to find us washed, clothed, fed and sitting on the mat in his office playing with his sons. Knox wouldn't dare raise his voice while his boys are around because his mother and Lake would beat the brakes off his ass."

These people are fucking weird!

After showering and shaving for the first time in two weeks, I feel a whole lot livelier. Lakeland even prepared a hot meal for us, which Xander and I both shoveled into our mouths like wild animals. I wanted to feel bad that I was eating like a pig in front of Lake but I couldn't because food never tasted so fucking good. Once we were finished, Lake told us it was time to meet her boys.

I can feel the tension wafting off Xander as we follow after her, he keeps clenching and unclenching his hands. Lake opens a door and steps inside. Children's laughter can be heard from inside but Xander is frozen on the spot and won't move. Lake shoots him a concerned look.

"We'll be right in, just give us a second," I say with a smile. She nods and leaves alone in the hallway. "What's wrong?" I ask him.

His shoulders deflate as he faces me. "Those are my best friends' kids in there."

"Yeah?"

He scrubs a hand down his face and shakes his head. "I ran Lakeland down with my car the night I thought she left Wave to die. I didn't just hurt her, I killed their baby!" Sorrow churns inside me for him. Lakeland and Knox suffered a great loss at his hand but I also know he has been beating himself up about this for years, you can see it in the way he refuses to hold eye contact with her for too long.

"Yeah, you did!" We both spin around to find Knox, Taylan and two of Knox's men standing a few feet behind us. Xander remains frozen at my side as he stares at his best friend.

"How can we move past this—"

Xander cuts Taylan off before he can finish speaking. "Saying I'm sorry won't change what I did, I can't replace what I took from you and Lake and for that I will never forgive myself." Surprise ripples through me at hearing Xander speak so emotionally.

"If you could go back, would you change it?" Knox asks.

Xander sighs and shakes his head, surprising not only me but Knox and Taylan as well. "No."

"Come again?" Knox grits out.

"I wouldn't change it because if I did, then you wouldn't have those two kids in that room. Call me heartless and hate me all you want but no, I wouldn't change what happened because it would mean that you wouldn't have Rave and Axlyn."

Knox's brows raise before he slowly turns to the side and glares at Taylan, who shoots him a toothy grin. "You told him their names?" he forces out.

Tay shrugs. "I'm sick of being your messenger. You claim to hate him but every month you track his whereabouts. When he went off grid a few weeks back, you lost your shit. You still care about him, Knox, and I think it's time you admit that to yourself because he isn't going anywhere, not this time." Both Knox and Xander stare after Taylan as he brushes past the both of them to go inside the room where Lakeland and her sons are.

"I'll give you guys a minute—." Knox pins me with a dark look that has me clamping my mouth closed.

"You stay the fuck away from my wife and kids," he snarls.

"And you can curb your anger, right now!" Knox's features harden as Lakeland comes to join us. "Knoxville Bronson, you will let go of this grudge, right now, because I won't bring my best friend back here with you hating the man—well, one of the men she cares for." Knox flinches in disgust.

"They are not going near you or her!" he snaps.

"With all due respect, fuck you," I say, earning a gasp from Lake and a cruel smirk from Knox.

"My twin not enough for you?" he taunts.

"You make another joke about your sister not being enough again and I'll break your fucking jaw!" Xander says in a tone so fucking cold and menacing that Lake takes a step away from him. "You can hate me, say whatever you want about me, but you will not talk about Wave in that way again. You don't know a fucking thing about what she went through."

"You don't know her at all," I add.

"What the fuck is this shit, Xander? You both think I'm going to stand back and let you, what? Date my sister, sleep with her?" Knox sounds like a prick.

"Enough!" I turn in time to see a woman and man exit the same room Lake came from. I step aside to allow them to pass and notice immediately how Xander softens at the sight of her and Knox tenses. "Hello, my boy," she says lovingly as she gazes up at Xander with a warm smile that is filled with love.

"Hi, Mom," he rasps out before he engulfs her in a hug. She begins to weep in his hold.

"That's Clara, Knox and Wave's mom but she is also Taylan and Xander's mom," Lake whispers. I reel back in disgust.

"Xander and Wave are related?" I hear the disbelief in my

own voice and feel bile rushing up my throat at the thought of them being siblings. Lake chuckles and shakes her head.

"No. Clara raised Taylan and Xander as her own and I guess in a way she sort of raised me and my sister as well. She may be blood related to Knox and Wave but she is all of our mother and that man, that's Roberto Da Luca, their father." My eyes widen.

"Doxy took his last name," I whisper.

"The fuck did you just say?" Knox snaps, garnering all our attention.

"Your sister doesn't go by Waverly Bronson anymore, she is now known as Doxy Da Luca." Knox's face pales, I look to his father to find he is shocked by my revelation.

"Why?" Roberto asks, speaking for the first time.

"Waverly Bronson died the night her son did, forcing her to become Doxy Da Luca," I answer. A sob tears from Clara and Lake covers her mouth as tears fill her eyes. Knox darts forward and wraps his arm around her shoulders drawing her into his side.

"My baby had a... baby?" Clara chokes out. Xander rubs her back and tries to offer her comfort. I look to Xander asking without words if I should continue or not, his subtle nod is all I need.

"Yes. She said she had a beautiful baby boy but unfortunately that is all I can say, it isn't my story to tell and honestly, I think I pissed your daughter off enough already," I say with a guilty smile.

"What the fuck did you do to my sister, asshole?" Knox snaps.

"Called you," I say with no emotion in my tone.

Chapter Twenty-Six

Xander

I stand here staring at Rave and Axlyn, they are so big!

Rave's seven and I am only just meeting him for the first time. I hate that I missed so much of his life. Axlyn is five and looks so much like his dad. Rave is a spitting image of his mother but I can see the devil in his eyes which is all his daddy. I've been standing out back watching the two boys play with Taylan, Clara and Roberto and can't help but smile at the sight. I never thought I would be back here or even have the chance to meet my nephews or see my mom's eyes have some life back in them.

"Here." I turn and grab the beer Knox offers me and nod my thanks. We stand here side by side, sipping our drinks as we watch the kids jump all over Tay who pretends to be injured from them bouncing on him.

"Roberto, huh?"

Knox groans and scrubs a hand down his face. "I was out voted in my own fucking house. Lake and mom moved him in while I was in the states meeting up with Chaos and Artemis." I had heard from Taylan that Knox has grown close with Chaos Murdoch and Artemis Argyros.

"You forgive him?" I push.

"Yes and no," he answers. "Yes, because he makes my mom happy and my boys get to have their grandfather around. No, because..." He lets his sentence trail off.

"Because you didn't have him around when you were growing up, you blame him for not being there to protect Wave," I finish for him.

"Yeah," he breathes out.

"She's not the same person you once knew, Knox."

"It doesn't matter—"

"It does to her. I love your sister with every beat of my fucking heart, Knox—"

"Stop–"

"No, you need to hear this!" I face him so he can see the seriousness in my eyes. "I've loved her since we were kids, I never stopped. There will never be another woman for me aside from her. You are my brother and I love you but if there is a war coming between you and her, I will choose her, always." His mouth parts and his brows raise as he searches my eyes for any sign of deceit.

"You mean that, don't you."

"Yes."

"Is my sister coming to kill me?"

"Yes."

"Why?"

"Because she blames me, you and Taylan for not finding her."

Guilt swarms his gaze. "I thought she was dead," he whispers brokenly.

"It doesn't matter what we thought. She thinks she is too damaged to be Waverly again but she's wrong. Trey and I know she can be her again."

He pushes his lips to the side as he studies me. "What's the deal with you and him?"

"No deal. We both love her. Trey has proven that she is the center of his world and shown it many times. He is the one who was there the night she escaped and whisked her off to a safe house where he helped her train and plan to take back her freedom and overthrow his father."

Knox frowns. "Who is his father?"

"Uh shit, I forgot you didn't know. Karl is his father."

"You brought a traitor into my fucking house?" he roars.

"No. Trey hates him and he is the reason we were able to put an army together and help Wave raid the clubs and free the girls. He knows she has his father and what she is doing to him. He won't betray us because he is in love with your sister. Make no mistake though, if there is a war, we will both stand with Wave. I'm sorry, brother, but you chose Lake and I chose your sister years ago." I wait for him to break out into a fit of rage and curse me out for having the balls to dare to touch his sister much less fall in love with her.

"Do you swear to protect her no matter what the cost is, even if that cost is our brotherhood?" His question surprises me but my response is instant.

"Yes."

"Is Trevante good to her?"

"Yeah, he soothes the darkness inside her. I force her to face it but together we both get her to feel without her even realizing it. I think seeing you again will make her admit to herself that she isn't an emotionless bitch."

"Boss!" Knox and I turn to see Marco, Chris and Drew rushing toward us. Marco shoves an iPad into Knox's hands. "A convoy was spotted leaving a private airstrip in Winnipeg. I checked the flight manifests and the plane came from Ireland sir."

"You confirm this?" Knox asks Marco.

"Yes, sir. I had Chris and Drew cross check my searches and they confirmed the same thing, the plane that landed was your sister's." Knox and I share a look.

"Get the men ready, we fly to Winnipeg as soon as the plane is ready." The three of them rush off to carry out Knox's orders. "Looks like I won't have to fly back to Ireland after all, she kept her word and came back."

"I'm coming with you to get my girl." Knox scrunches his face in disgust which has laughter bursting out of me.

"That shit sounds so fucking ugly coming out of your mouth," he grumbles as he stalks away.

Trey and I are both tense but excited at seeing our girl again, two weeks without her has been fucking hell. I miss the touch of her skin, the feel of her lips, the scent that lingers in a room after she leaves it. Fuck, I just miss her. Knox has been shooting Trey subtle glares every chance he gets, the plane ride was fucking awkward but being in a car with them both is suffocating.

"What's the plan?" Tay asks, breaking the tension-filled silence.

"We couldn't track her so we have no choice but to go in blind," Knox answers.

"What made you think you could track her? She has been a ghost most of her life, she knows how to disappear." Tay shoots Trey a filthy look over his shoulder before focusing back on the road. There may only be the four of us in the car but the amount of alpha energy in here can be felt.

"We thought making it look like you and Xander were tracking her that she would leave you some bread crumbs to follow but turns out, she didn't." I grind my teeth hating the gleeful way Taylan says that shit.

"That was your first mistake, you think you know her but you don't," Trey counters.

"And what would you have done differently, asshole?" Knox bites out.

"I would have created a fake club that held women and leaked its location, she would have come to you. She will do anything to help a woman in need which is why you are fools." We don't get a chance to answer, Tay slams on the brakes. I lurch forward and smack into the back of his seat with a grunt.

"Spikes, Wave has fucking spikes down!" I smirk, my girl is smart. I jump out of the car with Trey following after me, ignoring Knox's calls for us to stop as I stroll across the bridge, not giving a fuck about all the guns her men have pointed at us. She looks like a dark angel standing there in the center of the bridge with Anna, Kimber, Nano, Brett, William and Calvin forming a semi-circle around her. Her face is a picture of rage and fuck me, that look has my cock twitching in my pants.

Before I can get more than ten feet near her, Brett and Calvin step forward with their guns raised.

"Close enough," Brett barks out earning a scowl from me.

"You ready for the war pulling that trigger would start?" I taunt.

"Yes. I have my orders and will obey them." I purse my lips and nod my head at William's answer, respecting him for obeying her.

"What about me, Wavey baby? You gonna let these fuckers put a bullet in my chest?" Taylan asks as he takes a step past me. All the men cock their guns but the sound of Knox's guys mimicking their moves has everyone on edge. All it would take is for one of these guys to get jumpy and pull that trigger accidentally before a war would break out and lives would be lost.

"Yes," she answers without hesitation. Taylan's face falls.

"What about me, sister?" She snaps her gaze to the other side to watch as her brother stalks toward her, paying Brett and William no mind as he passes them.

"You shoot him and I will kill your families while you watch!" Taylan vows when Brett shifts his finger on the trigger. Wave raises her hand, halting her guys as Knox comes to a stop a couple of feet away from her. The dead look in her eyes tells me everything I need to know, this is a set up.

"Knox, move!" I roar as I try to reach him but I'm too late, she pulls her gun on him.

Chapter Twenty-Seven

Doxy

I press the barrel of my gun into the center of his chest, loving the dumbfounded look on his face at my move. This fucker really thought I would be happy to see him.

"What are you doing?"

"Did you really think that me coming back here was to reconnect with you, Knox?" I don't give him a chance to reply. "I brought you here to the place where my life ended and yours began so I could take it all away from you."

"You've changed," he whispers.

"A lot has changed *me*."

"If you want to kill me, then do it but I won't lift a finger against you, I would never hurt you Wave."

"Don't call me that!" I growl.

"What the fuck should I call you then? Doxy Da Luca?" He scoffs before continuing. "You were never and will never be a Da Luca. You are a fucking Bronson through and through. Don't ever forget where you came from."

"Forget where I came from?" I taunt. "You mean like how you forgot about me and moved on with your life like I was nothing but a bad dream?"

"I never forgot about you!" he shouts. Fuck this. I shift my gun and shoot him in the shoulder. He cries out and stumbles back a few steps. Taylan and Xander are held back by my men. Knox's guys rush forward but freeze when I point my gun at his head. "Any of you make a move and I'll shoot him," I warn. Taylan raises his hand and orders them back.

"Don't do this, baby, you don't want to kill him," Xander tries to reason.

"Doxy, he's your blood," Trey pushes.

I snort. "I told you before, Trevante, my tampon has blood on it every month and I still throw that shit away, he's no different than a used tampon."

"I take offense to that." I stiffen at the sound of her voice. My men swivel around and shout for her to stop.

"If they shoot her, Waverly, I'll kill them all!" Knox screams as he pushes to his feet. "Put your fucking guns down now!" Knox roars.

"Wave?" I close my eyes and fight back the emotions her voice has rising inside me. "That tampon with the bullet in his shoulder is my husband, your brother and the father of my sons." I snap my eyes and flick my gaze to Knox. Worry lines mar his face as he darts his gaze around at my guns, clearly panicked that Lake somehow managed to get here without him knowing.

"Stand down!" I shout.

"Doxy—"

"I said stand the fuck down, Nano!"

"You heard her, stand down now," Nano orders. My

breaths are erratic as I try to gain control over myself but I'm failing.

"Lakeland, get the fuck out of here now!" Knox barks. "Marco, get my wife and take her home now."

"Shut up, Knox," Lake snaps back. When the guy I assume to be Marco moves to pass by Xander and the others, I shift my sights on him.

"Touch her and I'll kill you," I declare. Marco looks to Knox for confirmation. I look to Knox to find his gaze already on me. "I may want to kill you but that bloodlust doesn't extend to her." He searches my eyes for a second, trying to decipher if I am lying.

"Kill me but don't touch her, Waverly, please don't hurt her," he pleads.

"I saved her life and sacrificed my own fourteen years ago," I snarl before spinning around to face the girl I could never bring myself to hate. How could I hate her when I chose her a long time ago. She loves Knox but he isn't her soulmate, I am. Lake is leaning against the railing that has flowers and a stupid cross attached to it, gazing out over the river. I slowly make my way toward her and rest my arms on the barrier, the same barrier I fell through over a decade ago. We stand here silently staring out at the river that is lit up by the moon in the sky.

"If somebody had asked me fifteen years ago where I thought I saw my life going, I would never have picked this." I snort a laugh but say nothing. "Eight years ago I found out I had been living a lie for six years. I didn't believe Riverland when she told me but I started getting these glimpses in my mind like flashbacks and I saw you a few times." I remain silent even though her revelation has shocked me. I can feel everyone staring at us but none of them move or utter a word. "I wanted my memories back so bad but the moment they returned, I was on this very bridge and screamed for *you*." She slowly turns to face me.

"I can't—"

"You can look at me, Waverly." I shake my head, fighting back the emotion trying to overcome me. For years I had nothing, I've been numb to everything in this world after the death of my son but just the sound of her voice has me wanting to crumble. "Look at me!" she screams. I stumble sideways and manage to catch myself on the barrier before I fall.

"I can't!" I yell, hating the watery tone of my voice. I watch her through my lashes, step forward and crouch down in front of the cross that has my name and date of birth but...

"It doesn't have a death date," I mutter as she grabs something off the cross and stands holding it out to me. I hesitantly reach out and grab the weathered looking piece of jewelry that is covered in grime and moss. It's a locket.

"I had that cross made eight years ago because I refused to come out here every month and look at a death date when I knew you were alive." I finally lift my gaze to hers and see tears trekking silently down her cheeks. Her green eyes hold so much love in them that it has a lump forming in my own throat.

"Why come back here?" I whisper brokenly.

"Because I couldn't let you go. I come here every month to bring flowers and have a team of Navy Seals that Knox has on his payroll drag this river. I needed them to find a bone or something so I could finally let you go but I couldn't let go because I knew you were alive. I would have felt it in my soul if you were truly dead."

"I did die."

"No you didn't. You just took a small vacation from being who you truly are because you needed to heal."

"Why the fuck did you do all of this?" I shout as I wave my arms around. "And what the fuck is this?" I snap, dangling the locket from my finger in front of her. She reaches into her shirt and pulls out a locket that looks the same as the one on my finger, albeit the one on her neck is clean.

"Knox gave this to me when I was sixteen and had it inscribed. This locket brought me back to him. I hunted for months to find you the exact same one and had it inscribed so you would come back to me!"

I bring the locket closer and brush my thumb over the locket, clearing away the grime to read the message.

I'll never give up, I'll find you.

I flick my gaze back to hers and frown. "You had this made for me?" I whisper. She nods and sniffs as she swipes away her tears with the back of her hand.

"I never gave up on you, Waverly. The moment my memories returned I began searching for you all over the world. Every day after I finished work I hunted for you. Knox and Taylan helped. I need you to know that I never gave up on you! I will always find you, Wave, because I fucking choose you." She sobs out. "I will always choose you, Waverly Bronson, because you are my fucking best friend, my soul mate." She is full on sobbing now. "I love your brother and would die for him in the blink of an eye but you are my soulmate. My person."

I don't realize I'm crying until I feel the tears hit my cheeks. I reach up and catch a tear on my finger, I haven't seen my own tears in... years. I haven't felt anything aside from rage for so long I forgot what it felt like to feel something other than that.

"Please, come back to me, Wave, because I can't lose you again, let me help you."

I shake my head. "You can't help me, Lay," I say as I hold her locket out to her. In a move I did not see coming, she slaps me. I stumble sideways and it takes me a second to register what the fuck just happened. My men are shouting and threatening to shoot but I ignore them and Knox's guys fighting as I turn back to Lakeland who is standing there looking like a lioness ready to charge.

"You fucking coward!" I gape at the audacity of this bitch.

"You have no fucking idea what I went through," I scream, the anguished tone of my shout has everyone around us falling silent. "You lost your memories, big fucking deal. I lost everything."

"Stop being a coward and running from the pain of your past and face it. You aren't here to kill Knox and take Canada."

"Yes, I am," I sneer. She closes the space between us and presses her head into mine, her eyes are filled with pain. Good, she deserves to hurt after what she just said.

"No, you're here for me because I made it out of that car and you didn't. You are here to punish me by hurting him because you and I both know that I could have easily been you if you didn't save me." I shake my head but she pushes on. "You. Saved. Me."

"So what?" I bite back.

"You want to punish me, then do it but don't hurt him, Wave. The day he thought you died he did as well. He tortured me and blamed me for years, thinking I killed his twin, his baby sister. He never let you go, Waverly. For fuck's sake, your face is tattooed over his heart." I reel back earning a smirk from her. "That's right, your face is tattooed over his heart because there is no one in this world that means more to him than you do." I shake my head. "Don't deny it because you would just be lying to yourself."

"Stop talking," I grit out past the lump in my throat.

"We named our son after you and River. We have two beautiful baby boys, Wave."

"At least your sons are breathing!" I scream. Before I can stop her, she has arms around me and is holding me tight against her.

"I'm so sorry, Wave," she chokes out. I try to push her away but she won't fucking let go.

"Get away from me," I shout.

"No."

"Fuck off, Lakeland."

"I'll never let go," she vows. Fuck, I can't stop it, a sound so horrendous and painful rips out of me.

"Argggh," I scream out as I collapse in her hold, taking us both to the ground but still, she won't let go as I break in her arms. I try to fight back against the emotions bursting out of me without consent but now that they have finally emerged, I can't shove them back in the box I have kept them in for years. "He died!" I cry out. "They took him from me." Now that the tears and the sobbing has begun I can't stop it.

"I got you, Wave. I'll never let you go. I'll put you back together, one beautifully broken piece at a time." I grip the back of her shirt and claw at her, needing to keep her close, terrified that if an inch of space comes between us that I will fracture and shatter into a million pieces that I will never be able to patch up again. I'm not strong enough to save myself twice. I can't do it again. The first time nearly killed me and I was emotionless then but now, she has forced me to face the feelings I had buried which means I wouldn't be able to save myself from hell a second time.

"It hurts, Lake!" I scream out. Her hold on me tightens as she pulls me as close as she can to her.

"Knox," she screams his name and within seconds I can hear people surrounding us but I keep my face buried in the crook of her neck as I fall the fuck apart. "Xander, Trey and Taylan are going to carry us to a car and you and I are going to stay in a hotel."

"No the fuck you aren't!"

"Shut the hell up, Knox. She needs your wife and you are going to let Lake help or I'll break your fucking jaw," Xander vows.

"And I'll shoot your other fucking shoulder," Taylan adds a second before Lake and I are lifted awkwardly. I refuse to even chance a peek, getting in the backseat isn't an option so they lift us onto the bed of a pickup and wrap some blankets around us.

"I love you, kitten." I hear Knox say to Lake.

"I love you too. Call the boys and tell them Mommy loves them and I'll speak to them soon," she answers.

"We won't come in but Xander and I will be keeping watch outside the hotel and so will the rest of the Da Luca... family," Trey announces.

"Fine, now piss off so we can go," she snaps at the guys.

"I love you, Wave," Xan mutters.

"What he said, Doxy," Trey tacks on.

"Well I refuse to be left out so I love you both and will see you soon," Taylan the twat bucket says.

Chapter Twenty-Eight

Doxy

When we arrived at the hotel, Lake led me to a room that she somehow miraculously had the key for and then dragged me into the large bathroom that had a jacuzzi size tub in it. She ran me a bath, then undressed me without uttering a single word. She placed me in the bath before disappearing for a few minutes only to return with two bottles of vodka. I shook my head when she stripped off her clothes and climbed into the bath with me, handing me a bottle and keeping one for herself. I can tell from the way she keeps eyeing me that the tattoos I now have are making her curious. I know Lakeland and it is just a matter of time before all the question bursts out of her so I pop the cap off the bottle and take a long pull.

After the first drink I can't seem to stop myself from drinking more or maybe I don't want to stop, I just want to feel numb again. It's fucking terrifying feeling again after so long. I thought I was dead inside but turns out all it took to shatter the carefully crafted walls I had built inside myself was the sound of my best friends voice.

"I saw them, Wave," she whispers hesitantly before taking a drink of her own bottle.

"Saw what, Lakeland?" I bite out.

"The scars," she whispers brokenly with unshed tears in her eyes. "The tattoos are beautiful but they don't hide the raised skin."

"What the fuck do you want from me? Do you want me to tell you that they were kind, loving and never laid a hand on me? Do you want me to make up a fairytale story so you can feel good about the past fourteen years and not feel guilty because you were happy and I was being treated worse than a dog and fucked like a pig?" Tears trail down her cheeks and I hate I just said all of that and want to blame the fucking vodka for loosening my lips but that's a lie. I was never good at holding back when it came to her. No matter how hard I tried to keep things from her, I couldn't. The only thing I managed to keep hidden was my relationship with Xander because I feared she would tell Knox and he would take him from me.

"If hating me is what helps you, then hate me because I can take it so long as you don't leave me. For years I envisioned you being laid up in a hospital in a coma or something like that but I never thought..." She shakes her head and takes a deep breath. "He came to the meetings with the head families, went to Switzerland with Knox and the others to play mediator for the Argyros and the Murdochs and never once did Knox suspect that his sister's tormenter was right there beside him."

"Why the fuck would he suspect anything? My own twin thought I was dead!" I hear the bitterness in my own voice.

"He didn't know, Wave. You know him, there is no way he

would have stopped searching for you if he thought you made it out of that car. Xander jumped in after you and searched for hours and no one could locate you. How the fuck did Karl find you before us?"

I purse my lips and ponder her question for a second. "I actually don't know how he found me." We remain silent for a long while as we get lost in our own thoughts and drink. I'm starting to feel light, like I can almost float.

"We need to get out before we get too drunk and drown." Laughter bursts out of me the second she finishes speaking, I have no idea why I am laughing. It feels weird to do it and even hear the sound. "Why are you laughing at me?" she snaps, clearly getting annoyed.

"After everything I have been through, it would wound my ego so badly to die by drowning." She eyes me for a second before she begins to laugh, we sound like fucking hyenas but neither of us can seem to find the strength to stop, that is until my laughter morphs into sobs.

"Fuck, hang on," she says before she is emptying the tub, then leaping out to dry herself and then comes to help me out. She wraps a robe around me, then I'm crushed against her as she holds me while I cry. I see nothing through the haze of my tears as she leads me from the bathroom and helps me onto the bed. She climbs in, spooning me from behind as she wraps her arms around me and holds me close.

"I can't stop crying," I choke out.

"Then don't stop, let it all out. You don't need to be strong in front of me, Waverly. I will never judge you, but just don't push me away, let me be your anchor. Let me hold you and be here for you." Her stupid fucking words have me sobbing harder. For years I was alone and had only myself to rely on. I became my own savior, my own white knight because I thought no one cared or even wanted me to be alive. I thought they gave up on me but Lay didn't, she has been searching for me since she got her memories back.

"Why am I so angry at everyone except for you?" I rasp out, my voice is hoarse from all the tears but I don't care.

"You are angry at me the most and that is why it's easier to project that anger onto everyone else because you don't want to hate yourself for hating me because you saved me."

"I don't hate you."

"A part of you does and that's okay because I hate me too for not finding you." I roll over and face her. She smiles sadly and reaches up to swipe away my tears with her thumbs.

"I don't hate you, Lakeland. I could never hate you but it seems I don't have that same issue with my brother." It feels weird calling him my brother or my twin after so many years of refusing to acknowledge that we were even related. I guess in some way she is right. It was easier for me to hate Knox and blame him for everything if I didn't think of him as being related to me.

"Give it time. What you went through, the horrors you endured at the hands of that cunt will last a lifetime. There is no time limit on healing from trauma."

"I have a family to run. I don't have the luxury of staying in this hotel and pretending that the world outside doesn't exist."

"Yes the fuck you do. Your guys are handling all of that stuff for you, Knox will help them."

"No—"

"It doesn't make you weak by allowing others to help you, a great leader knows how to delegate and that is what you are doing." I mull over her words for a minute before relenting, I can take one night to myself. I also know Kimber and Anna won't let Trey and Xander fuck shit up.

"So... Xander *and* Trey, huh?"

I narrow my eyes. "What are you, the twat swat?" She chokes on her own spit for a split second before she begins cackling like a damn hyena again. I find myself smiling at the sight of her curled into a ball laughing her ass off.

"The twat swat," she wheezes out, then goes back to laughing like an idiot while I lay here staring at her for a second before laughter begins to work its way out of me. Before long, we are both curled into balls facing each other with happy tears rolling down our cheeks.

"You're an idiot."

She smiles. "I know but you love me anyway."

All traces of humor vanish from me as I stare into her eyes. "I always will."

Her features grow taut as she reaches out and cups my cheek. "I never gave up, I found you."

"Technically, I found you."

"Knox and I had talked about leaving Canada after Rave was born and moving to Spain but we couldn't do it."

Frowning, I ask, "Why?"

"Because I knew one day I would find you and you would want to come home. Not only that, what if you did find your way home and we weren't here? I couldn't take that chance."

Realization crashes into me. "You put your life on hold for me, didn't you?"

"No. I went to nursing school and studied hard so I made something of my life so you didn't sacrifice yours for nothing. I married the only boy I have ever loved and we have two beautiful little boys who are named after our four favorite people."

"Xander told me what happened, what he did to you."

She takes a shuddering breath and nods. "I wanted to tell you that night. I tried but then we got run off the road."

"It was my fault that you lost your baby," I whisper.

"No. Don't you do that. None of what happened that night is your fault. Do you hear me? Our baby paid the price for my father and your uncle's greed. Xander had no idea I was pregnant and it doesn't change the hideous thing he did but I get why he did it. I'm at peace with it, Wave. God needed another angel so he took the best. I will see my baby again when I get to the pearly gates and... you will see yours as well."

Pain explodes in my chest. I slam my eyes closed and try to breathe through it. "I named him Laiken Knoxville Bronson, after you and Knox," I choke out.

"Oh, Wave." She cries as we hold each other, tears trailing down my cheeks.

"He was so beautiful, Lake. He had a button nose and the most angelic face."

"I'm sorry I never got to meet my nephew."

"He was born sleeping." I can't bear to tell her the rest. I may have told Trey and Xander but I will never tell another living soul.

"God must have needed another angel."

"I needed him more." I sob. "I was fine, I could take every-thing they did to me and compartmentalize it, they were hurting Doxy not Waverly. I kept Wave safe. But that all changed the day Waverly gave birth, she died with her son and Doxy took over. Doxy feels nothing. She's strong, doesn't need anyone, she just wants them all to fucking pay for what they took from her!"

"Doxy became your savior, she was your redemption, she is your superpower."

"My what?"

"Becoming Doxy Da Luca is what saved you. She gave you the power you needed to survive hell, she brought you to the other side and kept you whole while your world was falling apart. You gave your alter ego a name so it would help you process but make no mistake, *you* are Doxy but you are also Waverly Bronson."

"I don't know how to be Waverly again," I answer truthfully. "I haven't been her in years. Xander has tried to push me to be her—"

"Because he fell in love with Waverly Bronson."

"Trey has never pushed me to be her—"

"Because he is in love with Doxy Da Luca." The twinkle of mischief in her eye has me wanting to groan but I refrain.

"Can you stop acting like you aren't loving my misery?"

"Oh, I do not love hearing about your past at all but I do want to hear every single detail about you, Trevante and Xander. You have those boys eating out of the palm of your hand."

I scoff. "There is nothing to tell, we fuck and that's it."

"Oh, that is a load of crocodile shit!" I scrunch my face.

"Who the fuck says *crocodile shit*?" She waves me off.

"I have a five-year-old son who is obsessed with them and thinks Knox and I are rude because we won't buy him a pet croc for his birthday." A smile scratches across my face as I picture what their sons must look like. "Axlyn is a plague. Rave lulled Knox and me into thinking kids were easy, he was such a good baby so we had another. Ax has put us off having more children." Laughter bursts out of me. "I'm not kidding, I love being pregnant and going through labor but I don't have it in me to raise another mini Knox. These boys have a complex, and it's all their father's fault!"

"I want to meet them," I blurt out, her eyes soften immediately. "I-if... that's okay?"

Anger flashes through her eyes. "Don't you ever for a fucking second think that it wouldn't be okay. You never have to ask to see your nephews."

"Thank you."

"I missed you," she whispers brokenly as her eyes begin to fill with tears again. I clasp her hand in mine and place a kiss to the back of it.

"I missed you too." She sniffles and tries to smile but fails. "I never thought I would feel a semblance of Waverly inside me again but just hearing your voice had her spurring to life. I've felt nothing for years, Lake, not since my son died."

"I will be by your side as you face your demons, I will never leave you."

I hope she means that because I have more demons than Lucifer does in his army.

Chapter Twenty-Nine

Trevante

"How long do you think they can stay holed up in that room?" Taylan asks from the back seat. I rub my jaw and stare at the hotel in front of me as I answer.

"They've been in there for three days and the only people they have let in are Kimber and Anna."

"Wrong. Mom flew in with the boys yesterday and brought them here to see Lake and Wave." I turn in my seat to face Knox in surprise.

"I never saw them."

He rolls his eyes. "That's because they arrived when Xander forced your nasty ass to go take a shower," he bites back.

"Mom and the boys are still in there with them, so are Kimber and Anna," Xander adds.

"How long are we going to let them hide in there?" I ask the three of them. They all pin me with a weird look.

"Go knock on the door and see how well Lake takes to seeing you," Taylan says.

"I would love to see my wife rip you apart." Knox's tone is filled with excitement.

"Fuck this," Xander clips out a second before he shoves his door open and steps out, the three of us quickly chasing after him.

"What the fuck are you doing?" Knox calls after him but Xander doesn't slow his steps as he makes his way toward the lobby.

"Not letting my girl hide from me any longer," he answers as he reaches for the door but Knox shoulders him out of the way, then pins him against the glass wall.

"She needs time."

"Fuck you, Knox, you have no idea what she needs. If she is hurting, I want to be there with her and help her. I won't let her think she is alone again. I will never leave her." He shoves Knox off and marches inside, I follow after without saying a word because I agree with him. I haven't been able to relax since she left us that night on the bridge. I've sent everyone back home, except for Nano, Brett and Calvin. William will oversee everything until we return.

Are we going to return to Ireland?

I push that thought from my mind as we step out of the elevator. Xander pounds his fist against the door as nerves thrum through me at the prospect of her turning us away. What if she doesn't want us anymore? Could that be the reason why she is hiding away? When the door finally opens it's Clara who stands before us with a warm smile.

"I wondered how long it would be before you came and busted down her door." Her tone is filled with mirth and love.

"I just need to know she's okay, Mom," Xander says quietly. She reaches out and clasps his hand then leads him into the room. Knox, Taylan and I get into a shoving match as we all try to fight over who gets to go in next.

"Fuck off!" Knox snaps.

"Suck a dick, she's my sister too!" Taylan shouts.

"She's my girlfriend!" I snarl as I elbow Knox in his shoulder, the same one Doxy shot, knocking him out of the way, loving the sound of his pained groan as I rush into the room only to come to a halt a few feet inside the room. My eyes widen at the sight in front of me.

"It's a set up!" Taylan mutters. Xander, Knox and I all shoot him a glare. Kimber, Anna, Lake, Clara and Wave all sit on couches facing us while Rave and Axlyn play with their toys on the floor.

"Daddy!" Rave cries out at the sight of his father. Knox pushes past us and drops to his knees as both his sons run to him. I smile at the sight. He holds both his boys close and places kisses to their heads, all the girls melt at the sight but not *my* girl. She looks fierce and shows no emotion as she keeps her gaze on Xander and me.

"Daddy, come see Aunt Wave," Axlyn says as he tries to drag his father to his feet. Knox helps him out and stands slowly. Wave tears her gaze from us to face her brother and I see a range of emotions flicker in her eyes. Axlyn keeps trying to drag his father toward his aunt but he doesn't budge.

"Anna, would you and Kimber mind taking my boys for a walk?" Lake asks the girls.

"Yeah, I saw a park down the street, we'll take them there," Kimber says. The boys hug their mom and dad before the girls take them out. The moment they leave, the tension in the room soars to new heights as the siblings continue to stare at each other. Lake climbs to her feet and closes the space between her and her husband. He instantly wraps his arms around her and pulls her in close when she is within reach.

I envy them.

I know Doxy feels something for us but she won't fucking admit it no matter what we do!

"Go to her," Lakeland whispers low enough for only us to hear. Knox pulls back and stares down at her. She smiles encouragingly at him. "She needs you." Knox swallows and stabs a hand through his hair and nods. He steps around his wife and moves toward Doxy, slow enough so she has every chance to stop him. Her mother sits beside her, rubbing her hand up and down her back. In a move I didn't see coming he drops to his knees in front of his sister. He tentatively reaches out and grabs her hands, holding them in his as he looks up at her.

"I'm here." Two words, two words that mean nothing in any other type of situation except for this one, and has my girl's eyes filling with tears. Xan and I share a loaded look, she's displaying emotion and it's a sight to see. We are so used to her being cold, reserved and keeping everything locked down inside her. Knox drops her hands, grips the hem of his shirt and yanks it off. Her eyes zero in on the ink that covers his chest. "You have my heart. You are the first girl I loved aside from our mom. I had your face inked on my chest because the day I thought I lost you, I stopped loving everything in this world. I even forced myself to feel nothing toward Lay. There was no light without you in my life, everything was so fucking dark without you. I took over the Da Luca family so I had the manpower to search for you. I made up a fantasy in my head that you got out of that car, ran away and married some rich guy, then had a couple of kids and were happy. I had to tell myself that daily so I wouldn't break down."

"Why?" Knox jerks at the sound of her voice.

"Because you are my womb mate, my best friend, my twin. You are my exact other half, Waverly. I was cold and alone for years until I got my girl back, but she couldn't let you go when she got her memories back. I had to be the strong one and let her search so I didn't break down every time the Seals didn't find a body in that river. I had to hold her together and be strong for our boys." He reaches up to cup her cheek. "If I had to choose between loving you and breathing, I would use my last breath to tell you I choose you."

My heart lurches inside my chest when I see a tear fall from her eye. Xander's shoulders hunch forward, just like me he is feeling pain for her. I hate that we can't go to her and hold her. She is too strong and proud for that to happen, she needs this moment with her brother so she can let go of all the anger inside her. Spending these past three days with Lake have really helped her, I can see it in the way she doesn't sit so straight and tense, and her eyes don't hold that same haunted look like they always had.

"I'm... sorry," she chokes out as she pushes forward and falls into Knox, hugging him. His shoulders shake with silent tears as she sobs in her brother's hold. I look at Clara who has her hand covering her mouth, crying at the sight of her children embracing. It brings warmth to my heart seeing her making up with Knox and letting go of her anger, that shit was eating her up inside.

I hate that uncertainty is warring inside me, what if what we shared means nothing to her and sleeping with me and

Xander was just a way to pass time. If she admits to feeling nothing for us, I don't know how I will heal from that wound. I love her, I fucking need her and I don't need anyone. If she chooses to go her own way, then I will continue to work for her just so I would be able to catch glimpses of her and see her happy. I just want to be in her orbit.

Chapter Thirty

Xander

I haven't spoken a word since we got to her room. She's been talking to Knox and Taylan and even including her mom and Lake in some conversations but never me and Trey. We are sitting in the corner of the room like children who have been placed in a time out. I can feel the unease wafting off him as he worries over what she will decide to do with us.

Will she choose us? Send us away? Finally fucking admit to loving us as much as we love her?

Questions like that have been swirling in my mind for hours and I can't get them to stop, nor can I stop staring at her. She appears lighter, almost like the weight of the world has been lifted from her shoulders. It makes me happy to see some type of semblance of *my* Waverly in her eyes or in the way she gestures. I had an inkling that it wouldn't be her twin to break through her walls, which is why I had Trey call Lake and tell her to follow us when we left for Winnipeg. Lake and Wave share a bond like I do with Tay and Knox, we aren't just friends we are... family. No, we're closer than that, I would die for my brothers as I know they would me. Lake and Wave are the same. They proved that the night Wave sacrificed her life to save Lakeland.

"We should get the boys and head back," Lake says, drawing me from my thoughts.

"Yeah, it's getting late," Knox agrees as he climbs to his feet. Tay mimics him.

"Will... you come home with us?" Clara asks. A whoosh of air escapes Wave, she flicks her gaze to us for a split second before looking back to her mother.

"I need a night to... speak to *them*." The way she says *them* has dread pooling inside me. Knox turns to face us, I don't shy away from the bitter look on his face.

"Why?" he grits out.

"Knox, that is none of your business," Lake scolds. "Wave will come to us when she is ready." She looks to Wave as she asks, "Right?"

"Yeah. I swear I won't leave without coming to say good-bye," she answers.

"Wait, you're leaving?" Knox's voice booms around the room.

"Son, you can't force her to come with us," Clara tries to reason.

"I am not leaving her here with them, she comes or we stay," Knox retorts, sounding like spoiled fucking brat.

"You don't have a choice, it's her call to make," I snap as I climb to my feet and stare my best friend down.

"You stay the fuck out of this—"

Trey cuts him off before Knox can continue yelling. "We have never hurt her. You make her feel weak by thinking she can't defend herself. She doesn't need anyone to protect or shield her. She's fucking strong and will do as she pleases but if you want to push her away, then by all means keep going on like you are, because she will leave you and make no fucking mistake, Knox, we will be by her side when she does but you won't." I'm awed by the dominance and protectiveness in Trey's tone. Knox flicks his gaze between us, whatever he sees in our eyes has him deflating.

"Wave, please don't make me leave you," he begs his sister.

"You're not leaving me, you're just taking your family home so I can deal with my... guys." Yeah, I am man enough to fucking admit that hearing her call us her guys has pride swelling inside my chest and my heart racing. Maybe, just fucking maybe, this conversation we are about to have won't fracture my heart and she may just choose us.

"Knox, get your ass moving now because you are not ruining this for her. Say see you soon to your sister, she is a grown woman and doesn't need you trying to play big brother when it concerns her private life." I shoot Lake a thankful nod. Knox grunts and grumbles about everyone being assholes and not understanding as he says goodbye to Wave. He leaves the others to say their goodbyes before coming over to us.

"You hurt her or don't bring her home I will come after you both. I will make it the main mission for the Re Della Strada to hunt you fuckers to the end of the world." In true Knox fashion he doesn't wait for a reply as he storms out of the room, making sure to stomp his feet loudly so everyone knows he is in a shitty mood.

"My turn." I turn to face Taylan and fight the smirk from breaking free. "She may share his blood but she is my sister as well. Hurt her and I'll peel the fucking flesh from your bones with a rusted pair of pliers." I lose the battle, I smile wide.

"Does that threat ever work?" I throw back at him.

"I'd say to ask the fuckers that have heard it before but you can't because they are all dead so, yeah, it fucking works."

"You have my word, we will bring her home, Tay."

"Good." He hugs me goodbye then looks at Trey. "I don't know you so I am trusting Xan's judgment of you. Fuck her over and I'll make your nightmares appear like a daydream." I shake with silent laughter as he turns and leaves, following after Lake and Clara. The moment the hotel door clicks shut, we are bathed in tension—some of it bad but a lot of the tension vibing between the three of us is sexual. Wave keeps her back to us for another minute before slowly turning around. I take in every subtle detail as I drink her in. She is still the most beautiful woman I have ever laid eyes on and that will never change. She robbed me of my heart when we were just children, she is my middle school sweetheart and I will do anything to keep her with me.

Trey and I stand shoulder to shoulder as she assesses us with a keen look in her eyes, my nerves are getting the best of me. I have hope sprouting it's ugly head inside me that she is going to choose to be with us and make a life together, but I also know this is a huge fucking step for her. She has spent so many years at the mercy of a man, never having a say in anything but that isn't how it is with us. Trey and I only want to protect her and make sure she is safe, we don't want to control her or change a single fucking perfect thing about her.

SAMANTHA BARRETT

"What if we order some food and relax a bit before we get into... this conversation?" Trey asks. Wave nibbles her bottom lip nervously and nods.

"Order food, I'm going to take a shower," she mutters. Like the love sick fucking dogs that we are, we watch her walk away, close the bathroom door and groan when we hear the shower running. Both of us are picturing her naked with droplets of water cascading down that perfect body.

"Food!" Trey shouts, shocking me out of my wet daydream. I shoot the smirking fuck a glare before ordering room service, the moment they ask if I wanted it charged to my credit card, I smile wide and say a silent thank you to Lake for booking the room and I double the order and tell them hell yes. It's the least Knox can do.

The food arrives before Wave is finished, I ordered way too fucking much. All of it covers the small dining table, the coffee table and two trays are left against the wall since we ran out of space. I rub the back of my neck and shoot Trey a sheepish smile.

"I think Knox may lose his shit when he gets the bill." Trey bursts out laughing, I follow suit unable to hold back.

"Fuck it," he wheezes out as he snags a fry from one of the plates. He and I fall into easy conversation as we stuff our faces. It's strange how easy it is for me to talk to him, it used to be like this with Knox and Taylan. I could speak to them about anything and never fear being judged, but that is no longer the case. I will always love my brothers and have their backs till the day I die, but Trey and I share something different—we share a love for a woman who is the center of our world.

"I never thought I would be okay with... sharing a woman," I say honestly.

Trey's face turns serious as he regards me. "I didn't either. I always thought I would be alone given the life I lead but the day I saw her..." He sucks in a deep breath before continuing. "It's hard to explain but it felt like I was missing something inside myself but the moment she and I locked eyes, a part of her leapt inside me and made me whole." I nod my head, understanding exactly what he means.

"For fourteen years my heart has been fractured. I never thought it would heal but the moment I saw her again, it healed and started to beat again. My heart has always belonged to one woman, not only my heart but my body as well. I never slept with another woman in the fourteen years she was gone, I couldn't do it. It always felt like I was betraying her memory and diminishing what we shared together."

"If she tells us to go, I won't leave her. I'll stay by her side and help her accomplish her goal of setting all these women free."

"I will do the same. Knox knows my loyalty lies with his sister. If it comes to a war between those two, I will stand by her side and fight my brothers."

"There will be no war." Trey and I both jump to our feet and face her, she stands there clutching the towel that is wrapped around her body. Her hair is wet and loose. I fight the groan from breaking free as I picture gripping those silky strands in my fist as I slam into her from behind. The ink that covers her skin only adds to the sex appeal—fuck, she looks sexy.

"Okay," I rasp out awkwardly. She darts her tongue out to moisten her lips as she looks between the both of us, looking nervous and that is a look I haven't seen on her since we were kids.

"I..." She sucks in a ragged breath, squares her shoulders and tries again. "I'm a broken doll–"

"No, you're not!" Trey admonishes.

"Let me finish, if I don't say this shit then I never will." I shoot him a look of warning to keep his fucking trap shut. "I'm broken, I know it and so do the both of you, so don't deny it. I don't... feel things like others. I haven't felt anything for years until three days ago."

"Lakeland," I whisper, her eyes soften as she nods.

"She's my soulmate, you knew that, which is why you both called her to the bridge that night because you knew Knox wasn't the one to force me out of the darkness I was living in. I need time to... adjust to this whole feeling thing again."

"What does that mean... for us?" Trey hedges.

She blows out a loud exhale. "I won't lie to you both. I don't know where we go from here." Pain begins to seep through my veins.

"Are you sending us away?" I ask with a tone laced with anguish.

"No." My brows raise. "Well, the choice to leave is yours but do I want you to stay? Yes." That's all I needed to hear. I close the space between us, coming to a stop directly in front of her. I grip the back of her neck and force her head back so she can meet my gaze.

"We're yours," I say before meshing my mouth to hers and claiming her. She releases her hold on the towel, then grabs my waist, pulling me in closer. I feel Trey press against her back, forcing her to break the kiss and peer back at him.

"Tell us you want us, we want to hear the words—no, we need to hear them, Doxy," he whispers as he leans down and begins to nip at her neck, drawing soft mewls from her. Gripping the front of her towel I yank it open and watch as it drops to the floor. Her nipples are hard and begging me to taste them, so I do. The second I suck one into my mouth she moans. "We want every sound, you stop letting us hear those sexy sounds, we stop the pleasure." Trey reaches around to run his finger through her folds groaning. "She's fucking drenched for us, Xan."

I release her nipple with a wet pop and stare up at her, loving the sight of the heated look in her eyes. "I'm gonna taste you now." Trey removes his hand as I drop to my knees before her and lift one of her legs to throw over my shoulder as she leans back into Trey who claims her lips in a heated kiss while twirling her nipples between his fingers. Tearing my gaze from them, I stare at her weeping pussy, my mouth watering at the sight. I run my tongue along her thigh, relishing in the way she shivers. I run my nose along the seam of her lips and groan, fuck she smells so good.

"Eat her cunt," Trey orders and without hesitation I bury my tongue inside her, loving the cry that tears from her and the way her hips buck. Groaning at the taste of her, I continue lapping at her opening for a minute, loving how her body trembles and the sounds she makes when I suck her clit into my mouth.

"Grayson!" Hearing her moan my name is like feeling the sun kiss your skin for the first time. Hearing the way she says my name with such longing spurs me on, needing to hear her scream it as she comes all over my face.

"Take it, baby. I want to see you come all over his face before we fuck you." Trey's words have her burying a hand in my hair and holding me in place as she begins to ride my face, chasing her own release.

"Fuck, hold your tongue out like that," she orders. I do as commanded and allow her to take her pleasure from me. "Fuck, Xander!" she screams as she comes all over my face, tremors wracking her body. Needing to drag this high out longer, I suck her clit into my mouth, relishing in the sound of the scream that rips out of her at my unexpected move.

Chapter Thirty-One

Doxy

I'm floating.

Well, that's how it feels as I come down from the most intense orgasm. Xander brushes my leg from his shoulder and climbs to his feet, smirking down at me. If Trevante wasn't holding me up I would have dropped to the floor in a heap. I watch Xander strip in front of me, loving the sight of his naked flesh but my gaze is captured by his cock the moment he rids himself of his pants. I shiver when I feel Trey's lips against the shell of my ear.

"You want that cock inside your pussy, baby?" he whispers before sucking the shell of my ear into his mouth, drawing a strangled groan from me.

"Yes," I answer. Xander yanks me out of Trey's hold and lifts me. I wrap my arms and legs around him as I stare into his eyes, the loving look I see reflected back at me is like staring in a mirror because I feel something for them but I can't get my brain to commute with my mouth to tell them what they want to hear.

I'm scared.

"Get out of your head, baby," Xander whispers, then claims my lips in a searing kiss to distract me as he slowly eases his cock inside me, inch by glorious fucking inch.

"Fuck!" I cry out and throw my head back, breaking the kiss the moment he is balls deep inside me. I look back to see Trey standing there naked with his hard cock in his hand and a ravenous look in his eyes. He sees the look of want in my eyes and creeps forward at a leisurely pace, I shiver when I feel his hot heated skin pressed against my back.

He flicks his gaze to Xander and says, "Fuck her." Xander's grip on my waist turns punishing as he begins to lift me then slams me back down onto his cock. "Eyes on me, baby, I want to see it in your eyes the way he makes you feel." Something about this moment feels different. They're stripping away my layers and not giving me a chance to hide from them as they play my body against me like it's their own secret weapon to do with as they please.

"Fuck, baby, you're so tight," Xan grits out as he continues to fuck me. Trey shifts and grips my throat in his hand, forcing me backward so I am leaning against him making it easier for Xander to fuck me harder.

"Oh, fuck!" I cry out at the new angle.

"You like taking that dick don't you, Doxy?" Trey huskily whispers.

"Yes, I fucking love it," I cry out when he hits that fucking delicious spot inside me. I feel an orgasm cresting and know without a doubt Xan is close as well, I can feel his cock swelling inside me. Before I can grab onto that orgasm Xander comes, roaring my name. Before disappointment can wash over me, he pulls out and I'm passed to Trey. Xander mimics the position Trey occupied a second ago, then Trey's cock is slamming into me. "Yes!" I scream out.

"I got to taste your cum on my tongue so it's only fair he gets your cum on his cock, baby." I stare up at Xander in shock. The fucker smirks at me. "Yeah, baby, I stopped you from coming. That was your punishment for leaving us behind and thinking you could escape what this is."

I can't focus clearly on what he says, Trevante is fucking me too good and hard for that conversation. "Fuck, baby, I can feel you clamping down on my cock," Trey grits out.

"I'm so close," I whimper. He pulls almost all the way out of me before slamming back inside me, forcing me to arch off Xander who is pinching my nipples between his fingers. Fuck, this is perfect.

"I can feel his cum on my cock, baby. I need to fill you with mine so we can both be inside you, do you want that?" I can hear the strain in Trey's voice as he continues to fuck me at a relentless pace.

My orgasm slams into me with such force it robs me of air for a second as I scream out. "Yes!" Trey's hold tightens on my waist as he slams into me over and over again, chasing his release. I scream out as another wave of pleasure rips through me. I hear him shout my name as he comes but it sounds so far away. I feel so weightless, so full and *protected*.

I moan, feeling sated and... *happy?*

I snap my eyes open and look around the room in fright, then gape at the sight of Trey and Xander sitting on the couch with concerned looks on their faces. I look down and see I'm on the bed with a sheet pooled around my waist. They both stand and cautiously make their way toward me. I frown at the sight of them dressed in their jeans only as they both drop down onto either side of me, looking worried.

"What happened?" I ask.

Xan shakes his head. "You passed out." I recoil and shake my head.

"I think my cock knocked you out," Trey says, earning a glare from Xander.

"I passed out?" I say aloud as I'm trying to come to terms with it.

"Yeah, baby," Xan says quietly as he reaches out and cups my cheek in his hand, drawing my gaze back to him. "Are you okay?"

I hate that I worried them but it's not like I could have helped passing out. "Yeah. I'm fine."

"We cleaned you up," Trey says and nods toward the shirt that I am wearing, which is his. "Did... did we hurt you?" All traces of humor are gone from his tone.

I shake my head. "No. I've never passed out from sex but that shit was... a lot." They both chuckle. I scowl at the both of them when they high five each other. Fucking men and their egos!

"We ordered food but it's cold now... we thought you might have been hungry earlier but clearly you weren't hungry for a range of pasta, you just wanted sausages." Xander glares at Trey but I can't help but laugh at the idiot, they both stare at me with odd looks.

"What?" I snap.

Xan shrugs. "It's good to hear you laugh." I roll my eyes and shove them away as I climb off the bed and head for the food that covers the dining table. There is a fuck load of food here so I grab a spare plate and pile it with a range of different foods before claiming a seat on the couch, tucking my legs beneath me as I dig in.

"Did you want us to get the kitchen to reheat it or anything?" Trey asks.

I shake my head as I bite down on my chicken wing. "Nah, anything tastes better than dog kibble," I say without thought, the horrified looks on their faces has me sighing and dropping my wing back onto my plate. "I won't tell you everything at once, some days I will let shit slip so you need to deal with that. Okay?" Xander grinds his teeth while Trey looks murderous. I choose to ignore them both as I go back to eating my food. By the time I'm done stuffing my face, I'm in a mood because I can feel both of them still staring at me. "Make yourselves useful and go run me a bath," I snap. If I wasn't in such a sour mood, I might actually laugh at the sight of them rushing off to do as I asked.

I snag a cream filled cupcake off the coffee table and bite into it, moaning at the taste, then wipe the corner of my mouth, sucking the cream off my finger.

"Fuck."

"I'm hard." I snap my head with my finger still in my mouth to see them both standing there staring at me with desire in their eyes.

An idea peaks into my mind as I make my way toward the bathroom, eating my treat and shooting them a wink as I pass by. I hear them pushing and shoving each other behind me as

241

they follow like love-sick pups. I push the last bite into my mouth before gripping the hem of the shirt and yanking it over my head. I love the sounds they make. Hearing how much they appreciate the sight of me regardless of all the scars hidden beneath the layers of ink makes me feel desirable. I step into the large tub and moan, then peer at them over my shoulder and quirk a brow.

"You coming in..." It takes them two seconds to digest my words before they are racing each other to get their pants off. I move to the furthest side and remain standing as they both step into the tub. Before they can sit down, I clear my throat. "Sit on the edge." They share a look with each other before obeying my demand, looking apprehensive. I would be lying if I said I could live this life without them, they have given me a strength I didn't know I had. I may not have realized it before but I do now.

They saw the real me beneath the darkness.

Chapter Thirty-Two

Trevante

I can't stop my cock from growing hard at the sight of her. She is fucking perfect and that stunt she just pulled with the cupcake nearly had me jizzing in my pants like a fucking sixteen-year-old kid.

She darts her gaze between the both of us, smirking at the sight of our comfortability. Fucking her together is one thing but sharing a bath is different, the reward clearly outweighs the awkwardness for both of us. When she moves toward us, I stiffen in anticipation.

"You both may get to call the shots when we fuck..." Her tone is filled with need, then she surprises the both of us when she kneels down in the water and grips both of our cocks in each of her hands. I hiss at the feeling of her dainty hand wrapped around me. Xan groans when she begins to stroke us as she continues. "But I'm the boss outside of the bedroom, am I clear?"

"Whatever you want, baby, just don't stop," I grit out.

"Yeah, Wave, you're the boss out there but in here, *we* call the shots. Now suck my cock." Her eyes sparkle with desire as she shifts and moves between his legs and sucks him into her mouth while stroking me at the same time. He throws his head back and moans. She uses her hold on my dick to drag me to my feet. she releases Xander, then turns to me, wrapping her lips around the head of my dick and sucking me into her tight, wet, little mouth—fuck this shit feels amazing. Before I can get lost in the feeling, Xander grabs her by her hair and forces her mouth back onto his cock. I open my mouth to have a go at him but he speaks. "Lean forward, baby, you're going to suck my dick while Trey fucks that greedy little cunt." She moans around his shaft as she obeys his order and lifts onto her knees resting her hands on the top of his legs.

I lower to my knees behind her and run my hands over the globes of her ass, loving the way she shivers under my touch. My cock is aching and begging me to slam inside her. Gripping my shaft, I line it up with her entrance and slowly ease inside her, loving the sounds she makes as I glide inside her wet little pussy. I match my thrusts to the tempo in which she bobs her head up and down on Xan's cock.

"How does she feel?" he asks.

"Like home," I grit out as I slam into her, relishing in the strangled sound she makes. She tries to lift her head but his hold in her hair keeps her in place.

"Take me as far as you can, baby." She does as he asks and gags around his length, choking. The sound has us both moaning. Fuck, seeing her choke on his dick has me increasing my pace needing to empty myself inside her again, marking her as mine. "Like that, baby, stay like that while I fuck your mouth," he grinds out as he thrusts into her mouth, chasing his release.

A moment later, he's throwing his head back and coming with her name on his lips. He doesn't pull out of her mouth until he's sure she has swallowed every last drop of him.

"Fuck that was hot to watch," I praise as I continue to slam into her cunt. Xander pulls back and bends down, placing a kiss to her lips. Giving him a taste of his own medicine, I reach forward and grab her hair yanking her back until she is flush against my chest. I rest my chin on her shoulder as I meet his gaze and smirk. "Bounce up and down on my cock while he watches, baby." Xander's eyes darken at the sight of her riding me, her tits bounce up and down, drawing a groan from him.

"Fuck, Trey, I need to come," she cries out as I thrust up inside her.

"I got you, baby," I whisper as I reach around her and circle her clit, drawing a sharp cry from her.

"Fuck, like that, I'm gonna come," she cries.

"Not yet, baby, I want you to come with me," I grit out through clenched teeth. She whimpers but does as she's told. I feel my balls begging to tingle and I'm a second away from coming, when I order her to come under Xander's watchful gaze.

"Fuck!" she screams as we both come, shudders tearing through me. I'm panting and fucking breathless. Her pussy is clenching the shit out of my dick and milking it for everything it's worth. I place a kiss to the side of her neck before burying my face there.

"I want you both," she blurts out, causing me to tense for a second before I pull out of my hiding place and out of her as I shift so I can see her face. She looks scared and unsure. Xander drops into the tub beside me. We stare at her for a long while, waiting for her to gather her thoughts and elaborate. "I-I don't want either of you to go. I... I want whatever this is if you both want it... want me?" she whispers, the uncertainty in her tone and the worried look in her eyes kills me. Without thought, I grip her face and pull her to me, kissing the shit out of her before pulling back and resting my forehead against hers.

"You have me, baby."

Xander pulls her to him and kisses her before mimicking my move and resting his head against hers. "You've always had me, Wave."

She pulls back from him and looks between the both of us. "I know you both have said those three words but in my family we don't say them." Xander sucks in a sharp intake of air. "When we feel that way about someone we tell them that we... *Choose them.*" Xander's face softens as my heart beats wildly in my chest. "Alexander Grayson, Trevante Kane, I choose you."

We have spent four glorious days in this hotel room exploring every inch of Doxy's body, she's had time to explore ours as well. She even grew confident enough that last night she fingered herself while we jacked off watching her. Fuck, it was sexy and something we will be repeating, a lot!

"You need to answer it or he will fly back here," Xander says from the other side of the bed as her phone rings again for the thousandth time. Doxy groans from her position in the middle of us.

"I'll suck your cock if you answer it?" she volleys back. Xan lulls his head to the side and pins her with a deadpan look.

"That may have worked the last three times but it won't this time." She pouts at him before rolling over to face me and batting her lashes.

I snort and shake my head. "Nope. Answer the call, Doxy. He just wants to know you're okay." She groans and holds her hand out for me to place the phone in her palm. Being locked up in this room has been amazing, getting to know her and seeing this softer side, but Xander and I both know she is also using this as a time to hide because she's scared the moment she leaves this room, all the bad things that she escaped are going to come back and swallow her whole.

"Knoxville?" she says when she answers the phone.

"I've been calling!" he shouts loud enough for me to hear.

"I know," she bites back.

"Why didn't you answer?"

"Because I'm not a fucking child and also not your concern. I told you I would see you before we leave and I meant it. Stop calling, Knox!" she snarls before ending the call and throwing her phone across the room. It doesn't shatter against the wall which just seems to piss her off more.

"Baby—"

"Don't, Xander, I don't want to fucking hear it," she snaps before she climbs off the bed and dashes into the bathroom, slamming the door behind her.

"We need to go," I say.

"I know."

"Nano and the guys aren't willing to make a move on any of the clubs until she is back in Ireland and gives the okay."

He sighs and runs a hand through his hair. "We leave tonight," he says as he grabs his own phone from the bedside table and calls someone. "Lake?" My eyes widened in surprise that he called her. "Yeah, she's fine. Knox is just being overbearing and it's pissing her off." He pauses to listen to what she says. "Can you get him to send the plane, we're coming tonight. Yeah, but, Lake, she is gonna need you." I tune him out, climb out of the bed and get dressed. We sent our clothes to be laundered downstairs, it feels weird wearing them again after being naked for days.

A short while later Doxy comes out of the bathroom, showered and dressed with a scornful look on her face but her eyes betray her, I see the fear.

"Don't let me lose myself," she whispers. Both Xan and I rush forward, hugging her between us both.

"Never," he vows.

"We will always bring you back because we choose you," I say as I place a kiss to the top of her head.

Chapter Thirty-Three

Xander

The entire plane ride was filled with tension. Wave couldn't sit still and paced the length of the plane, driving both Trey and me mad. Trey finally lost it and forced her ass into a seat and told her if she moved he wouldn't eat her out for a week. She tried to drag me into their disagreement but I backed Trey. She refused to speak to both of us after that and has retreated back inside herself. When we landed, she practically ran off the plane and climbed into the waiting car, making sure to take the front seat, leaving Trey and I to sit together in the back.

She can try to play off that she isn't worried or even scared but I can see her gazing out the window and squinting her eyes to try to get a better look at certain things. As we pull into Knox's drive, she grows stiff. When the driver brings the car to a stop out the front of the house she doesn't move. Leaning forward, I tap Marco on the shoulder indicating for him to get the hell out and give us a minute, which he does.

"We're here, baby," Trey says softly.

"Going in there and seeing the life they have created without me..." She lets her sentence trail off.

"There was no life for any of us without you in it. Their son is named after you and River. Pictures of you hang on the walls of that house. I have photos of you and me together in my room. You were never forgotten, baby, I swear," I reassure her.

"I'm scared to be alone," she blurts out.

"You will never be alone again, Xander and I will always be with you. I know it's just words but give us time to prove to you that we mean what we say. We will never allow you to feel nothing again. It's going to take time for you to feel like your old self, Doxy." She sighs as she shifts in her chair to look back at us.

"If that's the case, then I need you to do something for me." Trey and I both nod our heads. "To all my men and the girls I will always be known as Doxy because that is who I will be when they are around but to you both... I want to be Waverly." Pride swells inside me, fuck she is so strong. She doesn't wait for a reply from us, climbing out of the car. Trey and I follow after her in time to see Clara and Roberto exiting the house. At the sight of her father, Wave slams to a stop. Both me and Trey flank her on either side, showing her without words that we have her.

Roberto slowly makes his way to us with Clara at his side. He stops a few steps away from us, tears clouding his eyes as he looks at his daughter. I discreetly interlock my fingers with hers and give her hand a squeeze.

"God, you're beautiful," he says quietly. She sucks in a sharp breath at the sound of his voice.

"Is it true that you were there that night to save Lake?" Wave asks.

"It wasn't just her I was trying to save, Waverly," he answers honestly.

"If you're looking for me to drop to my knees and weep because my daddy has suddenly come home, then you are fucking mistaken, old man. I lived my life without you, we didn't need you because we had her." She flicks her chin toward her mother as Roberto's face falls. "If you're here to make amends and try to form a relationship with me, then let me drop a bomb on you before you try to play the daddy card. I'm fucking both of them and if you have a problem with that then you can eat shit." She doesn't wait for a reply as she grabs Trey's hand and drags us inside the house with her mom and dad's laughter following after us.

"I see she takes after you," we hear Roberto say as we enter the house to see Knox standing there with a sour look on his face.

"Did you put him in his place?" he asks Wave.

She snorts. "You took over being my dad years ago, that fucker has his work cut out for him if he thinks he is sliding back into my life without working for it." Knox shoots her a wink as he tells us to follow him out the back. The second we step out the back the three of us slam to a halt at the sight of Taylan, Lake, Kimber, Anna and the two boys standing out here under fairy lights. Wave's face is a picture of horror as she wheels around on both Trey and me. "Tell me this isn't where you drop to your knees?"

Trey and I both laugh and shake our heads. "I will get on my knees for you anytime you like but we aren't proposing." Trey turns to me looking confused. "Are we?"

"No. I had nothing to do with this," I answer.

"Say you'll get on your knees for my sister again fucker and I'll break your teeth," Knox sneers.

"This was all me and the girls," Lake says, drawing all our attention to her. She motions for Wave to come to her, which she does with us following behind. Lake pulls Wave in for a hug then releases her and places her hands on her shoulders and smiles lovingly. "I love you, Wave, we all do, which is why we thought it was important for you to have a place to visit."

Wave frowns and cocks her head to the side. "A place to visit?"

Lake nods and clasps her hand as she leads her further into the garden which has a large fountain in the center of it. Taylan told me about the shrine they had built for her and Knox's baby that she lost because of me. I feel like I shouldn't be here and stop moving but Knox pushes me forward.

"Trust her," he mutters. I nod and follow after the girls who come to a stop next to a white sheet that is covering something. Beside it sits a headstone that reads.

Your wings were ready but our hearts weren't.
Beloved baby of Knox & Lake.

Guilt churns inside me at the sight of that headstone, that baby should have been here but my grief and anger took its life. I will spend the rest of my days trying to make up for the innocent life I took.

"I know you're strong and fuck, I admire that strength, Wave, I always have but I need to be the strong one now," Lake says in a watery tone. I spy Roberto and Clara entering the garden from the corner of my eye.

"Why?' Wave whispers clearly feeling uneasy.

"Because you were always the one to hold me up and be my rock, it's my turn to be yours." Lake looks to Taylan and nods her head. He grips the sheet and yanks it off exposing another headstone. Waverly tears her hand from Lake's as she stumbles back into me. I grip her waist, holding her up when she begins to tremble at the sight before us. The headstone has a statue of a baby with wings above it but it's the inscription on the stone that has Wave shaking and gasping for air.

My heart breaks for the moments we will never share.
My arms ache for the cuddles we will never have.
My soul longs for its forever missing piece.
The moment your heart stopped mine changed forever.

Laiken Knoxville Bronson.
Beloved baby boy of,
Waverly 'Doxy' Bronson.

Lakeland moves to stand in front of Wave who is full on shaking in my arms now. "He deserved a place to rest. I always dreamed we would have children together and they would grow to be best friends like us. Our babies will grow up together but in a better place where they will be waiting for us to join them one day. You lost your son and we know that you're devastated but let us share in your pain and mourn the loss of the beautiful boy we never got to meet with you because we love him too, Wave, and we are here for you." A sob tears out of Wave. I wrap my arm around her waist as I anchor her to me. Trey reaches out and rests a hand on her shoulder, Knox steps forward and gently pushes Lake aside so he can grab his sister's face in his hands.

"It is the greatest honor I have ever had in my life to have my nephew named after me." I swallow past the lump in my throat at the sight of Knox fighting back his tears. "I never got to meet my namesake, my nephew, but I fucking choose him, sister. That little boy may never get to meet us but he sure as fuck will feel how much we love him from the afterlife." When Knox pulls her to him, I release her without a fuss. She clings to her brother as she cries and he buries his face in her hair. "I choose you, Waverly."

"I choose you, Brother," she chokes out. I move to Lake and wrap my arms around her, she melts into my hold and returns my embrace.

"Thank you for giving her this, Lay, she really needed it," I say as I pull back and stare down at her.

"I think we all did. Laiken is our family and it seemed only right that he has a place here with his cousin." I drop my gaze to the ground in shame. "Xander?" I slowly lift my gaze back to hers. "I believe that you did what you did that night for a reason." I reel back.

"What?"

"I believe that my baby wasn't meant to be here with us because he or she was meant to be waiting for Laiken at those pearly gates." Fuck, I can't stop the tear that breaks free from rolling down my cheek.

Chapter Thirty-Four

Waverly

Three months later...

Xander, Trevante, Kimber, Anna, Nano, Calvin and Brett all stand there, staring at me like I have lost my fucking mind.

"Say that shit one more fucking time for me, Doxy?" Xander grits out through clenched teeth.

I pin him a warning glare. "Don't fucking push me, Grayson. I want all the clubs reopened but not as strip clubs. I want them to be normal night clubs that the girls can work in. They are to have security manning inside and outside at all times, all of the girls will be escorted to their cars after each shift."

"You want to reopen the clubs that were targeted by enemies of Karl's?" Trey barks at me. I shoot him a scathing look that has him narrowing his eyes.

"If any of those soft cocks want to come after us, then let them. I run Ireland not them. My girls need jobs and I won't have them turning tricks on a fucking corner. Get it done now. Anna and Kimber will be overseeing the everyday operations while Nano runs the rest of the business while we are back in Canada." At the mention of why I am doing this, both my guys relent and nod their heads. We have been playing clean up since we got back here months ago. We've had old enemies of Karl's trying to push me out but the moment I was appointed as the head of the Irish at the meeting in Switzerland two months ago by the other head families, the attacks have died down.

"When do you leave, Doxy?" Brett asks.

"Tomorrow morning, we'll be gone for two weeks," I answer.

"What do you want done with the *pigs*?" We no longer call Karl or the other's by their names, they are just known as the pigs. Every day they are visited by men who have loved destroying them, it's a beautiful sight to see.

"I want pictures of them taken and emailed to Ian. I want him to know that this is how we treat anyone who deals in the skin trade and if he doesn't want to make an enemy of me he will hand over a list of girls he has sold or we will take England from him." Pride shines in Nano's eyes as he smiles and nods.

"On it, Doxy," he says as he, Brett and Calvin leave but not before wishing me, Trey and Xan good luck. Only Kimber, Anna, the three of them and William know why we are going back to Canada.

"I'll call Davis in the morning and have him send through a report of the damages to the clubs from when we took them down and figure out the cost of the repairs."

"Thanks, Kimber."

"Also, Taylan and I were talking about a new business venture if you are interested?" I purse my lips and fight not to roll my eyes. Since they met, Kimber and Tay have become close and I worry his stupid ass tendencies will rub off on her.

"What is it?" I ask.

"How would you feel about setting up arenas here and in other countries for MMA fights?" I reel back in shock.

"Who came up with that idea?" Xan asks.

She shrugs and nibbles on the corner of her lip. Anna sighs and answers for her. "Kimber did, she talked it over with Tay who thought it was a fucking great idea and if you didn't jump on it he would take it to Knox." My jaw unhinges.

"That slimy motherfucker!" I growl. "Change of plans, Anna you take over meeting with Davis. Kimber make some calls and figure out what we need to do for these arenas. Pick the most profitable countries and send me a list. I'll bring it to the heads of the families when we meet next. We'd have to give them kickbacks but I'm good with that as long as it brings in a large profit." Kimber beams and nods her head eagerly. Anna shakes her head and waves us off as she leaves. The minute she's gone, I look at Kimber. "Any luck with the search?"

The happiness melts off her face as she shakes her head. "Not yet," she mutters. I reach into my back pocket and pull the slip of paper out and hand it to her. "What's this?" she asks as she takes it.

"The number on that paper is for Chaos Murdoch, he's good friends with my brother. He's part of the *Memento Mori* and they are said to be the best trackers. Chaos has even offered to call in his uncle who is known as the Bloodhound to help search for your daughter. Vincent Murelo is the best at his job and if we have any hope of finding your daughter, these people are the ones who are going to be able to do it." Her bottom lip trembles as tears fill her eyes.

"Thank you!" she chokes out before launching herself at me and crushing me in a hug that I return. "I mean it, Doxy, thank you." I tighten my hold on her as I answer.

"I gave you my word I would never give up and I meant it." She pulls back and smiles.

"I'm so proud of you, Dede," she mutters before placing a kiss to my cheek and leaving. I stand here shocked and feeling slightly weird over her being so emotional. Kimber is like me, she's cold and constantly in bitch mode so this is weird. I snap out of it when Trey comes up behind me and wraps his arms around my waist, then places a kiss to the top of my head.

"We're proud of you as well." I tilt my head back and smile up at him.

"Thanks," I breathe out a second before he kisses me. I melt into him groaning at the taste of him on my tongue.

"Hey!" We snap apart and turn to Xan who stands there with his arms crossed over his chest, looking at us with a stern look. "Your cock is staying in your fucking pants, three days is what the doc said." Trey and I groan.

"This fucking blows, I'm horny," I whine and stomp my foot.

Xander smirks cockily at me. "Sorry, baby, doc said no sex for three days before we have to jizz in the cup. Believe me, I am dying to be balls deep in that tight little cunt but I want our baby." My heart softens in my chest. Eight weeks ago, Lakeland flew here with my brother and a huge stack of papers. They sat the three of us down and slapped the papers on the table in the middle of us as Lake looked me dead in the eyes and said.

"I want to have your baby." The guys and I were stunned silent as she proceeded to explain that she would donate her eggs to be implanted with Trey and Xander's sperm and even carry the baby for me. I looked to my brother expecting him to be against this but he smiled and nodded his head, telling me he was completely on board with this plan.

I cried.

I can never have children, that was taken from me but to have my best friend be so selfless and offer not only her body but her eggs to give me and my guys a baby is something I would never have had the balls to even dream of. We fly back to Canada tomorrow to start the first round of treatment. Lake has been taking injections every day and now that she is ovulating it's the perfect time for the guys to come in a cup and implant their sperm in Lake. We are choosing to not find out whose sperm takes, as far we are all concerned we don't care who the baby's father is. It will have two daddy's and a mommy who will love it so fucking much.

"Hold off until tomorrow night, baby," Xan pleads as he leans down and kisses me softly.

"We're going to have a baby," Trey breaths out. I smile and nod my head.

"We're going to have a baby. Fuck, I want this baby so much," I admit.

"I know, baby. This time we'll be with you," Xander reassures me. We have a rule, every Saturday night no matter what is going on the three of us sit down and eat dinner while we share stories of our past. We made a deal to always be open and honest no matter what. Well, except for when one of them corners me and fucks me without the other around and then I'm forced into secrecy. I swear they know the other is fucking me because you can guarantee within the hour I'm being fucked by the other. They are so keeping score!

"I choose you both," I say before turning around and trying to flee.

"I saw that look," Trey shouts after me as I rush through the house heading for our bedroom.

"Get her, she's going for the rabbit!" Xander yells. Fuck, I run as fast as I can to save my vibrator from being taken from me. I never thought my life would end up like this. I never thought I would love or feel anything again but here I am stupidly in love with these two idiots and about to have a baby.

I was forced to become Doxy Da Luca to survive but I choose to be Waverly Bronson now.

Epilogue

Taylan

Four months later...

Leaning against the bar, I bring my Jack and Coke to my lips and take a long drag as I watch Lake and Knox dance. They look at each other with such adoration that it makes anyone around them jealous. I look beside them to see the three stars of the evening. Wave is sandwiched between Trey and Xan as they dance. It brings warmth to my chest to see her happy— fuck, it just makes me happy to see her again, point blank period!

This wedding isn't exactly legal but no one in this room would dare to tell them otherwise, as of today Wave officially became Waverly Grayson-Kane. They wanted to be 'married' before the baby arrived. Oh yeah, Lake is two months pregnant with their baby and we all couldn't be happier for them. It makes me fucking ecstatic to see them all happy.

"Bartender?" I dart my gaze to the side to see a stunning

leggy blonde with... fuck are her eyes gray? She flicks her gaze to the side and sees me staring at her. She scrunches her face in disgust.

"Can I buy you a drink?" I ask after finally finding my voice.

She scoffs and shakes her head. "There's a bar tab, you dumbass." My jaw unhinges.

"That's not very polite," I tease. She turns to face me and fuck does my cock grow hard instantly at those perfectly full, pouty lips, I picture her on her knees with them wrapped around my cock.

"And what makes you think I give a fuck about what you think?" My brows raise in surprise.

"Common courtesy?" I try.

"How about you go die and I'll pretend to shed a tear," she snaps before she walks away. Fuck, the black dress she wears hugs her figure perfectly, fucking hell her ass is perfect.

"You are never going to bag that kitty." I wave Kimber off as I watch my new conquest slide up beside London Murdoch. Huh, that makes total sense why she has such a bad attitude. London isn't exactly known in my world as being kind and of sound mind.

"I'm so getting her in bed," I declare.

Kimber snorts, earning a scowl from me. She and I have grown really close, especially since the building of the arenas is going ahead and we are both working on them for Wave but I don't like her like that. I look at her the same way I look at Wave, I would kill a cunt for Kimber no questions asked.

"I bet you 100K you will never bag that blonde."

I shoot her a devilish smile and nod my head eagerly. "Oh, Kimmy, you know I never lose."

She rolls her eyes and shakes her head. "Trust me, Casanova, this is one bet you will never win. Bow out now and save yourself the shame."

"When have I ever backed out of a bet?" I hedge.

"Ohhh, fine, you have a month to bag the blonde or you owe me 100K." I laugh and rub my hands together as I turn back to look for my girl. I look around the room but can't find her anywhere. I frown as my gaze collides with Gage Murdoch's, who is... what the fuck?

"Is it just me or is Gage glaring at me?" I ask.

Kimber chuckles. "Hand over that 100k now." I look at her and scrunch my face.

"Why the fuck would I do that?"

"Because that blonde you are trying to bag is Gage Murdoch's only daughter, Destiny." My face falls as Kimber laughs at my expense.

"Laugh it up. Fuck Gage, the bet is still on," I vow as I walk away.

Murdoch or not, I'm banging that blonde and making a hundred k. I don't do feelings like my brothers so this will be easy. Find her, feel her, fuck her and forget her.

The fucking end...
Until book 3!

List Update

Daniel- Trevante shot him

Jackson - shot in the mouth

Donald - killed at the club

Lionel - shot in the head

Mike, Tom, Aaron, Jones - Blown up on the boat

Ed - shot in the head

Stephen - slit throat

George - shot in the neck and chest

Frank - killed with a knife

Thank You

Book 2 is motherfucking done!

Writing Waverly was fucking hard and broke me at times but my God was it worth all the tears and pain.

I know you hate me for *another* cliffhanger but I promise I won't make you wait years for book three. I have to write Damned By His Angel and then I will be writing *Tainted Essence- book 3 in the Re Della Strada* series. Thank you so much for reading Wave's book, it means so much to me that you took you a chance on her.

I cannot thank you enough for reading *Fractured Heart*, it means the world to me that you have taken a chance on reading one of my books!

If you would leave a review that would be amazing!

ACKNOWLEDGMENTS

I suppose I better thank my baby daddy even though the fucker doesn't read my books! Thank you for dealing with our demons as I wrote this one. I know it wasn't easy considering I had to go to dark places to channel Wave. Love ya, daddy D!

My demon spawn, you two are all the inspiration I need to write these torture scenes. I joke, you two are the best story I have written. Keep being crazy, keep being you and always being true to yourself. Mommy loves you to the devil and back!

Leah, my friend, my designer, my plot partner, my sound board, the one who helps me spend money! I fucking love you and appreciate you so much, babe. I couldn't do any of this without you and I mean that!

Jaye Pratt, the woman who threatens to become besties with my daughter to spite me! Thanks for formatting all my books and dealing with my moaning daily because I didn't want to work even though you didn't either, haha.

My alpha's, Debbie, Clare and Sarah, you three are my Musketeers! None of these books would be what they are without you, I mean that shit. You three make my job so easy and polish these books to perfection. Thank you from the bottom of my heart, I love you.

My beta girls, Erin, Rizzo, Morgan and Patti, you ladies are the core of this whole book journey, without your hype, love and constant support I don't think I would be where I am today. I love each of you so fucking much for all you have done and continue to do for me.

My Army: Alicia, Amber, Angel, Ash, Barb, Charlotte, Cyndi, Debbie, Jasmine, Jen, Kahanna, Katelyn, Lakshmi, Lora, Lyndsey, Sarmi and Tess. Thank you ladies so fucking much for being the best freaking team an author could ask for. I owe you all so much for the love and dedication you give me.

Lizz, my friend, my editor, my fucking Bible! Thank you for all that you do for me and continue to do. I wouldn't be able to publish any of these books without you so thank you from the bottom of my heart.

My darling dark delicious readers, you are the most amazing bunch of humans I have ever had the chance to interact with and also being able to meet some of you has been the highlight of my year. Thank you so much for taking a chance, reading these crazy motherfuckers and loving them as much as I do.

Sam xxx

Also By Samantha Barrett

Mafia Romance

Murdoch Mafia Series

Played By The Bishop

Tormented By The King

Tortured By The Knight

Tempted By The Queen

Turned By The Pawn

Ruined By The Rook

Murdoch Mafia Novella

Stalemate

Memento Mori Series

Reign Of Royal

Broken By Sin

In Havoc Lays Chaos

Godfathers of the night

London has Fallen

Re Della Strada

Shattered Soul

Fractured Heart

Fairytales With A Twist

Condemned Beast

Sports Romance

Playing For Keeps

Offside

Touchdown

End Game

Hail Mary

Blindside

RH Sports

Hate Us Like You Mean It

MM

Love Me Like You Mean It

Paranormal Romance

The Dream Series

A Beautiful Dream

A Twisted Fate

A Beautiful Nightmare

Redemption

Anarchy

Brutal Savages

Savage Lies

Brutal Truth

Savage Beast

Brutal Beauty

ABOUT THE AUTHOR

Samantha Barrett is originally from Auckland New Zealand
but living in Brisbane Australia.
Sam writes all things dirty dark and delicious with a side of
twisted mind fuck.
She is the love of all things red flags and an anti-hero is a must.

www.ingramcontent.com/pod-product-compliance
Lightning Source LLC
Chambersburg PA
CBHW030619170726
48283CB00002B/663